# Bed Time Stories for Adults:

*3 Books in 1: Self-Hypnosis for Deep Sleep, Guided Mindfulness Meditations, Overcoming Anxiety, Insomnia & Stress Relief for Stressed Out Adults.*

# Table of Content

# Bedtime Stories for Adults

*Relaxing Deep Sleep Hypnosis. Reduce Anxiety, Stress, Depression, and Insomnia. Mindfulness to Heal Your Brain.*
*Book 1*

# Table of Contents

# Introduction

Have you ever been lying in bed at night, staring at your ceiling and wishing that sleep would come for you? Maybe you were stuck there, desperate for that sleep to arrive, but no matter what you did, it was impossible. Your mind continued to race, and you couldn't slow it down. Insomnia strikes when we least expect it, and it can have all sorts of sources. Commonly, it is found in those suffering from anxiety and depression. However, just because you are suffering from that doesn't mean that you have to lose out on your sleep as well. Are you stressed out? Are you tired? Worried about the world? In a world filled with as many unpredictable variables, that comes as little surprise. However, we can overcome it.

Ultimately, if you are currently suffering from anxiety, depression, or even struggling from insomnia for reasons unknown to you, you are strongly encouraged to talk to your doctor. There may be underlying causes that this book will not be able to address. However, you can learn to begin mitigating the symptoms. This book is here to help you alleviate your insomnia through the use of mindfulness. It is not a cure, but it is a way that you can find some support for yourself if you need it, and it is here if you want to make use of it.

At the beginning of this book, you will be treated to seven short, slice of life stories that are there to be relaxing. They are designed to help to draw you into these worlds where your own personal worries can begin to melt away. Through listening, you will realize that you are at ease and at peace. As you read through these, you will be following Sophie, a young, relatable woman who doesn't quite know what she wants in life. As you read her slice of life stories, you will watch her enjoy herself, solve minor problems, and, more importantly, find ways to relax and enjoy the moment with those that live around her.

Then, as this book comes to a close, you will be treated to two guided meditations. They are there to provide you with a calming guide into that state of mindfulness. As you follow the instructions, you will feel your mind, your body, and your spirit beginning to relax. You will feel your worries fade away and your stress dissipate. They will gently ease you into a receptive and calm state so that you will be able to focus on the story and eventually fall asleep. These two meditations should help you begin to relax just enough that you feel far more receptive to that state of sleep that you have been yearning for, and hopefully, you will find that you can rest well.

Each and every story is designed to be compelling to slowly lull you into that state of mindfulness so you can focus on the story provided. Mindfulness is a state of quiet, calming awareness. It is a state where you can simply be in the moment. You let go of your judgment, your worries, and your discomfort in favor of being able to release the struggles that come with them. You are able to heal yourself from the inside out, defeating those negative thoughts that are probably holding yourself back. As you do so, you find that you are in peace with yourself. You find that you are content at the moment. You find that you are comfortable as the person that you are.

It might seem strange to listen to these stories to try to help yourself fall asleep, but they are there to be a gentle guide for you. They are designed to be something that you can rely on to better yourself, to feel calmer and more content in yourself as you head into this process. They will guide you into that calming state so that you can be certain that you are calm and ready to go.

Before you begin, however, there are a few key skills that you will need that will be addressed in the first few stories. These will come up in the meditative bedtime stories that you hear. You will need to know how to use mindful

breathing to guide yourself into focusing on the right state
of mind. You will need to use calm breathing to help
yourself settle down. This works because it triggers your
vagus nerve, which reminds your body to settle down. Deep
breathing changes the pressure in your chest, and as a
result, your vagus nerve reminds you to slow down. Your
heart rate slows, and your blood pressure will settle down.
Your stress hormones will begin to lower, and you will feel
at peace. This is the key to relaxation before these stories,
and it will take you far. You will also need to understand the
idea of a body scan and how to perform them. Finally, you
will need to understand what an affirmation is.

## Mindful Breathing

Mindful breathing is the act of being able to breathe
mindfully. It is to focus on your breaths as they come in and
out without worry. When you do this, you are to focus
entirely on your breathing without exception. Typically, this
is done with one long breath in through the nose, usually for
about five seconds. Then, you breathe out through your
mouth. You do this more and more in order to calm yourself
down. The purpose of mindful breathing is to focus entirely
upon your breath without anything else. Every time that
your thoughts drift from your breath, you gently and
without judgment, push your attention back to it.

## Body Scan

A body scan is a meditative technique where you go over
your whole body, place by place. Usually, you start at your
toes or your head and slowly work to the other end,
stopping your awareness at each of the different areas of
your body. Every part of you should be focused on one at a
time before you move to the next. This is often joined with
relaxing each part as you do so, but other times, it is simply
becoming aware of the feelings at the moment in every part
of your body.

# Affirmations

Affirmations are a repetition of speech that is used to remind you of the critical points that you will need to remember. They are to help you to find calmness, peace, or even just to keep your mind focused on something that you are pursuing. When you use affirmations, the idea is that you are able to focus entirely on the moment on making something true. If you want to create your own affirmations for anxiety, stress, or depression to help yourself to manage them, you would repeat these phrases to yourself to sort of ground yourself at the moment. They should be personal, positive, and present-oriented so you can assert that they are true in their moment.

Ultimately, those are the most important aspects that you will need moving forward as you read through this book. You should find that you get plenty of information through doing so, and you should find that the process is simple enough. For the best impact, consider following along with a guided meditation to help yourself begin to relax so you can then move on to reading the stories if you are still awake. Hopefully, by the end of it, you will feel your own personal insomnia start to melt away. So, sit back, relax, get ready for bed, and let's begin!

# Story 1: The Path Less Traveled

*Sophie heads out for a nice, leisurely hike through the mountains with her German shepherd, Bella. However, things take a turn for the worst when she heads down the wrong road. Will Sophie learn to embrace the road less traveled and appreciate the beauty, or is she going to find herself miserable the entire time she tries to find her way back to the trail?*

*Beep! Beep! Beep!*

"I'm up! I'm up!" shouted Sophie as she sat up, unceremoniously, in her bed. Her long, dark brown hair was all over the place as she pushed herself up, and next to her, Bella gave her what Sophie could only describe as a dubious look. Bella's black ears were cocked to the side, and she almost looked like she was raising an eyebrow at the utter lack of grace that Sophie had exhibited pushing herself up. She had practically tumbled out of bed entirely!

Sophie stuck a hand out to swat at the beeping alarm clock on her nightstand, blinking blearily. It had been yet another long night of struggling to sleep, and now that she had heard the alarm, she knew that she would never get back to sleep, no matter how exhausted she was. The clock's LED face was shining exactly 6:03 AM as she stared at it, and she sighed. As much as the appeal of bed was begging her to get back under the covers, she knew that it would be for the best if she got up and out of bed. She swung her feet over the edge and patted Bella on the head.
"Well, Bells, what do you say we go hiking?"

Just the word "go" had led to the pup's ears to perk up even more, and she sat up with a doggy grin, mouth agape and tongue lolling out the side as she waited for her owner to actually get up and get moving. After all, Sophie wasn't always the most motivated person. 27 years old, still single, and working as a freelance article writer for her local newspaper, Sophie wasn't what most people would call conventionally all together, especially at her age. However, she also knew that she wasn't driven to follow the main path through life. Her path may be unconventional, but she was still fond of where life was taking her. Sure, most of her girlfriends were off getting married, buying houses, and settling down to have kids, but she still had years to think about that—she was more interested in enjoying life. Besides, no one she met ever seemed to enjoy her lackadaisical attitude, so why bother settling down if they aren't going to appreciate her in the first place?

Within an hour, bellies were full, bags were packed, and Sophie was taking Bella into the passenger seat, buckling her harness in, and then hopping into the driver's seat. With the music on and nursing another coffee the whole way there, they made their way out of town and up toward the local state park. The park itself was just outside of town, thankfully, but felt so isolated where it was. It was up at the edge of the foothills, and the park itself was miles and miles of winding trails through a massive forest. It was usually a pretty popular hiking destination, but something about 6 AM on a Wednesday morning seemed to clear it out well. After all, it was work time for most of the population. Sophie smiled to herself. She knew that she was lucky to have an unconventional schedule that meant that she had no competition when it came to doing things. Errands to run? She could run them during business hours while most people were at work or school. Is it an opening day for a popular movie? She could get the matinee showing and be one of maybe ten people in the theater. It certainly had its perks to be out and about during those business hours, and she could not deny the value.

Just as quickly as Sophie and Bella had hopped into the car, they hopped out and stood at the trailhead. "What do you think, Bells?" she asked, glancing down. Bella was standing next to her, perfectly obediently. The German shepherd looked up at her and met her gaze for a moment, tail swishing lazily behind her back. *Of course, you didn't answer,* Sophie found herself telling herself, mentally rolling her eyes. What did she expect? If she wanted a chatty hiking buddy, she would have had to wait for the weekend to go with a friend or something.

Rather than bothering to waste the mental energy on thinking about that, she looked up at the trail instead. The forest was a vibrant green—almost too green to be real, and yet there it was right in front of her. It was beautiful as it stretched out and up the hillside. The trees grew together so densely that the entire forest was deeply shaded. Very little of the sunlight actually managed to filter through the verdant foliage, but Sophie preferred it that way, anyway. She was pale and had a tendency to burn, so the added protection of the shade was a net positive for her.

Off they began, walking through the trail. As soon as they rounded the first bend, it was like they had been transported to a whole new world. Without a clear line of sight to the parking lot that she had left her car in, it was like they were really engulfed in the wilderness. The trees grew so thickly that any sounds of people were drowned out. All she could hear above and around them were the sounds of hundreds of birds chirping away that fine morning.

She knew that they were flitting about—they were all over the place. Occasionally, the sound of rustling feathers would cut through the melodies of their songs, and the quick blur of a bird darting across their path would grace their view. It was utterly peaceful as they walked. The trail, though somewhat rough and steep at times, wasn't too difficult to get through, and she could see that Bella was having a great time. The pup was happily walking alongside her, tail wagging and without so much as pulling.

As they walked, Sophie found herself getting lost in her mind. She watched the trail in front of her, simply letting her mind wander from place to place. It was easy to let herself get lost in thought as she walked. It was peaceful to simply allow her thoughts to drift endlessly. The more that she did so, the more she felt like she was calm. Being in nature had that effect for her—the more that she wandered about inside of it, the more at ease she felt like she was. The ground underfoot felt somewhat soft, she realized as she continued along.

Soon, Bella and Sophie found themselves at a cross-section. She looked to the left and to the right. Neither trail was marked, and she was unsure which was the right way. "You know," she murmured to herself thoughtfully, running a hand through her hair, "I'm pretty sure that Emma from work told me that if we took a right at the fork, we'd end up heading right back to the parking lot. She said it was a loop or something." She looked left, and then right once more, and then set down on the path. "It's only a mile or so back to the car... So we should be there in the next twenty minutes?"

This path was markedly denser than the one that they had been walking down—it was much more crowded with trees, and the further they walked, the thinner the trail itself seemed to get. She looked around, seeing that even the trees seemed to change—though before, they had been mostly around trees with soft leaves, it seemed like the further they went, the more the trees shifted into being more pine instead. They were beautiful, and the scent of sap and soft earth filled the air, but Sophie found herself worrying a bit.

"It's probably nothing, right?" she told herself, shaking off that doubt. She didn't want to give up on that gorgeous trail just because of that nagging feeling that they were going the wrong way. Bella simply wagged her tail in return, perfectly content to be walking about in the forest.

To help herself pass the time as they walked, Sophie turned her attention to her breathing. It was ragged as their path slowly became much more uphill suddenly. Strange, she thought to herself—why would it go uphill when they were supposed to be heading back to the parking lot?

Then, it dawned on her: They weren't heading to the parking lot at all. They were going deeper into the woods. Sophie stopped in her tracks, arms hanging limply at her sides, and she looked at Bella in disbelief. "Bells!" she announced incredulously. "What happened to that master sniffer of yours?!" She rubbed at Bella's head and groaned, and the German shepherd licked her hand as if trying to make her feel better about the situation. She looked around herself and realized that she had no idea where they were, and she had turned several times since getting to that point. She had no idea how they were going to get back to the car.

Pulling out her phone revealed no signal, so using GPS wasn't exactly an option. She also didn't have a printout of the map of the area, nor would that have helped since she had no clue where she was at that point in time. She looked around and sighed. It was just her luck to end up lost. What if she was lost forever? What if a bear found her? Or worse, a serial killer? The thoughts raced through her head, and she felt herself break out in a cold sweat, goosebumps breaking out across her arms as the hair on the back of her neck stood on edge. Suddenly, that peaceful getaway in the mountains was anything but.

"Get a grip!" she told herself firmly, forcing herself to take a deep breath. "There are no bears here, and they're certainly aren't any serial killers," she told herself feebly as if to convince herself through sheer willpower. It didn't work. She breathed deeply, in and out, and looked around the area. If they had been hiking up, going deeper and deeper into the park, then the logical answer was to head back down toward the foot of the hill, right?

Tightening her grip around Bella's leash, Sophie took in a deep breath and turned around. "No big deal," she told herself. "Just gotta backtrack!" And so, she set off, heading back down the mountain. At the very least, it was easy to tell when she was going down based on the slope.

Before long, however, she felt like she was even more lost than before. But, this time, she heard something other than the sounds of the birds or the wind rustling the leaves. It was the sound of gently bubbling water over rocks, not far from where they were. It sounded incredibly close. What a relief, she told herself as she looked for the source. She remembered that there was a creek not too far from where they had parked—perhaps this source of water would lead to it. She moved her way through the woods carefully, trudging through the path with determination. She wasn't willing to allow the fear at the moment to keep her from getting back down the mountain, and off she went, heading toward the sound.

It didn't take long before the trees separated to give way to a beautiful little creek. It wasn't much—maybe three feet across and just a few inches deep, but it was a welcome sight after so much wandering about aimlessly. Bella barked once and wagged her tail, looking up at Sophie with pleading eyes. She wanted to splash in the water a bit, and quite frankly, Sophie couldn't blame her. She wanted to do the same thing. Her feet were starting to get sore too. She slid her shoes off, quickly discarding them and her socks to the side, and took a step into the cool water.

The water was chilly at first, and she gasped at the sudden shift of temperature before breaking out into a big grin. Bella pounced into the water too, happily splashing about with her large paws. Her tail wagged furiously, sending droplets of water splattering everywhere. The rocks in the water were smooth, worn down over the years of water running over them. They were gentle under her feet, and she was thankful for that. She was thankful for a whole lot at the moment. Turning around to look around her, she saw that there was so much more to see. She could see that the

trees, though verdant and green, were also standing tall. Their branches were intertwined together as they stretched together, blocking out the sun. Occasionally, she could see the quick glimpse of beautiful, crystal-clear sky shining behind the leaves, only for it to fade away behind another leaf.
It was beautiful, and at that moment, as the cool water gently caressed her toes and lapped up against her ankles, Sophie was at peace. Suddenly, her troubles melted away. She was there, in that moment, privy to a beautiful scene of trees that were thriving, with a clean creek of water. She was there with her dog, loving the moment, and she found herself so happy to be there in the moment. Yes, it had been a struggle to get there, and yes, it wasn't where she was heading to originally, it was still worth it in the end.

She smiled down at Bella and patted her on the head, and Bella returned the gesture with a puppy grin. They spent just one more moment lingering there, taking in the peaceful moment. The birds continued to sing. The trees continued to rustle together, creating a beautiful percussion behind the sounds of the trees.

Bella barked loudly and pounced at something in the water.

And just as suddenly as the moment of peace came, it was gone.

Sophie turned her attention just in time to see Bella chasing after a frog that was swimming as quickly as it could downstream. "Bella!!" she cried out with a grin in faux exasperation. "Leave it!" Laughing, she tugged at the leash to guide Bella out of the water. She dried off her feet with a spare towel she kept in her hiking pack and slid her socks and shoes back on. They followed the creek, and sure enough, it brought them right back to the parking lot that they had been in.
Disaster averted!

When they were settled into the car, Sophie let herself flop against the back of the seat and sigh. Though she was mentally at ease and feeling recharged, her entire body, every fiber of her being was exhausted and ready for a nice, long nap as soon as they got home. She was ready to cash in on that extra sleep that she had been wanting but putting off, and by the looks of Bella, who quickly curled up, somehow not falling off of the seat, the sentiment was shared.

# Story 2: Airport Antics

*It's vacation time! Sophie is ready to head out to the airport to travel to Greece with her good friend, Cara. But, she has to get there in time! Sophie's got to move quickly if she wants to make it to the airport and onto her flight on time to enjoy the vacation of her dreams, but everything seems to be working against her. Will she make it to the terminal on time?*

It was a surprisingly drizzly day on that fine morning. The sky was overcast, swollen with the threat of rain ahead of what would be a busy day. The sun was completely obscured, and the darkened sky sort of lingered over everything. It was definitely not the bright, cheery day that it should have been, and it almost made everything seem a bit less exciting than she felt like it should have been. She was thrilled—in less than six hours, she would be on a plane headed to Greece—but she had to get there first, and it was looking like it would be a long day full of more than she expected.

Sophie sipped at her coffee as she looked out the window over her lawn. It was quite flat back there, with the occasional hole dug out by Bella, and without her trusty German shepherd running about, it felt almost empty out there. But, Bella had been left with Sophie's mother the night prior so she'd be supervised during the vacation. After all, Sophie had a feeling that if she had left the pup to her own devices all alone for a week, she would be returning to utter destruction throughout the entire house, and that was not something that she was really interested in dealing with at that point in time. Who had time to clean up all of the torn-up carpets that a bored dog would inevitably leave behind?

As Sophie finished up her last sips of coffee, she turned her attention to the list written on the purple sticky note sitting on her table. Along the lines, in bubbly letters, she had written her to-do list for the day:

- *Pack carry-on bag*
- *Fill automatic plant waterers*
- *Make sure ALL lights are off*
- *Put passport in purse*
- *Lock door*

It wasn't much of a long list, but all week long, she had forgotten to pick up her passport from her drawer. She kept forgetting all about it, and she knew that if she made it to the airport without her passport, all bets would be off. She'd let herself down, she'd miss her plane, and both she and Cara would be miserable. She couldn't do that to everyone! She really wanted to make sure that the entire vacation was as easy as possible to get through so they could have as much fun as possible. That meant making sure that everything on her end was as impeccably managed as it could be, and she was determined not to leave anything up to chance or fate—she was determined to make sure that everything about her trip was perfect.
It didn't take long for her to knock everything off her list, and that was with even remembering to slip her passport right into place in her purse as well, next to her phone and her keys. Just as she finished making sure that her purse had everything she needed all packed up, she heard a knock at the door before it opened up.

"Hell-oooo!" she heard cried out in a falsetto downstairs, and she grinned in response.

"I'm upstairs!" Sophie called back from her room, not even bothering to poke her head downstairs to see her friend downstairs. She closed up her purse and looked to the clothes that she had lined up on her bed. She had picked out a cute flowy skirt that hit her knees, made of ruffled material in a bright, floral yellow print. It was definitely on the side of bohemian casual, especially when paired with her white off-the-shoulder top. It was comfortable, breezy, and plenty flexible so she wouldn't be miserable as she sat on the plane. After all, from their local airport to Athens was roughly 13 hours, not counting loading, getting off the plane, getting through customs, or anything else. It was going to be exhausting—but hopefully worth it to have that time to unwind.

Cara poked her head into the door to Sophie's room and looked shocked at what she saw. "Sophie!!" she gasped in shock. "Surely you're not going like that, honey. That will... Not do. Not at all!" With a sigh, Cara stormed right into the room, shaking her head and tutting her disapproval. "Honey, how many times have I told you? No white after Labor Day!" She rushed into the room, her blonde hair bouncing behind her in perfectly groomed waves. Cara was, as she liked to refer to it, as a "connoisseur of fashion," and her wardrobe definitely screamed as such. Even today, she was wearing a strappy dress in black with geometric circles patterning across it in white. Around her waist was a thin black belt, tucking in and showing off her curves. Over her shoulders was a small, black blazer with ¾ sleeves. On her feet were two heeled, strappy sandals in shiny black leather, and she was walking around with a strappy black purse draped over her shoulder.

"What's wrong with white after Labor Day?" Sophie replied with a frown, looking down at the clothing hanging from her body. "I thought I looked great!"

"Yeah, maybe if you're just heading down the street for your morning coffee before you get ready for the day... You're going to ATHENS, BABY!! Dress the part!" With a dramatic flair of her arm, Cara tossed the bag onto the bed and immediately stepped into Sophie's walk-in closet, looking around for something. She rummaged around in the clothing, muttering to herself under her breath. Sophie rubbed the back of her head sheepishly as she waited around, catching only some of the quiet tirade that Cara was going on about. "No... No.... Not enough... Wrong..."

"You know, I think it'll be fine..." Sophie told her with a quick peek into the closet, but just as she put her head into the door to see what was going on, she had a bunch of clothing thrown right at her.

"No, it will not be fine! Be *civilized,* Sophie!" Cara tutted again as she walked out, looking at her handiwork that was currently draped over Sophie's face and shoulder. Cara had chosen out a casual dress made of navy fabric with a deep V cut down the neckline. It was held up by two straps over the shoulder, and the fabric had a pretty print of pale pink flowers growing across it. The dress was narrow at the waist and flared out toward the hemline, creating a bouncy swing to it when it was worn. "Wear this one!"

Sophie shrugged her shoulders. It really didn't matter that much to her, but if Cara cared, she'd deal with it anyway. She tugged her shirt and skirt and then put on the dress. The fabric was smooth as it gently clung to her waist and hugged in all the right places, and she loved the feeling. The shoes, white pumps, were pulled on with it, and she picked up her purse. "Fine, fine, ready?" she asked Cara, who clapped her hands and squealed in delight before heading down the stairs head of Sophie.

"I'll be waiting outside!"

Sophie nodded and looked out the window. It was still overcast and looked like rain would start at any point. Briefly, she wondered if what she was wearing would even be enough in the moment. Could she really wear that in the rain? "Well... I'll be inside most of the day. It'll be fine." She pulled her purse over her shoulder and ran down the stairs and out the door, locking the door behind her. She was ready!

Cara was already sitting outside in her shiny silver Prius, car running to warm up. The first drops of rain were beginning to fall. As Sophie dragged out her luggage and loaded it up in the trunk, she looked at the time—they had an hour to get to the airport and another two to get through customs and boarded onto their flight. Thankfully, their airport was only precisely 52 minutes away, according to GPS, and they'd be able to get there rather quickly—they'd just have to hope that traffic agreed with them.

With both of them in the car and ready to go, Cara was off. The rain picked up quickly as they went down the road, and Cara groaned. "We're going to be late..." she mused as she ran a hand through her hair and looked over her shoulder as she switched lanes on the interstate, dipping into the carpool lane in hopes of shaving off even a few minutes. Glancing at the clock, Sophie could see her doing mental math as she tried to calculate just how quickly above traffic speed she'd have to go if she wanted to get to the airport with any time to spare.

The rain was harder now, thudding against the roof of the car like drums as they drove. In the distance, they could hear a summer thunderstorm rumbling away, and occasionally, the sky, far from them, would flash for a moment. "What a day for a storm!" Sophie said as she looked out the window listlessly, chin resting on her hand and her other hand resting on her lap. She watched the rain drifting off the window absently as traffic slowed to a crawl. As the rain picked up, driving conditions continued to drop, and soon, it felt like it would be too dangerous to keep going at that rate. They had to slow down, or they would have been in an accident.

But then traffic fell to a standstill. Cara slammed her hand against the car's steering wheel. "We're going to be late!" she growled under her breath, leaning over to try to peer ahead of the car in front of her. Traffic was barely moving at all, and her GPS was reporting that there had been an accident not too far from where they were at that moment. "What are we going to do?" she lamented, glancing over at Sophie.

"Well…" Sophie began, deliberating over her words as she looked over at her friend. Cara looked incredibly stressed out at the moment—her eyes were wide, and her lips were tense. "We'll be okay. I'm sure they'll be able to clear the accident quickly, and we'll be on our way in no time."

"I hope you're right," Cara sighed as she slumped against her seat, letting her hands fall off the steering wheel. She turned up the music a bit, and gentle music played in the background, not really exciting enough to catch their attention, but it also made the car's silence just a bit more tolerable as the rain continued to pound, harder still this time.

"I am," Sophie said with a resolute nod, though the waver in her voice betrayed her nervousness. Still, she had to be strong—she had to be convincing enough for the both of them. Of course, she was not quite convinced anyhow—it was hard for her to believe that they would make it on time with the slowdown, especially when they heard the sirens approaching, and the ambulance and fire truck made their way past them to presumably where the accident had occurred. They could see the flashing lights ahead, so it must have been incredibly close to where they were. Had they left a few minutes earlier, they probably would have been caught in it. At the very least, she told herself, they were safe. They hadn't been hurt, and if the worst thing that happened to them was that they missed their flight and had to book the next one, then their days were still going better than the people who had been in that accident. Their inconvenience was better than the pain that would be felt in an accident.

Traffic slowly began to move, crawling through just one lane that they were able to merge into slowly. They crept along until they finally passed the wreckage. A red SUV's front was crumpled in, and the other car, a small silver sedan, was slammed into the concrete divider to the left of the freeway. EMTs were tending to people who were all sitting up, looking shaken up but ultimately, okay as they passed.

"Wow…" Cara breathed out as she glanced at the accident. She was uncharacteristically at a loss for words as she looked at the scene. It looked awful. Both cars were almost certainly a total loss.

"They're lucky…" Sophie whispered as she eyed the carnage. Aside from being shaken up, it looked like everyone was doing okay, especially since both ambulances that had passed them earlier were still there, doors open, with the paramedics doing rounds between the people. Both Sophie and Cara fell silent, radio still gently playing the music and rain still thundering on the roof.

The rest of the drive to the airport happened in relative silence with just the melodies coming from the speakers and the cadence of the rain rapping at the roof. Cara was driving notably more carefully as they made their way there, and though they were running a few minutes late, that scene seemed to give her pause when it came to rushing through the rain. It certainly was not the weather to be trying to speed across the street.

Before long, they made it to the airport and got parked. They were still two and a half hours before their flight would leave—giving them plenty of time to get through customs. They dragged along their luggage behind them as they walked through the rain, with Cara holding an umbrella precariously in one hand while trying to pull two-wheeled luggage containers behind her.

Entering the airport was the easy part. What came next, the constant waiting, was the worst of it. They had to wait in line to check-in, causing Cara to tap absently at the handle to her black luggage. Sophie tugged at a strand of hair, curling it around her hair as she people watched. There were all sorts of people out and about, and they were all going in a different direction. Some were dressed for sheer comfort, wearing sweats and a t-shirt while others were dressed for business, prim, and proper. It was interesting to see all of the different people going in, as well as seeing the people of all walks of life going out as well. Some of them were clearly foreigners, rubbing heads and speaking in different languages as they looked around in confusion and attempted to piece together English sentences just enough to get a cab while others were eagerly following their tour guides who seemed ready to take them to wherever they were planning to head first. There were some groups of young adults as well—likely college students heading out for spring vacation.

The people-watching was always Sophie's favorite part of being at an airport, and it helped her to pass the time. She'd imagine all of the different situations behind the different people. She'd start imagining whole lives for these people. She'd think about the people's vacation plans as they came into town. She imagined that they'd go to all the famous tourist sites in town—they'd go and see the restaurants and the beach as well. She assumed that they'd all have a grand time, looking over the city in their hotel rooms, or that they'd be spending time at a rental home.

Before long, she felt Cara tapping her back to the real world, snapping her out of her reverie. "Ready?" she asked Sophie, who blinked in surprise. She hadn't realized that she had been spending so much of her time just thinking about other things, and she nodded her head, pulling out her passport and letting the attendant see it.

Checking in and handing in the luggage was simple—then it was time to wait for boarding. They went through the security gates and stood in line at the boarding gate for their plane. The line was already quite long, and they still had another 30 minutes to boarding.

"Are you ready?" Sophie asked Cara as she fiddled with her purse strap, grinning at her friend.

"Oh, am I!" Cara echoed with a thumbs up. "I'm so ready!"

"Same! Greece, here we come!" Sophie was thrilled—she was so ready to go through the different sights they had to see. She wanted to see the ruins of Acropolis and get to eat all of the god food. She was thrilled about the beach that they'd get to go visit, and being able to go through it all on their own was something that was thrilling to her—she was so ready to be able to go through it all. Her dream as a child had always been to go to Greece, and she was finally living that chance.

Before long, the line to board was moving, and they were in their seats. They had first-class seats, at Cara's insistence. Once they were on the plane, they realized that it was absolutely worth it as well—the seats were massively luxurious, comfortable, and absolutely worth every cent that Cara had so generously paid.

The seatbelt light came on, and the voice of the flight attendant came on the overhead, informing everyone of the rules, regulations, and what to expect, and before they knew it, they were up in the air, high above the world beneath them and heading toward the open ocean.

Cara and Sophie toasted to each other with the complimentary glass of wine that they were each given. "To safe travels!" they said as their glasses clinked together. They both sipped and laughed at each other. It was going to be a long flight—but at least it was a flight in luxury!

# Story 3: Acropolis

*Sophie and Cara have made it to Greece on their vacation, and after their resting day to catch up on all the missed sleep, they are ready to get going and finally start exploring. This day is Sophie's turn to choose what they do for the day, and she has chosen to explore the Acropolis of Athens, getting a glimpse at the past first hand.*

Sophie yawned as she rolled out of bed. She was in one room of the two-room suite that Cara had insisted upon for their vacation, and so far, she loved every moment of the luxury. The flooring was a soft, plush carpet that squished so comfortably underneath her feet, almost just as invitingly as the bed had gently squished underneath her as well. The suite was overlooking the gulf to the south of Athens, and her window gave her a beautiful, breathtaking view of the bright, clear water. Across the sea, she could see land gently rolling toward the horizon as well, and there were tiny, bright sails lit up all around the water. It was a wonderful start to the morning; she told herself as she looked out at the view.

She watched for another few minutes before taking a shower in a wonderful stall, carefully tiled with beautiful marble. Getting ready in luxury was a breeze, and she was utterly relaxed as she washed the last of the soap through her hair. She was up early—her night-owl nature was really helping her out during the travels—jetlag meant that she was perfectly content being up in the daylight hours since she already normally was awake at that time, relative to her home, anyway.

Stepping out, she was greeted by a plush robe that she wrapped herself in to dry off, and she brewed a coffee using the small machine provided in her hotel room. The wondrous scent of coffee filled the air, waking her up more as it brewed. It smelled roasted and comforting—a bit of familiarity in her travels abroad, and she was thrilled to have that opportunity afforded to her in the first place. She was thrilled that her time was going to be spent enjoying the moment and actually having some peace and quiet to herself for a while. It was nice being able to take her time without waking up and immediately rushing to her computer to look over everything. It was nice being able to simply go throughout her day without being so overly concerned with everything that she was doing at any given point in time. It was enjoyable being able to go through her morning routine in leisure at her own speed.

By the time that she had finished up her coffee, she noticed that Cara had finished getting herself ready as well. She stepped out of her own room in a nice, airy blue dress that gently clung to her waist, and half of her hair tied up and back, out of her face. She wore tan strapped sandals that somehow managed to be the perfect blend of functional and attractive at the same time, and her black sunglasses were carefully perched atop her head. Her makeup was impeccably done, perfectly put on while still somehow managing to capture that natural look to it as well. She looked great. Even on vacation and even when their itinerary for the day involved walking, she still managed to look wonderful. It was a wonder she was still single, Sophie marveled as she looked on toward her friend. "You're not ready yet?" Cara asked, raising a perfectly sculpted eyebrow up in surprise.

Sophie grinned back. "I'm enjoying taking my time for a change! I'll be ready to go in a few minutes." All she really had left to do was get dressed, and she'd be good to go, too. She wasn't nearly as particular about her looks as Cara tended to be. So, while Cara sipped at her own coffee on the balcony overlooking the gulf, Sophie got ready to go. She tossed on some khaki high-waisted shorts that came just above her knees and a white chiffon top, tucked into the waistband. She was comfortable, yet functional as she also tied on her walking shoes and picked up the wide-brimmed hat that she placed atop her head. She walked out to meet Cara, waving for her to follow.

Cara stood up and put away her cup. "That looks quaint," she acknowledged with a smile.

"Thanks," Sophie said, choosing to take the comment as a compliment rather than bothering to say a word about it. She grinned and bounced as they walked down the hall together. She was brimming with excitement—heading to visit Acropolis had been one of her lifelong dreams that she had for herself, and she was finally living it! She was so happy to do so, and even though she knew that it would be crowded and nothing like it once was, there was something thrilling about going somewhere that was built nearly 2500 years ago. Though it was beginning to crumble, it was a real testament to the power of humanity, even that long ago.

Sophie was incredibly impressed with what she had seen in the books—every time she ever looked at the pictures of the ruins, it was gorgeous—tall, crumbling, and flawed, but that made it so much more awe-inspiring to view. It was made before humanity had levels and laser pointers to help them measure our angles just right. They built them before people had machines to help lift these massive behemoths of stone and marble. They were so immaculately and impeccably carved for people that only had their hands and small hand tools to work with, and she couldn't help but be fascinated with them. She loved being able to explore them, to learn about the world around her, and to learn how to better begin to relate to how people used to live.

Cara might not enjoy exploring around as much as the shopping and the sightseeing, but for Sophie, being able to see just how humanity used to live was so worth every moment of travel that came with it. She didn't particularly enjoy flying, but getting to go around all of the different historical sites gave her a great perspective over everything and everyone involved.

Stepping outside of the hotel had them immediately hit with warm, humid air that smelled of the beach and of promise for a day of fantastic exploration and sightseeing. It smelled of excitement and of being able to meet those lifelong goals once and for all, and Sophie was entirely ready to throw herself into it all. Even Cara, who was typically uninterested in such events and fun, had a smile on her face as they walked out. Even though Cara had a tendency to be very set in her ways, she had a huge soft spot for making sure that her dear friend was happy, and this day was no exception to that matter. She was willing to put on a happy face to go through everything with her friend if it meant seeing Sophie's dream come true.

"Did you know that Acropolis is referred to as the crowning jewel of Greece, *and* it is the birthplace of democracy?" Sophie practically squealed as she walked through the path. "It's such an important site! AND, even though it was damaged, it is still there for us to see now."

"Really?" Cara asked in return. It was hard not to feel excited when she watched Sophie bubbling over the words that were being said. She grinned back at her friend. It was always pleasant to see just how worked up Sophie would get when she was talking about something she loved. "What happened to it anyway?"

"What, with the damage?"

"Yeah. It's pretty broken down now, isn't it?" Cara replied as they made their way to the site.

"It is! So back during the Morean War, the war between the Turkish and Venice, Acropolis held the gunpowder that they would use. But, during a battle in 1687, the Parthenon, the main building that everyone thinks about when they're thinking of the Acropolis, was hit with a cannonball. When that happened, it kind of all blew up! And now, it has that broken down look that it had. But, there's more to Acropolis than just the Parthenon, too. It was a great big citadel built atop a big hill. It was called acropolis because it is so high—did you know that acro means extreme or high, while polis means city? It's high up in the city, and the one in Athens is the most popular." Sophie was bouncing along with every step as she talked away. She knew her Greek history and mythology and was not afraid to show it off.

"Wow, that's... A lot of a lot!" Cara said, patting Sophie on the shoulder. "But I'm really excited to go see everything. It should look great."

"Me too!" Sophie squealed.

It didn't take them long to arrive at the location where their tour bus would pick them up, and they waited among the small crowd of people, happily chatting. The Acropolis was in the center of the city, overlooking everything around it. It had once been the home of some of the most important parts of the city, dedicated to Athena, the patron of the city, and it was an incredibly popular tourist site year-round. This meant two things: One, that they would have to be around lots of people, but two, that they would be able to get to the site without having to walk all across Athens. The bus was filled up, and before they knew it, they were being addressed by the tour guide. He was a tall, thin young man with beautiful olive skin. His hair was trimmed at the sides and slicked back, and his face was impeccably sculpted. His eyes were kind as he talked to them, and he appeared to be genuinely passionate about his heritage as he spoke to them.

"Ooh, look at the eye candy," Cara said, nudging Sophie on the bus with a sly smile on her face and giggling.

Sophie looked at her with a scandalized expression. "Shh!!" she shushed her friend, giggling quietly as well. Cara was not wrong—he was a very handsome man, and even better, he was telling them all about everything that they would be learning about on the tour. But, what he had to say was mostly just the same details that Sophie had parroted about the entire walk to the stop. He mentioned the history and what they could expect, as well as some rules that they would all have to follow to ensure that everything went smoothly.

"The hill was picked out," he said through his Greek accent, "Primarily because of the fact that it sat so high up. It was the area where the locals settled down to live, and the rock at the top was deemed where the ruler would live. It was not until later that it gained recognition as being associated with the goddess Athena, and it was not until the 8th century. Athena gained her own temple on the northeastern side of the hill." He looked around the tour bus, seeing that most of the people were only mildly interested at best. "But, the Parthenon is the most popular of all. It has withstood over the centuries, surviving fire, earthquakes, wars, and even explosions while still standing. It was once a powerful symbol of religion and culture of Athens, and today, it still endures, showing the true perseverance of the Greek people and of the Athenians themselves."

Sophie grinned at the man, glad to hear someone else sharing her passion for the history of such a magnificent building, but she was not interested in approaching him, even with Cara's incessant nudging. Yes, he was good looking, but she didn't really want to go through the hassle of an international fling, even if it were just a temporary ordeal. That didn't sound particularly appealing to her, even if they both shared a certain appreciation for the Greek culture.

Before long, they had arrived. The bus slowly squealed to a stop, and they all unloaded, one by one, to get off the bus. Then, Sophie got her first glance of it all. They were down toward the bottom of the rocky wall that built up the city. They were in for plenty of walking, but still, the sight was breathtaking. Against the blue sky, she could see the buildings, all aligned. The Parthenon's stark white walls and pillars clashed against the sky, and she could see that the line was already building up.

"This," the tour guide called out, pointing to the entrance to the area, "is the path to the center of it all. It is here that you will be able to follow the path that thousands of years ago, the ancient people of Athens walked when they entered this sacred area. This is the road to the Parthenon, to the altar of Athena, and more. As you enter, remember to remain respectful. This area is ancient—it deserves the respect that you would have in any ancient relic. It is a part of my people's history, and if you cannot honor the rules. Where you are standing right now is the gate to the Acropolis, the Propylaia. It was here that people were able to enter, and in order to pass through, in the time when this sanctuary was dedicated to the great Athena, only certain people were allowed to enter. You must take nothing, and you must leave nothing but your footsteps behind in this great, sacred place. Now, are you ready?"

The group of people in the tour all gave a weak cheer and chuckle, and off they went into the site. It was beautiful, Sophie marveled as they finally took their first steps in. The stones were surprisingly lightly colored underneath her feet, and she looked up at the eight massive pillars supporting the beam that undoubtedly once made up the building's roof in front of her. Sophie was practically bouncing in excitement as they stood outside under the sun—she was thrilled to see everything in front of her, and she was ready to dive in. Of course, the tour had different plans.

As they toured the structures, they slowly traveled from ruin to ruin. Their tour guide was happy to explain to them everything that they would be doing and why he loved each and every building. He was quick to provide information about every single building.

The first stop was the Erechtheion, a temple located in the northern part of the Acropolis. As Sophie gazed upon the building's crumbling walls and the strange sculptures of women on one end, she listened closely. "The Porch of the Maidens," her tour guide begun, "Was added there to hide the beam that supports the southwest corner of the building. Due to budgeting constraints after the beginning of the Peloponnesian War, the building's size was cut, and as such, they had to find a way to disguise the pillar. Thus, the caryatids were built to create something beautiful to view and look at them!" All six women stood there, balancing the roof of the building on their heads, and yet, each and every single one looked graceful.

Before long, they had moved on to the Temple of Athena Nike. The massive temple stood tall on the stretch of land. It was built to provide a place to honor Athena Nike, the goddess of victory. It was a beautiful temple, complete with a beautiful carving of Athena herself trying to adjust the strap of a sandal.

They made it through several of the buildings, but the last one that they approached was the one that Sophie had been looking forward to the most: The Parthenon. "The Parthenon was created," the tour guide begun, "Primarily to provide people with a place to gather. It was the hubbub for all religious life in Athens, and the temple itself, built by Pericles, was believed to represent the power, lavish culture, and wealth that Athens enjoyed during the time. Today, it has remained one of the largest and most recognizable buildings that exist. It was eventually overtaken by the Byzantines after their conquering of Greece and was turned into a church. Then, again, it was converted when another empire, the Ottomans, took over Athens. It was converted then into a mosque. However, upon the war in 1687, the building was detonated when a cannonball from the Christian Holy League, attempting to reclaim their land, hit the ammunition depot and caused a detonation."

"Oh, so you were right!" Cara said with a grin.

"Shh!" Sophie hushed her as she marveled at the building. Though in ruins now, it was still magnificent to look on to. It was huge—a massive testament to human ability and skill, and something about it was absolutely amazing to behold. Her heart was happy—she had finally managed to check another item off her bucket list.

# Story 4: Rainy Day Blues

One of the worst parts about living in the Pacific Northwest, Sophie had to admit, was the rain. Yes, it had its place. Yes, it was beautiful when she was inside, looking out at the vibrant green of the leaves and grass all around her. Yes, she felt like the luckiest woman out there to be able to live in such a beautiful, diverse, and welcoming area. But, she couldn't stand when the rain never relented.

On days when it rained, Sophie felt stuck. She felt like he had no choice but to stay indoors, and sometimes, she was simply restless. Sometimes, she just wanted to get outside and enjoy the day. Sometimes, she wanted to work on exercising her weary bones and body, and she wanted to find somewhere nice to do so. Of course, when it's constantly drizzling rain, it is hard to find somewhere comfortable to go jogging or to go hiking outdoors, and that constraint could be frustrating.

Sophie sighed as she sipped into her mug of tea. It was the cusp of autumn, and she could see it in the faintly yellowish tinge to the trees outside. It was on the slight chill that she felt in the air whenever she stepped outside, or the scent of leaves starting to die on the air. It was in the shortening of days and the lengthening of darkened mornings. It was in the fact that pumpkin spice was suddenly everywhere, even if it didn't always belong. It was something that brought the smell of cinnamon and spice or apple pies, but she couldn't help but sigh to herself. She loved summer. It was the short reprieve from the constant rain and drizzle that was all she could get in the area most of the year. It was the time when she got to really enjoy the weather and the climate, from kayaking on the lake to be able to hike through the mountains.

Next to her, Bella was curled up, fast asleep. She had done her business like normal, but rather than taking advantage of the time to go outside and play, she seemed more interested in sleeping more than anything else. Maybe the cold was getting to her too, Sophie mused as she took another sip of her tea before looking outside. Despite the ample watering, the grass on her back lawn was already starting to yellow, and there was not really anything that she could do about it but shrug and move on. It wouldn't be worth the hassle of trying to fight off the inevitable shift to winter.

With a sigh, Sophie finished up her tea and put the mug away. She knew that she had to work, but for some reason, she just couldn't bring herself to do so. She wanted to sit and enjoy the day, but to enjoy the day, she wanted sunlight and warmth. Unfortunately, the sky said it had vastly different plans, judging by the grey clouds, pregnant with rain, and ready to spill at a moment's notice. That meant that her original plan of walking through a local park known for its immaculate landscaping was out. She had been looking forward to looking at the different plants that were thriving in her area—she was hoping to figure out what she would plant in her own garden as she was pretty sick of looking at all of the grass all the time.

"I guess I could watch a movie..." she murmured under her breath as she stood up to wash her mug. But, a movie didn't sound very fun at all. She wasn't really interested in sitting around and watching what other people were doing. She was much more interested in finding a way to get moving. Even as she scrolled through the recent new additions on her streaming app on her phone, nothing stood out to her. She had seen most of the mainstream movies, and it didn't look like there was anything that was actually compelling or interesting to her in the theaters at that point in time either, so a movie was out, and honestly, she didn't mind at all.

Reading a book was usually her second pick, but she was feeling somewhat burnt out over reading after spending extra time reading over and editing some books on the side that she normally would not have been responsible for. She chose not to bother with reading at all, feeling that her eyes and mind needed a bit of a reprieve from written words for a while. After all, when you live and breathe writing at all times, you are bound to get bored.

Playing video games was out too—she had never really been one to play video games, and the idea of sitting around to do so was something that she had very little interest in, all things considered. She didn't even own a video game console in her home, nor did she care to do so.

She sighed again as she settled down into a cozy recliner in her living room, tucking her legs up and wrapping her arms around them. She was totally lost at what she should do with herself, and no amount of thinking seemed to be enough for her.

Pulling out her phone, she shot a quick text to several of her friends, but none of them seemed like they wanted to get together. With every rejection and every failed lead on something to do, Sophie sank deeper into her chair. It wasn't fun feeling like no one wanted to be around her, and in that moment, she was getting serious abandoned vibes and didn't know what she could do to make it better. She was stuck—she felt like she had no choice in the matter but to find something to do on her own since not even Bella seemed like she wanted to do anything.

Without a plan in mind, Sophie got up, went upstairs, and got dressed for the day. She was wearing the perfect transition to fall look for a dreary, drizzly, chilly day. Her top was a thin ombre sweater, starting with black around the hemline and sleeves and slowly fading into a purple, and finally, into a light grey. Throughout the sweater, there were other colors speckled into it as well. Her pants were a pair of dark blue skinny jeans, and on her feet were her trusty

boots that she rarely ever went without in the winter and
fall months—they were grey and up to her mid-calf.

Pulling her hair back and out of her face, Sophie picked up
her phone, her keys, and her purse, and off she went. She
sat in her car and turned it on, not quite sure where she'd
end up. She wasn't sure if she'd end up at a new restaurant
or anything else, but she had an idea: She had seen an idea
for exploring the town on social media not too long. All she
had to do was roll a dice a handful of times so she could
figure out where she would go.

The rule of the game was that if she got a 1 or a 2 when she
rolled, she would turn left at an intersection, if legal. If she
rolled a 3 or 4, she would go straight, if legal, and if she
rolled a 5 or 6, she would turn to the right. She was to do
this for 10 different intersections, with three intersections
passing any given direction before using the next roll. It was
something that was supposed to be a fun date night idea for
couples who are not really familiar with their area, but
Sophie figured the universe would allow her to make an
exception here—she didn't need anyone else to go with her
at all.

So, she rolled the app on her phone six times, and she wrote
down the following on her sticky note with her directions:

- *Left*
- *Straight*
- *Right*
- *Right*
- *Left*
- *Straight*

With that list in mind, it was time for her to explore. She
turned on her car and began heading out from her home,
thinking that every three intersections, she would follow the

instructions given to her by the dice. Risky? Sure, but she thought it would be worth it.

Sophie quickly ducked into her car, covering up from the rain, and turned on the engine. Her sticky note of directions was stuck to the dash, and she was ready to go. She got to the exit of her subdivision, and the instructions began. She turned left and headed down the road. It was quietly forested where she was—she lived just north of the main part of town, barely outside of city limits. She drove down the road for a while, counting the intersections as they passed. One... Two... Three... And then she had to turn left at the next intersection.

Sophie drove past a gas station, and a few bus stops shaded by trees as she drove down the dreary road. There were some dead-end streets that she passed that she chose not to count as intersections just due to the fact that she'd never get anywhere, and soon, she had crossed a little wooded creek. One... Two... And then there was a long stretch of road with nothing exiting off from it. It was nothing but trees all around, and while it was gorgeous, there would be no hiking through the mud for her. She finally made it to the third intersection, and her instructions sent her straight, so off she went.

This road found her on the ramp to get onto the freeway, and she shrugged. May as well see where it took her. She cruised along the freeway, counting the exits she passed. It eventually got to a place where there were four different split-offs, and a quick glance at her paper told her that she had to turn right, so she took the rightmost lane and found herself traveling south down the freeway. She passed the first three exits and then found herself taking a right turn off the road. A glance at her instructions told her she had to turn left and then go straight.

Following those instructions, she found herself on the southernmost outskirts of town—there wasn't very much out here but residential buildings and the occasional school or small building. It was cozy out there, and Sophie was actually quite unfamiliar with the area. She had never really had a reason to go through the area because she had never felt the need to. There really was nothing there if you didn't live there.

But, upon taking that final turn, she found herself in a parking lot. The parking lot led right into a cute little shopping strip. There was a small convenience store on one end, a post office in the center, and then a small local café on the other end. It was just the three buildings with maybe ten parking spots throughout the whole parking lot, and at the moment, four of them were filled up. She parked there and looked at the area that she had ended up in.

The café itself was called Coffee Maybe, and it was tucked underneath a big oak tree that was growing on the left, with a few small tables and chairs for people to enjoy their drink outdoors. Of course, this particular day did not lend itself to sitting outdoors, but it was nice that the option was there. She put her car in park and turned the engine off, then looked around. It was a nice enough area, that was for sure. The entire little strip of the building was impeccably maintained, nice and clean, and there was a cute little flower bed between the parking lot and the sidewalk leading up to the doors for each shop.

Sophie stepped outside, pulling her raincoat closer, and hustled all four steps to the entrance. She was ready to be away from the chilly rain, that was for sure. She walked right inside and dried her boots on the rug at the entry, and looked around.

The inside was surprisingly even cuter than outside. Along one wall, there were several coffee tables with reclining chairs, and on the left were walls of shelving, all filled up with board games and books for people to borrow if they chose to do so. The floor was a nice grey tile that was easily cleaned, and the entire place was dimly lit, but not in a bad way. It was very reminiscent of the time spent playing games in the late night at home at a sleepover as a kid, and she loved it. It looked like the perfect hangout place for the local high schoolers or college students, and though she was there alone, she felt herself wishing that she had brought some of her friends with her. Of course, she was there on her own, but that would be okay too. She was perfectly content to be there anyway. It was cozy.

The bar at the back of the café was immaculately kept. Shelves on the back wall were filled with just about every syrup type she could imagine. The whole place smelled of fresh coffee and pastries, and there was a big pastry case right in the front, with all sorts of sweet treats on display. In the back, she could hear the rumbling of a coffee machine as it brewed, and the whole place had quiet music, jazz it sounded like, playing to set the ambiance. The lights were pendant lights hanging down from the ceiling as well.

The cashier grinned and waved at Sophie as she looked around. "Thank you for coming to Coffee Maybe, where coffee is always a yes! Can I help you?" The cashier was a young girl, maybe 19, and she had her long, auburn hair pulled into a ponytail. She wore a plain black ¾ sleeved top and had an apron over it.

"Yeah, uh… Sorry, I've never been here before. Could I have a sec, please?" Sophie replied sheepishly, shoving her hands into her pockets as she stared up at the menu. It looked pretty typical—divided by mochas, cappuccinos, lattes, iced drinks, smoothies, and even frappes. It was too cold for anything iced on that rainy day, though, so she ignored the sweet treats listed there and focused instead on the other items on the list.

There were so many different combinations that Sophie felt a bit overwhelmed, and with every passing second, she felt a bit more anxious about how long it was taking her to look over the menu. She hesitated a moment before saying, "So, uh… What would you recommend? What's your favorite?"

"Oh, that's easy! I'm so glad we have our pumpkin spice flavors back in stock now that the season is changing! My favorite is the pumpkin spice latte or the pumpkin spice white chocolate mocha. It's delicious!" The young girl was practically vibrating with energy, and Sophie laughed a bit. She had clearly had her fair share of that pumpkin spice that day.

"Sounds good. Let's do a medium pumpkin spice white chocolate mocha." She had never tried combining the two, but it sounded promising—after all, there are pumpkin white chocolate cookies. Why not coffee?

"Great! Anything else? We have some delicious pumpkin pastries today, fresh from Bacrena Bakery down the street. They're freshly made and delivered still warm every morning, and oh man," she added, making the chef's kiss motion with her hands. "Delicious! You can't beat it, especially not with this weather. I can warm up one of the scones if you'd like?"

"Sure!" Sophie said with a quick smile back. She may as well—she was already there.

"Great! That'll be $9.42, please!" she cashier replied after punching the order into the computer.

Sophie passed her a debit card and looked around a bit more at the store. It was slow, surprisingly enough. There was an old man sitting at one table, looking out the window as he sipped at his coffee, just watching the rain and the occasional car drive by. It was a very sleepy area—not much traffic passed on foot or by car.

Upon receiving her card back, Sophie walked off, hesitating for a moment before approaching the lonely old man. "Excuse me," she said softly as she approached.

The old man didn't seem like he had expected to be talked to, and he looked up with mild curiosity. "Yes?" he asked. He looked excited to be approached, and he smiled at her.

"Mind if I join you?" asked Sophie, gesturing to the empty seat. "It's been a long, boring day without anyone to talk to, and I could use the company." She smiled shyly.

"Of course, dearie, make yourself comfortable!" He scooted his drink and book over to make space on the other half of the table. "It's definitely one of those days, isn't it?"

"Yeah, it's the rain, I bet! It's so hard to feel like there's anything to do when it's so soggy outside. That's why I came here. My wife and I used to come here all the time when it rained." He smiled wistfully, his gaze far away as he reminisced for a moment. "Her favorite was to come here in the fall when the leaves changed colors, and she would order herself one of those fancy pumpkin lattes. She loved the spices, she always said, and she would sip away at them. I always went with plain drip coffee. But... She loved the sweetness." He looked down at his drink for a moment and took a sip. "Now that she's gone, I like to come here from time to time as well to enjoy a drink in her honor."

Sophie nodded her head in understanding. "I'm sorry for your loss."

"Me, too," he replied, looking over at the barista, who was walking over with Sophie's drinks.

"I've got a pumpkin spice white chocolate mocha and pumpkin scone for Sophie," she said, placing them down on the table in front of her.

"Sophie?" the old man asked incredulously.

"Mhm," she said as she brought the cup to her lips to take the first sip of the fresh coffee, closing her eyes and savoring it. It was surprisingly delicious, she realized. The white chocolate added sweetness, but it wasn't overwhelming. She smiled at him.

"My wife's name was Sophie," he said, his eyes tearing up a bit. "Well, Sophie, it's very nice to meet you. I'm Al."

"Nice to meet you, Al," she replied softly with a smile. It sounded like she had ended up exactly where she was meant to be. And, for the rest of the rainy afternoon, she and Al spent the day chatting away as they enjoyed each other's company.

# Story 5: House Hunting

*Cara is house hunting! She's touring a local mansion that she is interested in buying, and she's bringing Sophie along for the ride. Sophie gets to spend the day exploring an extravagant, 10,000 square foot property on the outskirts of town, and she wants to make sure that she's not all alone while she does it. Sophie is thrilled! She loves looking at properties, and this one will be plenty of fun.*

"Are you ready, darling?" Cara purred as she peeked her head right into the front door of Sophie's home. She didn't knock—she never did, but Sophie didn't mind. Cara was like a sister to her, and she was thrilled to be included on such an important journey. But, she was running a bit behind, as usual. Bella woofed once in greeting before calmly trotting over to visit Cara as she popped inside, closing the door behind her. She petted the dog on the head and walked to sit at the dining table.

"Almost!" Sophie called back from upstairs. She was in her closet, getting her clothes for the day. They would be doing a lot of walking that day—Cara was there to pick Sophie up for a nice tour of a mansion nearby. The house was sitting on four acres of land, leading up to a strip of the Puget Sound, granting it instant beach access. From the pictures Sophie had seen, it was *gorgeous*. And she honestly hoped that her friend would buy it just because of the beauty of it. Cara was independently wealthy, having inherited her parents' multi-million dollar business that she had run for her, leaving her free to pursue her own interests in fashion. She was lucky, but she didn't let her wealth ruin her, either. Cara was very down to earth for someone who could literally afford to buy just about anything she wanted, and Sophie greatly respected her for it. Even now, with Cara sitting in her home, she knew that the entire downstairs level of the house was more or less the size of just one wing of that mansion they were heading out to look at, and she didn't mind one bit. Cara never gave her the impression that she thought that Sophie was incompetent or a failure. She never made Sophie feel like she was less than Cara due to money, either. In fact, Cara was actually incredibly generous more often than not, knowing that she was in a better financial position than most.

Within moments, Sophie was bounding down the stairs and to the main floor of her home. "Are you ready to go house hunting?" she asked with a big grin on her face.

"Am I!" Cara replied, flashing back a big smile as well. Cara was dressed impeccably in a nice baby blue pantsuit with a pair of flats that she slid onto her feet. The suit was clearly tailored to just her size, fitting just right on all the curves, and it looked great on her. Her blonde hair was neatly straightened, falling just past her shoulders, and she stood up from her seat at the table. "Let's get going!"

They hopped into Cara's car and were ready to go. The house wasn't too far away from where they were—maybe thirty minutes out of town, but it would be worth it. The day was sunny, and they would actually get to see the full beauty of everything in all its glory, and they were looking forward to it.

Before long, they had driven just out of town and had deviated off of the freeway to begin driving toward the Sound itself. The house was nestled against one of the dips inward, and as they pulled up to it, they were greeted with a wide expanse of forest. They were so far out that there was no way that they'd be seeing neighbors any time soon. The houses were on massive plots of land to grant that privacy, and they had been well planted to ensure that the privacy was maintained as well.

They pulled up to the parking spot, and both of them gasped in awe. They parked outside a garage entrance and saw that the walls of the house were beautiful white masonry, sculpted carefully, and kept clean. They were not even dusty or dirty, and they didn't even see a single spider web or anything. The roof was gently sloped, showing that the entire house was just one floor of expansive space in several different wings. The house's front was filled with arching windows that went up the entire expanse, ending maybe a foot from the room, and they were perfectly clear—no grime was present at all. Despite being outdoors, they were crystal clear, and they could see straight into what they assumed was a great room.

"You ready?" asked Cara.

"More than you know," Sophie replied, looping one arm into Cara's and off they went further into the room. They were incredibly excited to see everything within the entrance, and off they went. The ground underneath their feet was perfectly laid out concrete slabs with marble tiles shaping a path straight to the entrance. On either side of the entrance to the house, there were two perfectly cultivated gardens, complete with the most beautiful Japanese maple trees on either side, shielding over the entryway. It was a beautiful space, just walking up and inside was even better.

Right as they walked up, they saw the doors open, and a woman wearing a professional suit ushered them inside. "Welcome! Welcome!" she announced with a flourish of her arms. "It's nice to see you, Ms. Linn," she said, nodding to Cara with a smile. She clearly knew exactly who her customer was. "And you are?" she asked, turning her attention to Sophie.

"I'm Sophie Rogers," she replied with a smile and extended her hand. The realtor nodded and shook her hand.

"My name is Robin Evans," she replied curtly. She didn't seem nearly as interested in Sophie as in Cara, and Sophie couldn't really blame her. She wasn't the one about to put down money on a multi-million dollar property after all.

She was the one that was just there for moral support and to see the beautiful architecture throughout the house.

As they stepped indoors, they were surrounded by tile. It was gorgeous indoors, and the floor was the most beautiful red cherry that Sophie had ever seen. The trim on the walls matched the floors throughout everything that they could see in the area. Even the furniture was that beautiful cherry color everywhere they went. It was impeccably matched from item to item and from room to room, and she couldn't believe just how beautiful it was going through it all. She was in awe of the beauty all around her.

The great hall was the first room that they went through. It had vaulted ceilings with massive skylights filtering in as much sunlight as possible, and there were couches lined up all around on the ground. The floor was that same beautiful cherry wood, and the couches were each immaculately white—as if they had never seen a speck of dust before. They were perfect—they looked so nice that Sophie felt herself wondering if they were walking through a staged showroom rather than an actual home that had been lived in before. She was shocked—there was no way that this was a home that someone else lived in. There was no way that a home that actually saw usage would be so impeccably neat.

But, then again, there was so much space open throughout the whole place that it was entirely possible that they just never used the same areas enough to ever actually make much of a difference to it. Sophie looked around slowly. The art on the walls was abstract—lots of colors that seemed to clash together, and she wasn't quite sure she knew what to make of it. She looked at it for a long while, eyes slowly skating over the whole thing. There was so much going on that she couldn't quite tell what was what, and she was unsure how that made her feel. But, one thing was true—she had to appreciate that the colors were nice and they matched well with everything else that was there.

There was a sitting area next to a grand fireplace, built into the wall with immaculate masonry out of granite with marble white pillars and mantle surrounding it. There was no fire burning at the moment, and Sophie wasn't really surprised—it was hot. She had to wonder, however—if they used it, did it get soot all over everything? Did it cause problems for the staff that probably cleaned up the room?

Before she could really wonder about it much longer, she found herself being tugged away by Cara as they moved on to the next room—the kitchen. The kitchen was the most exciting part of Sophie. While she wasn't much of a cook herself, she loved seeing the grand setups that people came up with on their own. She loved being able to see what people came up with and kitchens, being one of the most commonly used rooms in a house, always felt like a great place to start understanding the mind of someone else when you were in them. Sophie looked around as they walked in. The floor was black and white tiles, something that she never thought that she would appreciate, but upon taking that closer look, she realized that she loved it. They weren't actually that ugly when they were done intentionally. The counters were made of granite as well. The cabinetry, however, was the best part of what she was seeing. As she looked up, she realized that the cabinetry was designed carefully, intricately carved to display some beautiful flower-like designs that curled up the cabinets and all around the corners. They were immaculate, and they looked hand-done, which was even more impressive. Each cabinet was painted a fresh white color, and stainless steel appliances filled the room. There was a double oven in one counter setting, with a gas range with six burners quite close by. The fridge was massive, with French doors and a drawer underneath for the freezer. Overall, each appliance

clearly was picked to match, shiny, and polished and
without so much as a fingerprint marring the surface.

There was a big island bar in the center of the kitchen space,
with barstools lining up on one side, and above it, there was
a rack that was designed to hold all of the pots and pans up
overhead. There was an assortment of gourmet pots and
pans dangling there, waiting for action, but Sophie felt like
they had never actually been used.

Again, Sophie felt Cara's touch, and when she turned to
look, she saw her friend tilting her head, ushering her into
the next room after they had undoubtedly finished
discussing whatever it was that they were there to talk
about. Off they went to the next room: A dining space that
appeared designed to showcase a massive table that was
almost certainly there to entertain people, judging by the
number of chairs. There were at least eight on each side of
the table, with two on each end as well, giving space for 20
people to sit and enjoy a meal.

The tabletop was granite, and there were massive pillars of
the most beautiful cherry wood legs there to support the
space. Each chair was a deep red leather, with brass legs,
and they were all pushed into place carefully. On one end of
the room, there was a massive cabinet that went up all the
way to the ceiling, made of the same deep red wood that the
rest of the house seemed so quick to showcase. In this room,
the tile was a light, sandy color, giving some brightness to
the space, and along the other wall, there was plenty of
space and countertops for more food to be stored if
necessary. The whole room was very well designed, and a
big chandelier hung overhead, each crystal sparkling
brightly and shining vividly.

They continued to go through room after room, but after a
while, Sophie found herself getting restless. She wanted to
find something else to do that would catch her attention
longer. So far, she felt like every room was just more of the

same, and after a while, she was simply bored. She didn't care to see three iterations of a kitchen in one house or so many rooms that she could hardly count them. Some of the rooms seemed just redundant—they would have similar setups in different colors or with different art up on the walls, and she found herself wondering what the point of so much space was in the first place.

But soon, they made it to the part of the tour that she found herself the most interested in seeing: The outdoors. They were heading toward the private beach that overlooked the Sound, and she was confident that it would be even more stunning in a real lie. As she walked out, they made their way to a beautiful porch overlooking the beach with a dock heading right out all the way into the water. It looked like a yacht could be parked there. The tile underfoot was smooth as well and looked almost wet—but it was simply the sheen that was on there. A hot tub sat underneath a large shade, and there was a nice outdoor dining set there as well. The view was unrivaled by anything else. It was gorgeous—the sun was starting to set by that point, and the sky was tinged a beautiful shade of magenta, with a sunburst orange color on the horizon as the sun fell behind the Sound.

"Wow," Sophie gasped as she looked out. "That view is *amazing.*" She smiled as she looked over it, wishing that she would be able to get a view like that more often. It wasn't often that a view made her stop speaking in awe, but this one did. It didn't get much better than that view right there, and she felt like anything else that they saw after that point would be a waste of time—she felt like that would be the best possible end to their tour.

The realtor came up behind her. "Sure is something, isn't it?" she said wistfully as she looked at the sunset.

Sophie glanced over in surprise that she was being spoken to. "Yeah, it's gorgeous." She smiled. "I'm sure you get to see views like this all the time, huh?"

"Something like that," she replied, glancing to the ground and smiling for a moment. "But being able to see the houses, walk through it all, and just envision what life is like on the other side... it's amazing, isn't it? It's so *luxurious*."

Sophie nodded her head in response. It really was. She couldn't quite imagine leaving her life behind to live in what amounted to almost ten houses the size of her own. She thought it was beautiful, but she felt like she would get lost with all of those rooms out and about. She loved to look at everything, but she felt like ultimately, her own home was better suited for her and was perfectly designed for the space that she would need for herself. She didn't want to be totally overwhelmed—she wanted to be comfortable in her surroundings, and her house was exactly right.

"So, ready to go?" Cara called out from behind Sophie, making her turn her head. Cara looked exhausted but happy after the long day of trekking through all 10,000 square feet of house and so much of the acreage outside.

Sophie nodded. "Thanks for your time," she told the realtor, who smiled and waved in return.

"You two take care. And Cara, dear, you know how to reach me if you need anything!"

Cara waved back as they left.

As they sat down in the car, Cara let out a big sigh and flopped against the back seat. "Man, that house was *big*."

"Yeah, it was!" Sophie chimed back. "What do you think about it?"

"I think I'd be too tired to walk around so much! It's much too big for me!" Cara wiped her brow off and closed her eyes. "I might stick to closer to the city—at least I can walk across your house without getting winded."

Sophie laughed. "That is true!" she said as Cara started up the car to head home. It turned out, even Cara thought that there was such thing as too much house, and that one was it.

# Story 6: Missed Connections

*On a cool autumn day, Sophie went out for lunch at a local bistro, only to find that her old college roommate was also there enjoying a meal! Together, they sat down and had a nice, long chat to catch up with each other and see what was up with each other's lives.*

Sophie closed up her laptop with a sigh to herself. Her stomach was rumbling, and even though she knew that she had more work to get through, she knew that work would be infinitely harder if she didn't take the time to eat. She needed to find a way to eat something to keep her energy up and keep her mind focused on the work that she needed to do. With a stretch of her arms, she glanced at the clock. It was lunchtime, for sure.

Standing up, she walked into her kitchen, opening up the fridge. It was shockingly empty—all that was in there was a half-gallon of milk, a small container of yogurt, some butter, peanut butter, and ketchup. It was a strange hodgepodge of ingredients, and she sighed. "Guess I shouldn't have skipped grocery shopping..." she told herself with a sigh as she closed the fridge door. It was pretty typical for her to run out of food—she was only one person, and she didn't eat nearly as much as many other people seemed to. Of course, not buying that food often led to her also having to deal with the consequences—primarily needing to order out. Of course, ordering out also usually cost more money that she would have to spend, but that was okay—at least she would have delicious food to enjoy without having to cook and without having to clean up the mess afterward. Win, win!

But, that also meant that she had to find something new to eat, too, and that was always the hardest part of it all. How did she choose out what to enjoy when there were so many different options? How could she choose out what her meal would be when there were nearly limitless choices around her? Just within a five-minute radius, she had a teriyaki restaurant, a ramen restaurant, a sushi restaurant, an authentic Mexican restaurant, a Chinese restaurant, an Indian restaurant, two Thai restaurants, a few burger joints, and just about every fast-food chain imaginable. There were so many options, and if she were to get just a bit further away from home, she would have even more options to enjoy as well.

With a sigh, she scrolled through a list of local restaurants on her phone. She looked over the, one at a time, and tried to figure out what the right one was for her. She wasn't totally confident in the choices—but then she realized that there was one name on the list that she hadn't recognized: Sunnyside Bistro. It was just five minutes away, and she remembered that it had been opened maybe a week prior. It was supposed to be locally sourced ingredients that would create delicious dishes. It was open for brunch, lunch, and dinner daily, and she had heard that it was supposed to be great. It was opened up by the owners of another restaurant that was delicious and did well in the area.

Well, it was always good to try new things, she told herself as she looked around. And this was the perfect opportunity to do so. After all, many of the blogs that she wrote on a regular basis would encourage people to try new things to enjoy life, and why not? Trying new things brought variety, and variety was supposed to be the spice of life, right? It sounded perfect and like a nice way to break up the monotony of her day.

After quickly getting ready to go and put on an oversized beige sweater to go with her skinny jeans and boots, she grabbed her purse and rushed out the door, keys, and phone in hand. The bistro was really just a few blocks away, and if it hadn't been so chilly, she would have considered just walking. But, given the volatility of the weather, she figured better safe than sorry. She didn't really want to get wet.

Within minutes, she was there, pulling her car into park and getting herself situated. She was ready to enjoy her lunch. She had spent the whole three-minute drive, thinking all about what she was going to eat and how enjoyable it all was going to be. Sophie's stomach gurgled and growled again, and she rubbed it absently for a moment as she pulled out the keys and stepped out of her car. Lunch was calling.

As she stepped into the little bistro, she noticed that it was mostly empty. There was only one other person there, sitting in a corner, head down and in a book. The waitress working, upon seeing Sophie, waved and ushered for her to follow. "Right over here, please!" she said kindly with a smile. Sophie followed readily as the waitress gathered up a menu and a bundle of silverware, setting it down in the table across from the one that the other person was sitting at.

As Sophie got settled, the waitress ran off to get her a glass of water, and she flipped through the menu. It had all the usual choices one would expect in a bistro. There were a maybe a dozen different choices plus a make-your-own-panini section listed as she skimmed through it. There were so many different options there for her to choose from—she just needed to figure out which one sounded the best.

The waitress came back with a fresh glass of cold water. "Do you need another minute to glance over the menu?" she asked with a smile.

"Mmm…. No, I think I'm good," Sophie replied with a smile.

"Oh, great! And what can I get for you today?"

"I'll take the turkey basil Panini, please."

"Great choice!" the waitress informed her, nodding her head sagely as she wrote down the order. "That's one of our most popular sandwiches, and it's delicious! Anything else for you?"

"Nope, that'll do it. Thanks!" Sophie passed the menu back over to the waitress and took a sip from her water, pulling her phone out to mindlessly scroll through social media. It wasn't like she had much better to do at the moment—she just had to wait for her dish to be brought out for her.

"Sophie Rogers is that you?"

Just as Sophie was about to read through her next image collection, she heard someone call her name behind her. Turning around, she was greeted by a young woman about her age, with pixie-short brunette hair, pale skin, and petite features. Her big, blue eyes looked at Sophie incredulously. But, it was the perfect little mole on the right cheekbone that jogged Sophie's memory.

"Wow, Sylvia, is that you?" She smiled at the woman sitting at the table. "Ohmigosh, it's been so long!!"

"I know! What have you been up to? You look great!" Sylvia replied, grinning from ear to ear. Sylvia always had that air about her—she was someone that was wrapped up in all levels of positivity, and her excitement was always contagious.

"Not much! I'm just writing articles these days. I've got an adorable German shepherd named Bella, but other than that, it's just me! How about you?" Sophie was glad—Sylvia looked like she was genuinely doing well. She looked healthy, comfortable, and even better, just as happy as she used to be. Her happiness practically emanated off of her, and Sophie was so relieved to see it. She always loved seeing people that she used to know doing well—it gave her hope.

"Come over here!!" Sylvia said, gesturing for her to come to the table with her, and Sophie obliged, hopping over to the other chair. She took her water with her and smiled, settling down and resting her chin on her hands with her elbows propped onto the surface. "So then, a dog, huh? No kids? No special someone?"

"Nope, just my dog!" Sophie smiled at her friend. "What about you?" She was more interested to hear about Sylvia than to talk about herself. After all, they had lost touch long, long ago. The two of them had shared a dorm together when they were freshmen in college. They had been quite different from each other, but they got along well. Sylvia was down to earth—she had studied mathematics with the goal of being a math teacher for middle school. She had always been someone that wanted to help reach out to those who needed it the most, and she loved the idea of getting through to stubborn children, teaching them to love something that they initially rejected. "Are you a teacher yet?"

Sylvia smiled and shook her head. "Nope! That line didn't really work out."

"Oh?" Sophie was curious—the Sylvia she knew was so passionately driven toward that degree path. She was so determined to be that teacher. It was actually mildly shocking to Sophie that she wasn't interested in the least. However, Sophie also knew that it wasn't really her business, and though it was surprising, if Sylvia had found something else to occupy her time, then that was great, too. After all, Sylvia had that sort of happy glow to her—Sophie couldn't quite put her finger on where it was coming from, but it looked good on her.

"Actually, I'm married now," she said, holding up a hand to reveal a wedding ring wrapped delicately around her ring finger. It was a beautiful rose gold ring that complemented her skin perfectly, and there was one diamond—not too big or too small—sitting right at the front of it.

60

Sophie gasped, pulling her hands up to cover her mouth while her eyes widened. "No way!!" She squealed, barely able to contain her excitement for her friend. "Congratulations!! So who's the lucky guy?"

"Do you remember Drake? The chemistry major?"

"Dorky Drake? The really shy one that always tried to avoid confrontations, even when he really shouldn't be?" asked Sophie, trying to remember.

"That's the one! He's not so dorky anymore, though." Sylvia smiled fondly as she pulled out her phone, unlocking the screen and turning it around to show Sophie. The picture had Drake, the same man she had remembered. But, he looked more mature. His skin had cleared up from the acne that it had been covered in before, and he looked like he was genuinely happy. He wore a confident smile, and his hair was slicked back. He was dressed in a nice pair of slacks with a white button-down shirt and polished shoes, and hanging to his arms was Sylvie, standing just barely at his shoulder height. She was looking up at him with an affectionate smile.

But, what stood out the most to Sophie was Sylvia's stomach.

It was round.

"Do you have a baby?" Sophie blurted out unceremoniously, eyes getting even wider as she looked at her friend.

"Not yet!" Sylvia said with a smile, pushing her seat back. Sophie hadn't realized it, but her old friend's belly was swollen with a baby. She looked about ready to pop at any moment!

"Wow!" Sophie breathed out. "You look so good!" It was true—Sylvia was carrying that pregnancy like a natural, and

Sophie realized that was what was giving her that joyful, youthful glow to her—it was the pregnancy glow. "Is it a boy or a girl?"

"Both!"

"Both?"

"Twins! One boy, one girl." Sylvia rubbed her belly affectionately. "We've got another four weeks to go before these two are done baking. Hopefully, it goes by quickly! I don't know if I could carry them for much longer at this rate!" She laughed. "I'm kinda starting to feel like I'm in beached whale form."

"No!" Sophie gasped. "You look fantastic! And besides, not everyone can carry a twin pregnancy. I'd say you're doing absolutely wonderfully." She nodded her head resolutely. So many pregnant women would put far too much pressure on themselves to look good, and it drove Sophie insane. There was no reason for her to feel so harshly about herself. "But, do you have any names chosen out?"

"We do!" Sylvia replied. "We're naming the little girl Luna Vivian, and the boy is going to be named Damon James."

"What stunning names!" Sophie replied after a moment to mull over the names. They flowed well off of the tongue, and both names were gorgeous. She loved them and could only hope that when it was her turn to name her own children, she could have as good of taste.

"Thanks!" Sylvia replied, taking a sip of her water as she smiled. She got a faraway look in her eyes before rubbing her belly again. "They're definitely going to be a handful," she mused.

"Oh, man, I bet. But you'll manage! So, are you staying home with them?" Sophie was definitely curious about her old friend's plans. She had always been the type to say that she had no interest in

"That's the plan! It'll be the three of us while Drake heads out to work every day."

Sophie nodded her head. "Makes sense! Man, the daycare costs... That sounds awful." She took another sip of water as she looked at her old friend. It was crazy to see just how far her peers ended up in life. It was interesting just how many different directions everyone would go down. Some would make the shift toward domestic life or having families, as Sylvia was doing. It was great to see them settling down happily, enjoying where they were with their relationships. Others were full steam ahead in their careers.

"I know! Plus diapers for two? It's crazy. But it'll be worth it!"

"I'm sure," replied Sophie. It certainly sounded like it would be. So many women felt that pull toward having children— they were driven by their desire to mother others. Sophie, however, wasn't sure she felt that pull. She didn't know whether what she wanted was to have her own children or to be her own person. It was hard to know where to fall between the two when she didn't feel a pull one way or the other. She wasn't quite sure where she wanted to be in life. She had her dog, and she had her home, and for the moment, that was enough. For the moment, she was perfectly satisfied with where she was, and she would have plenty of time to find her way later on.

Both Sophie and Sylvia fell silent for the moment. They both sat there quietly. It was slightly awkward and uncomfortable—the kind of silence that lingers just a bit too long with people who have grown distant. Sophie's gaze slipped away, looking out the window at the dreary sky as she spaced out, just watching the cars drive by, and Sylvia glanced down at her cup of water.

"Well," Sophie said finally, breaking the silence, "I'm glad that you are doing so well. It's really refreshing to see people living their best lives." She smiled genuinely at her friend. She really meant well for her dear old friend.

"It's nice to see you doing so well, too! We'll have to catch up again more often. Do you live here?" Sylvia asked.

"Yes, I'm maybe five minutes from here. Just figured I'd try a new restaurant today!"

"Wow! I'm maybe five minutes away too. We'll have to meet up more often. You'll have to come and visit when the babies come! I'm sure Drake would enjoy seeing you again, too. It's always nice to catch up with people after a while!" Sylvia picked up her purse. "But, I've actually gotta run—Got an OB appointment in a few! It was so nice to see you here again, Sophie!"

Sophie nodded in agreement. Meeting up again sounded great, and she was totally down to do so again. She scribbled her phone number down on a piece of paper from her own purse and passed it over to Sylvia. "Just send me a quick text when you're feeling up to another meeting!"

"Will do! See you later!" And with that said, Sylvia headed out the door and off to her appointment.

Sophie gathered her items up and turned back to her own seat, where she had been. She sipped at her water and went right back to scrolling through her phone. Just as she did, a message popped up:

*"Nice to see you again!*
*XO*
*Sylvia"*

Sophie smiled to herself. How nice! And, just as she read the message, the waitress came back with her sandwich. The panini was perfectly grilled, with a nice, generous helping of fries next to it. It looked great! "Thank you!" she told the waitress as the food was put right in front of her.

"Enjoy!" replied the waitress as she left Sophie to her own devices.

Sophie didn't need to be told twice—she was thrilled to have her food. Her stomach gurgled again as she took a big bite. It was perfect. The sandwich was cooked perfectly, and the taste was better than she could have imagined.

Of course, that could also have just been the hunger that she was feeling, too. She was *famished*.

# Story 7: Variety Is the Spice of Life

*After a few days of boring deadlines that had to be met, Sophie is ready for some real change! She is determined to make a difference in her day, and she has decided that she will do that by trying to do something new. Her new thing of the day is shadowing strangers in the park.*

"I'm so bored," Sophie moaned to herself as she threw herself onto her bed. She was tired of not having anything to do and was more than ready to find something exciting. She needs variety! She needed thrill! She needed *excitement!* Anything would do, so long as it broke the monotony of the day. She just had to find something. *Anything.*

Sighing, she stared up at the white, textured ceiling that she had meant to paint. She had been thinking about it for ages, but she had never bothered painting her master bedroom. White was good enough for her as far as she cared—at least it was painted. But, she knew that she'd have to get to it eventually. The task went onto her to-do list that she constantly had growing on the backburner. It would get done eventually, she told herself offhandedly as she looked around her room.

She pulled her phone over to herself and started scrolling through her usual sites. Maybe she'd find something interesting to do somewhere online; she thought as she looked through everything listlessly. She wasn't exactly having much fun as she went through everything. But then, she saw it: The thing that she would do to cure her boredom.

On a page of random ways to pass the time, she stumbled upon the shadowing game. The idea of the game was that she had to follow around someone in public for as long as possible until they noticed that she was. The longer that she could get with following them around, the better. It sounded fun! Vaguely creepy, she had to admit, but also like harmless fun. She wasn't going to be bothering anyone— she'd just be following them around for as long as possible to see what would happen. She figured that she might as well give it a shot—after all, she had nothing else to do.

So, Sophie set out to have a little bit of fun. She was determined to enjoy herself somehow, and a bit of a thrill was definitely in order. After getting dressed, putting on a white long sleeve shirt with horizontal stripes, a pair of skinny blue jeans, taupe booties, and a military green faded canvas jacket, she was ready to go. The best place she figured she could go to have some fun would be in the mall—there were always plenty of people wandering about, and she figured that she would have luck finding someone to follow there. With her purse over her shoulder and her determination steeled, she set off.

The mall was only ten minutes away from home for Sophie, and it was surprisingly empty. Or, maybe it wasn't surprising considering that it was early afternoon on a Wednesday. People were at work—it was normal working hours. But, Sophie wasn't willing to let that cause her any problems—she was determined to enjoy her day! She parked her car in the parking lot and figured she'd take the time to enjoy the moment. She set off, striding with purpose and determination that, as she got closer and closer to the mall's entrance.

As she got closer and closer, it felt more and more real, and she realized that she was about to start her game. She faltered for a moment. Was she being weird? She felt like she kind of was. But, that voice in the back of her mind pushed her forward. It told her that she had to at least try— may as well. She drove out all that way, and the least that she could do was make it a point to actually do something while there.

So, she went off and started looking around the mall. She needed to find someone that wouldn't be mean about things. It had to be someone who would be likely to laugh off what she was doing. Maybe someone looked like they weren't a very serious person. It would have to be someone that looked like they were going to be friendly, and someone who wouldn't be worried that she was trying to rob them.

Sophie looked around, trying to find a good option. There weren't many. She saw a woman walking with young children, but in her experience, they were usually the most likely to be offended or bothered by someone following them because they would be afraid that they were genuinely going to be hurt.

Sophie felt a pang of guilt at the thought—she just wanted to have some fun trying something new. This seemed like something spunky and spontaneous, and that meant that it had to be a good option, right?

She wasn't so sure at that point—she was starting to doubt that she had made the right choice at all. After all, these were just unsuspecting people out at the mall, looking to enjoy their day. With a sigh, Sophie plopped herself down on the nearest bench and looked at the people that passed by.

There was a mother toting two children along with her, both of which looked miserable. The boy was maybe 4, and he was pouting and whining about something that Sophie couldn't quite make out, but judging by the parent's reaction, was something annoying or something that had been argued several other times in the past, and she was having none of that nonsense. The daughter was in a stroller, grumpily rubbing her eyes. The mother was the walking definition of a mombie. Her hair looked frizzy, and she looked like she was in dire need of a coffee. At that moment, Sophie did not envy that woman, nor did she really feel the urge to follow along and see what would happen next. After all, that seemed like it was just asking for trouble.

The next person to go by was actually a group of people—they were 20-something men walking through the mall with a couple of bags from the local sports shop. They were laughing together about some sort of inside joke, judging by the exaggerated eyebrow waggling and the tilts of the head. Sophie sighed. They wouldn't have been much fun to follow either and, in fact, would seem like the kind of people that would do nothing but cause her problems. So, they were crossed off the list, too. Nope, no, thank you, Sophie told herself.

The third person she saw pass was a man all by himself. He was staring down at his phone as he walked by, with a serious expression on his face, and he looked like he really needed to get something off his chest, but he wasn't sure how to do so. He looked around at the surroundings with a sigh, wondering what he was going to do next, and Sophie quirked a brow. She kind of wanted to see what he was going to do.

Before she knew it, she stood up and started to follow him from a distance. He was walking down a major strip of the mall slowly, almost leisurely. His gaze drifted lazily from store to store as he tried to make out what he was looking for. Sophie wondered briefly what he was looking for, and she had to bite her tongue to keep herself from asking him. She didn't want to out herself; after all—she needed to make sure that he didn't catch that she was behind him. She would have to be very careful to make sure that she was unnoticed. If she could do her job the right way, she would be able to get through the whole mall and figure out whatever it was that he was looking for.

He stopped first at a store that looked like it was meant to sell trinkets in general. There were many little blown glass figurines hanging out in the front, and they sparkled in the fluorescent lighting of the mall. Sophie could admire them from her spot a few feet back. They were shimmering in the light, and in particular, Sophie found herself staring in awe at an owl that was suspended in the air, its crystalline wings sparkling as they refracted light and glimmers of sparkles all over the surrounding surfaces. The owl was gracefully swooping, wings spread, and eyes fixed on something as it did, and Sophie couldn't take her eyes off of it. It looked so great that she had to keep on staring. In fact, she stared so long at that adorable little figurine that she realized she completely lost where he was in the first place. She lost track of the man that she had been trailing. Inwardly kicking herself, she scoped out the area.

He was wearing a black collared shirt and slim-cut slacks that hugged his frame nicely, highlighting just how in shape he was. His sandy hair was cut relatively short, with a small flair of hair in the front that was slicked back. She knew that he couldn't have gone too far, and she looked around for black clothes.

But, she realized at that moment that black seemed to be as trendy as ever—there were a lot of teens and men wearing black shirts and black pants that appeared to be slim cut. And, he had been an average height in general—it wasn't exactly easy to find this man with is virtually basic look. With a sigh, Sophie shook her head. She had definitely lost that one.

"Excuse me, ma'am, you look lost," a deep voice purred from behind her, almost tantalizingly teasing as it spoke.

Sophie turned around in curiosity, only to find herself face to face with none other than the man that she had been following. He was smirking at her, almost playfully, as she watched him in embarrassment and horror. Her cheeks burned as they turned bright pink, and her eyes widened as she stumbled and tripped over the worlds that she had to say. How could she possibly explain the game that she was playing and how harmless it was when she had just been following someone around? How could she possibly spin this, so she didn't sound like she was absolutely crazy? It was difficult at best—especially because she *was* following him around.

He quirked a brow at her lack of a response, his smirk growing more satisfied as she grew more flustered. With a huff, Sophie crossed her arms. "Can I help you?" she asked him.

"I believe I should be asking you that question, not the other way around," he bantered back. He had a point, too. "Why were you following me? If you wanted my number, you could have just asked." He winked at her playfully. He was clearly enjoying every minute of her suffering, and he was dragging it out as much as he could, too.

Sophie huffed again and averted her gaze, arms crossing defensively in front of her chest. "It's nothing, really. It's a silly dare." She was really beginning to feel embarrassed the more that she spoke, and she had no idea how she was going to make it better. Ultimately, the best thing that she could think of to do was to tell him the truth.

"You see... I was actually just playing a game. I wanted to know how long I could follow someone before they noticed that I was. I saw it online, and I know that it was stupid, but I was bored and felt like it would help me to pass the time. I'm sorry for bothering you." The words tumbled out of her mouth before she could do a thing to sort of censor them, and she found herself staring at the ground, wishing that she could get it to open up from underneath her and eat her up. She really just wanted to disappear in the moment, but she had no clear escape.

"I see," said the man thoughtfully as he looked her over, head to toe. He seemed to be considering something, and Sophie hoped that he wasn't going to get her banned from the mall or something for harassing patrons. She loved the mall—she had just been bored and needed something to pass the time.

"I am really sorry," Sophie repeated again with a sigh.

"I don't believe I got your name," he replied almost coolly. Sophie was going crazy—she couldn't quite make out what he was thinking, and that made him next to impossible to read. His inscrutable gaze bore into her, leaving her squirming in her place. She was incredibly uncomfortable in the moment but could not think of a good way to break free. She felt stuck—after all, she owed him an explanation.

"Sophie," she replied shyly. She was shocked at the shyness—but she couldn't quite make it go away. She was *embarrassed*. She sighed to herself, running a hand through her hair. "Look, I'm sorry," she said, averting her gaze.

Sophie was expecting him to get mad or to yell or to tell her that she's a creep. But none of that happened. A long silence hung in the air for a few heartbeats, and then Sophie was surprised at what she heard: Laughter. She heard laughter.

The man was *laughing* at her.

Sophie looked up in shock, meeting his gaze. He seemed genuinely amused, and Sophie wasn't sure if she should feel relieved or disappointed as a result. She looked back down at her feet in embarrassment, unsure what to do next. But, then he spoke.

"Well, you were not very good at it." He quirked a brow at her and smiled. "You really have to work on that sneaking of yours. You were way too obvious, just slowly following me around. You didn't even look away! You were just staring right at me."

Sophie felt another, fresher wave of shame fill her. He had a point—she wasn't really careful at all. And, it backfired on her. She really was bad at this whole thing, and that was definitely something that she would have to deal with. But, more specifically, she knew that she would not be going out of her way to follow people again. Lesson learned. Experiment failed. She was entirely done with that line of thinking and action. It was time for her to go back to her boring life, doing boring things, and enjoying boring days. Variety might have been the spice of life, but really, Sophie had to admit that boringness was at least predictable. At least she knew what to expect, when to expect it. And, it wasn't as embarrassing.

"But, you know what? You'll have to learn from a pro next time. I like to make it a bit more obvious: I walk around and do something conspicuous just to see how long it takes for someone to realize that I'm following them. Sometimes I whistle a certain song the whole time. Other times, I will skip or ride a unicycle around. And even better—when they look at me all confused and wondering why I'm following them? I look around like they are, looking as confused as I can to see what happens."

Sophie was shocked. She hadn't expected him to be interested in some silly game like that—but she was a bit relieved that he seemed to think that it was actually funny. At least she didn't have him threatening to call the police or do something else that would have added a whole new layer of complications to the day.

"I'm Eric," he told her, holding out a hand to shake.

Sophie looked down at his hand and composed herself for a moment before taking it. "Nice to meet you," she said. She still felt embarrassed, but she was glad that things weren't a total problem for her. She was glad that he seemed like he was a lighthearted kind of person. He seemed friendly enough as well.

"So, bored, huh?" asked Eric. "That's something that can be fixed easier than stalking someone else through a mall, you know," he teased, once again smirking. He seemed amused by her internal squirming and her total embarrassment, and Sophie had to force her to take a deep breath and sigh.

"You're right. Next time maybe I'll just make it a point to just stroll right up and start a conversation!" Sophie told him with a smile.

"That's a wonderful idea, Sophie. We could have had a great, easy conversation that would have been a whole lot of fun. But now, you'll never know, will you? You really missed out, you know." Eric was watching her with a teasing expression.

"That's too bad, isn't it!" Sophie shrugged. "Well, Eric, I'll keep your suggestion in mind for the next time. I'll make sure that next time, I'll just walk right up to you. But, for now, I gotta get going. I've got things to buy and people to see."

"You mean that owl you were watching?"

Sophie was shocked—he had been paying enough attention that he had noticed her. Wow, she was worse at this than she had thought for sure. Not only did she fail to stay out of sight, but she was also so bad at this that Eric was able to see exactly what she was doing. "Yeah," she said with an embarrassed smile.

"Well, Sophie, you're in luck." Eric held out a paper bag to her. It was a nice, lavender-colored bag with white handles, and the name of the store that she had passed was scrawled out across the top.

Sophie's eyes widened, and she looked down at the bag. "What's this?"

"Open it and find out," Eric replied with a wink.

Sophie opened it up, and inside was a box. Inside the box was that crystalline owl that she had been eyeing. It was perfect—the wings were shimmering, and she *loved* it. Her eyes widened up as she looked at it, and she looked up to Eric. "What, no!" She shook her head. "I can't accept this!"

"Please?" asked Eric. He smiled at her. "Consider it payment for the awkwardness." He refused to take the bag out of her hands as she offered it back.

Sophie sighed. "Okay," she said. "If you insist. Well... Thank you." She smiled at him and looked down at the gift.

"Just promise me that you'll make it a point to talk to me the next time you see me instead of trying to shadow me, okay?"

"Will do!" Sophie nodded her head. She smiled.

"Well, Sophie, I'm heading out. I'll see you later, okay?" Eric smiled and waved at her as he turned around. "Enjoy the day!" She smiled

"You, too!" Sophie slid the owl back into the bag and turned around to leave her car. She smiled to herself as she walked away. While things didn't quite work out the way that she thought they would, she had met someone new that seemed nice in his own way. She was glad that she had the chance to talk to someone else. So, off she went, heading back home. She considered her lesson learned. No more crazy suggestions from the internet when she needed something to do for the day!

# Guided Meditation 1: The Plateau of Inner Peace

Close your eyes and take in a big, deep breath. Feel the air flowing through your nose. Notice how it feels. Focus on the temperature and the smells. Feel it filling up your lungs, with your lungs swelling up within you like great, big balloons in your chest until you feel like they can't swell up anymore. Feel the air warming in your chest and exhale slowly, feeling the air pass your lips gently and slowly. Is it warm? With each breath that you take, you feel yourself calming down.

You breathe in... And out...

Now, feel yourself. Focus on your center, the point just above your belly button. How does it feel? Is it tense? Tight? Stressed? Focus on this point as you inhale in. One... Two... Three... Four... Five... and out... One... Two... three... Four... Five... Focus on that spot for another breath or two...

Now, feel the tension in your body. Become aware of any tension you are holding in your head and face. As you breathe in, imagine that you are pushing the tension down to the center above your belly button. Let it gather there. Now, feel the tension in your shoulders. Focus on that stress and tension and as you breathe in, feel it moving down to your center. Let it gather there, imagining your tension and stress all becoming balled up in the center. Feel the tension in your arms and hands gathering and flowing into your center. Feel that center growing with the tension and allow it to build up. Then, take the tension from your chest and upper back, and flow it down toward your center.

Then, go down to your toes and feet, identifying the tension that is there. Push it up, feeling it flowing up your legs, through your pelvis and belly, and noting it as it arrives in

the belly. Focus on it as it grows within you and allow it to
flow.

Feel all of the tension in your body, all boiled up into one
big ball in your core. Allow yourself to feel the weight of that
tension and the burden that it has been putting on you.
Take in a deep breath as you focus on it. Then, bid it
goodbye and goodnight.

As you exhale, pull the tension out from your core. Envision
yourself picking up the ball of stress and tension and
holding it like a basketball. Feel its heft in your mind. Inhale
again. One... Two... Three... Four... Five... And as you
exhale, throw the ball away from you. Watch as the ball of
tension flies into the air. Watch it as it continues further
and further away, getting smaller and smaller into the
distance as you breathe. It is much smaller now, and soon, it
is so small that you can no longer see it, and then it is
completely gone.

Now, in that space where you pulled the tension away, in
your center, imagine that peace and calmness flow into you.
It is slowly manifesting within your core, filling you with
peace, comfort, and the feeling that everything will be okay.
You have a big, shining golden ball of peace and relaxation
within your core. Breathe in... One... Two... Three... Four...
Five... And out... One... Two... Three... Four... Five... As you
breathe in, imagine the feeling of relaxation extending
throughout your body. Feel it in your head. Breathe in... and
out... Feel the relaxation pulsating in your shoulders and
arms... Feel it spreading throughout your chest. Feel it
spread down to your legs and feet. It fills your whole body,
bringing you utter peace and relaxation. Your mind feels
incredibly open and ready to go on a peaceful, relaxing
adventure. Your body is ready to fall deeper and deeper into
your relaxation so you can become more and more relaxed.

As you breathe, you fade away until you are surrounded by
nothing but darkness. The darkness is friendly and calm,

and you feel utterly relaxed as you bask in it. It is inviting and familiar. You feel it calling to you, reminding you that you are always at home when you come to this place. This place is your imagination; it is your innermost part of your mind and is a place where you control everything. It is a place that you can visit whenever you are finding yourself feeling stressed or unable to relax. Here, you can be at true peace with yourself. It is a place of potential and possibilities. It is a place where you are the master. You are the creator.

Out of the darkness, you see a point of light on the distance. It starts out small, one tiny point of light. With every breath you take, it gets longer. It starts to get a little bit bigger. The light is golden and warm, and it spreads out. Its rays begin to radiate through the darkness above you, and you start to realize that the darkness above you is transforming. It becomes filled with radiant hues of reds, oranges, and pinks, as the light in the distance gets larger and larger. It is a great, big orb, rising up into the sky and illuminating everything around you. The sun is rising in your imagination, lightening up your surroundings. The sun is your inner peace and relaxation that you have summoned within yourself. With every breath you take, it pulsates stronger and larger as it slowly creeps across the sky.

As the light spreads across your inner world, you feel yourself at peace. Your innermost environment is being illuminated with the relaxation. It is warming your body, and as it continues to glow, you feel yourself basking in the warm, early light. You feel calm, and the sky above you has erupted, painted with streaks of pink chasing away the darkness in the dawn. You take in another breath, feeling that all is right within your world. In your heart, you know that you are safe. You are calm. You are relaxed. You are ready to explore this inner world within yourself that you never knew existed.

You realize that you can move around in this space within yourself. You become aware that underneath you, there is a surface that you can walk upon. You can feel it, sturdy and supporting your body, underneath your feet, and you can feel the faint tickling of fresh, dew-kissed grass against your skin. It feels cold for a moment, but then it leaves you feeling refreshed. You look down, and you can see the softest, most verdant grass you have ever seen. It spreads around underneath your feet and all around you as well. If you will it, you can move about the world as well. You can walk. You can turn. You can move. This whole world exists within you, granting you that power over yourself that you can use to embrace the world. Reach out and take it,

You take one step effortlessly. Even if your body has pain, in your imagination, within yourself, it is painless to move. Your legs are strong, and they can carry you. They are powerful and supporting you. Your body is there to help you. It is there to be there for you. It loves you as only you can love yourself. As you move throughout your body, you realize that you are at peace within yourself.

As you take a step, you see that there are flowers growing behind you. With every step that you take, flowers spring up in your wake. You can see that there are marigolds, beautiful and red there as you walk. You can see irises, blue and tall. There are tiny pinkish bells of heather and bushy bunches of pansies growing all around you. Each step you take brings more into the world to dance about. Each step brings more beauty into the world.

Your own steps in the real world bring beauty as well. As you walk throughout the real world, you leave a trail in your wake. Your existence, your actions, and your presence will influence those around you. You leave your own mark on every single person that you meet, but in here, within yourself, you can physically sculpt the land. You can see the flowers, and you can smell their soft, sweet scents starting to waft up, a beautiful, bright fragrance that reminds you of a time when you were able to be in perfect peace with the world. You can feel your own peace and harmony with the world and with everyone around you. You can feel your own ability to relate to everyone around you. You can feel that you are perfectly at peace in your moment.

Now, you take a step as if you are walking up a stairway, and as you do so, you manifest a step out of nowhere. The step is almost cobbled in appearance, made of perfectly smooth stones that are warm beneath your bare feet. The step is almost perfectly molded to your feet, and you can feel yourself in the moment walking up them. Around the edges of the steps, you can see more of the flowers—snapdragons with bright orange heads this time. They sway in a breeze that tousles your hair but leaves you invigorated and calm. You feel confident. You feel at peace. You feel ready to keep exploring.

You take in a deep breath, soaking in the scent of the flowers, and you step once more, knowing that you cannot let yourself down. You step, knowing that your mind will not let you fall, and you are not disappointed. Another step, just as curiously cobbled as the last appears, just a little bit higher up this time. You take the step and see more snapdragons spring up all around it. You look around yourself, and you see the world beneath you. You can see your entire world—everything that you are—sprawling endlessly underneath the sun in the sky above you.

You continue your way up the stairs, going higher and higher, not knowing what to expect. As you walk up the stairs, you get further and further from the ground, but you do not feel afraid. You know that you are safe as you continue to walk your way up the stairs. You feel totally confident that you are in control and safe as you continue your way up them. You know that you can get there if you just keep going a little bit further... You are not sure where you are going yet, but in your heart, you know that the steps are taking you in the right direction. The more you go, the more confident that you are in the right direction. You look around yourself, and you can see nothing. You have climbed so high that the ground beneath you is nothing but a big, green patch, and above you, all you can see is the warm, early dawn sky. The colors are beautiful as they paint the clouds above you, refracting the pinks and oranges as they shine. You see the clouds, and you know that you are going up to them. You can't explain it—you just must get up there. You have a feeling that there is something there that you must go and see. Up you go, higher, higher, and higher into the sky around you.

Every step fills you with purpose. It reminds you that you are on the right track to that success that you are looking for. You take each step, knowing that you will get to where you need to go, little by little.

Soon, you make it to a layer of clouds. You stand there, looking at it for a moment. The clouds look fluffy soft all around you, plush, white, and inviting. You take the step onto them, and you are pleasantly surprised by the sensations surrounding you. Your feet feel softly embraced by the cloud's surface. You sink a little bit, but you can still feel that the cloud is firm enough to hold you up. It feels almost like walking on a large plush rug. The cloud squeezes between your toes as you walk, softly rubbing against your skin. It feels surprisingly warm, and for the first time, you realize that despite the fact that you are so high up in the sky that you can see your breath as you breathe, you are not cold at all.

In fact, you are grateful.

The sun in the sky bathes you in its golden hues, and you feel entirely content in the moment. You take a moment to bask in its warmth, and you keep walking forward. The clouds tickle as you walk, and soon, you realize that the stairs continue on up. You take another step, and this time, you manifest a stair made of the same plush cloud that you had just left behind. You keep walking, listening to the sound of your own breath, even and steady, and the soft whisper of the wind blowing around you as you continue your way. You feel ready for whatever will come next.

You are grateful for the chance to explore the world, and even beyond the world, as you continue to work your way up the stairs. Soon, you find yourself at the edge of it all. You step, and suddenly, you realize that you are no longer stepping on clouds.

You are now standing atop a massive plateau, built of stone. Strange, you tell yourself, you couldn't see the stone when you had been walking up. And, looking down, you don't seem to see anything beneath it. It is almost as if this strange, stony point is hovering there in the sky with you. You take a step onto it, expecting it to wobble. You brace yourself, but then you realize that it is perfectly still. It is not moving at all, and you are standing atop it without a care in the world. You are perfectly at home in the moment, and you know that where you are right that moment is where you were meant to be.

From your vantage point, the entirety of your world, of your imagination is visible. You can see endlessly, and you can see that your imagination is limitless. If you want to see something, you can manifest it here. You can think about what you want to see, and it will appear for you.

On one side, you can see a blanket of clouds expanding across the sky. It is slightly underneath your position. The clouds reflect the light of the gleaming sun and appear almost golden in their color as they sparkle brilliantly. You can see the surface of the clouds rippling, almost like waves of an ocean as the wind slowly carries and molds them. They ebb and flow, rotating and casting light shadows across their surfaces as they do. They look smooth and flow as they move.

Above you, you can see some thin, wispy clouds in the pale blue sky. The sun is higher now, and you can see the blue coming clear in the distance. The wisps of clouds move in their tiny little tufts, carried on air currents. They dance above you, flowing and caught in their own personal world away from your own.

You sit down on the rock surface under your feet, letting your legs dangle off the edge. You are miles above the ground, but you are unafraid. You know that you will not fall, and you know that you are safe. You sit there, watching the clouds move about, and you realize something: The clouds' rippling appears to be in response to your own breathing. With every breath that you exhale, you see what appears to be another wave, radiating out from the point where you are, rippling away from your location along the sky.

The sun above you sparkles and gleams, and though you are right in its light, you feel only warm. It is not too hot nor too cold.

You lean back on the rocks, and as you do so, you place your hands against their surfaces. They are just as smooth as the rocks that you had climbed up earlier, though these ones are darker and harder to get past. They are comfortable in your hand, and you feel at peace holding them where you do. You take in another breath, watching the beauty of your world. You feel at home.

As your hands rest on the ground, you feel something sprouting up around you. It is soft and almost warm, and when you look down, you are surprised to find that you are surrounded by grass and flowers. Little yellow flowers have popped up all around you, soft and inviting. You find yourself driven to follow them. You are pleased with how they feel, and as you look over your shoulder, you realize that the entire plateau is covered in the lush blanket of grass that spreads everywhere. That is the power of your inner peace and your mind. It creates softness and comfort wherever you go. It is self-compassion, creating a comfortable spot for you to land. Even when things are difficult, you can find yourself here. You can find yourself able to relax in the moment. You can feel comfortable where you are, and you can understand that even when you struggle, this inner peace is here for you.

As you breathe, you can hear the whispering of the grass rippling around you. You can feel it tickling, gently, with hundreds of blades, all along your hands and wrists. You can feel it wrapping you, supporting you, and relaxing you.

You feel yourself lay down in the grass, and it immediately feels like you are in the right spot. You feel like you could remain there forever. You watch as the clouds come and go above you. You can see them moving about above you in their little wisps, free and unburdened by anything. The clouds above you are utterly free and able to flow, and you can see them. You can see them moving throughout the sky as naturally as fish in water.

The sun grows lower, and you realize that you have been there far longer than you thought. You are suddenly laying there with the edges of the sky, starting to turn a faint purple with the vaguest hints of the impending twilight as the sun continues to set behind you.

Soon, the sky is alight with the sunset. It is burning brilliantly in streaks of reds and purple. It is brightly lit, filled up with pinks, and burning with oranges. It looks as if the entire sky were ablaze, and yet, the longer it lasted, the duller it grew, until finally, the entire sky faded into the darkness of night.

This time, the sky looks different. It is not the same, vast nothingness that you were in when you first arrived. The sky is dark, and yet it is filled with endless stars across its expanse. There is no moon, but that brings the brilliant

pinpricks of light into even more view. You can see
thousands upon thousands of them, more than you ever
thought there were. They shimmer and flicker in the sky.
Some of them look brighter than others. Some of them are
closer to others.

A shooting star streaks across the sky almost leisurely,
trailing behind it the long, white tail as it goes. It fills you
with a moment of peace and calmness. Then, you see
another shooting star, and another, until it looks like all of
the stars are falling out of the sky. You can see them all,
gently cascading around you. You can see them becoming
visible, almost like glitter falling out of the sky.
Then, you realize that with every star that falls, your heart
beats. Every little streak of light across the sky is a pump of
your heart in your chest, calm, and content. You feel a
concentrated warmth, right where that point in your center
is. It is relaxing, almost heavily so. You can feel yourself
sinking deeper into yourself and your mind. You can feel
yourself growing more and more tired as you do so. You can
feel yourself relaxing, fading away, and wishing for it to last.

You can feel the feelings of joy within yourself. You feel love
for yourself and respect and kindness. You feel calm. You
tell yourself that you are safe in this world. You are
somewhere that you can be certain that you will be
comfortable, and you have no worries. Any anxiety that you
have is gone. It has been thrown with your tensions, leaving
behind only the quiet, soft blanket of your peace of mind.
All you feel is yourself within you. You feel at peace and at
ease, and you are ready for yourself to remain right there.
You get more comfortable and take a deep breath.

One... Two... Three... Four... Five...

And out...

One... Two... Three... Four... Five...

As you breathe deeper, you recognize that you are bringing yourself comfort. You feel sleepier. You feel ready to relax. You feel sleep starting to reach for you, and you welcome its embrace. Your whole body is deeply relaxed as you watch the stars falling around you to the rhythm of your heart.

You feel utterly calm in that moment, more than you ever have before beneath those stars, in your own personal paradise, nestled away from everything that may have been bothering you. You are safe, and you are so sleepy.

Across the sky, you see a great, big streak. It is silver, shimmering, and it flies through the stars, leaving a shimmering tail in its wake. You watch it, never taking your eyes off of it. The shooting star itself fades away, but you can still see the streak of its tail left across the sky, spreading all the way across. You watch it, and it looks almost shimmery as it is there. It remains right there for you to see, and you watch it closely.

It's time for another deep breath in…

One… Two… Three… Four… Five…

And out…

One… Two… Three… Four… Five…

With every breath that you take, you see the streak in the sky start to fade a little bit more. It slowly fades out, first at the edges, until the edges are hazy and beginning to blur. You feel perfectly at ease, and you are ready to begin the bedtime story.

# Guided Meditation 2: Counting Down to Sleep

Close your eyes and take in a big, deep breath. Feel the air flowing through your nose. Notice how it feels. Focus on the temperature and the smells. Feel it filling up your lungs, with your lungs swelling up within you like great, big balloons in your chest until you feel like they can't swell up anymore. Feel the air warming in your chest and exhale slowly, feeling the air pass your lips gently and slowly. Is it warm? With each breath that you take, you feel yourself calming down.

You breathe in... And out...

Now, feel yourself. Focus on your center, the point just above your belly button. How does it feel? Is it tense? Tight? Stressed? Focus on this point as you inhale in. One... Two... Three... Four... Five... and out... One... Two... three... Four... Five... Focus on that spot for another breath or two...

Now, feel the tension in your body. Become aware of any tension you are holding in your head and face. As you breathe in, imagine that you are pushing the tension down to the center above your belly button. Let it gather there. Now, feel the tension in your shoulders. Focus on that stress and tension and as you breathe in, feel it moving down to your center. Let it gather there, imagining your tension and stress all becoming balled up in the center. Feel the tension in your arms and hands gathering and flowing into your center. Feel that center growing with the tension and allow it to build up. Then, take the tension from your chest and upper back, and flow it down toward your center.

Then, go down to your toes and feet, identifying the tension that is there. Push it up, feeling it flowing up your legs, through your pelvis and belly, and noting it as it arrives in the belly. Focus on it as it grows within you and allow it to flow.

Feel all of the tension in your body, all boiled up into one big ball in your core. Allow yourself to feel the weight of that tension and the burden that it has been putting on you. Take in a deep breath as you focus on it. Then, bid it goodbye and goodnight.

As you exhale, pull the tension out from your core. Envision yourself picking up the ball of stress and tension and holding it like a basketball. Feel its heft in your mind. Inhale again. One... Two... Three... Four... Five... And as you exhale, throw the ball away from you. Watch as the ball of tension flies into the air. Watch it as it continues further and further away, getting smaller and smaller into the distance as you breathe. It is much smaller now and soon, it is so small that you can no longer see it, and then it is completely gone.

Now, in that space where you pulled the tension away, in your center, imagine that peace and calmness flows into you. It is slowly manifesting within your core, filling you with peace, comfort, and the feeling that everything will be okay. You have a big, shining silver ball of peace and relaxation within your core. Breathe in... One... Two... Three... Four... Five... And out... One... Two... Three... Four... Five... As you breathe in, imagine the feeling of relaxation extending throughout your body. Feel it in your head. Breathe in... and out... Feel the relaxation pulsating in your shoulders and arms... Feel it spreading throughout your chest. Feel it spread down to your legs and feet. It fills your whole body, bringing you utter peace and relaxation. Your mind feels incredibly open and ready to go on a peaceful, relaxing adventure. Your body is ready to fall deeper and deeper into your relaxation so you can become more and more relaxed.

With your core of relaxation, you can do anything that you want. You can fend off anxiety and worry. If you feel anxious in the moment, you can turn to the light of your inner center and have that guide you toward finding your inner success and peace. If you want to be able to ensure that you are at peace, you must first focus there. You must focus on what you want to be and how you can achieve it. If you want to be at total peace, you can be with ease. All you have to do is tap into that warm center that you have within yourself.

With your eyes still closed, relax your shoulders and chest. Let your stomach go lax. Breathe in deeply as you do so, allowing yourself to focus on the sensation within yourself. Tap into it closely, holding it close to yourself so that you can be certain that you are at total peace in the moment. Work to keep your mind nice and clear as you do so. Focus only on the sensation of your breathing and forego everything else. As you do this, you can feel your anxiety begin to fade away. Any anxiety that managed to remain in your body can be pushed away with this mindfulness. You focus solely on your breath.

You breathe in...

One... Two... Three... Four... Five...

And out...

One... Two... Three... Four... Five...

You breathe in...

One... Two... Three... Four... Five...

And out...

One... Two... Three... Four... Five...

Keep breathing until you start to feel more and more relaxed. You should notice that the anxiety starts to fade away. Now, it is time to count your way to sleep. With each breath, you must repeat to yourself these affirmations. You must say them as if you believe them, focusing on how they make you feel one by one. We will count down from 40 with each deep, long breath.

You breathe in...

One... Two... Three... Four... Five...

And out...

One... Two... Three... Four... Five...

We start at 40. You can see the number clearly in your mind as you sit there. You can feel it in your mind, and if you reached out, you knew you could touch it. You see fifty feathers, all floating around gently around you. Each feather helps to melt away your anxiety that you are feeling, and you say to yourself:

*I did my best all day long, and I'm willing to forgive my shortfalls. I did enough, and I have no reason to feel anxious.*

Now, we are at 39. Envision the curves of the 3 and the 9 in your mind, seeing them clearly. There are 39 flowers in your mind's eye, growing abundantly. They smell soft and sweet.

You breathe in...

One... Two... Three... Four... Five...

And out...

One... Two... Three... Four... Five...

*I am supported. I am loved. I am safe. I am ready for a restful night of sleep.*

38. You are calm as your breath fills your body. You can feel warmth emanating from your center, helping to push away the anxiety left over from a long day of stress around yourself.

You breathe in...

One... Two... Three... Four... Five...

And out...

One... Two... Three... Four... Five...

*I feel completely at ease as I lay in bed, ready to sleep.*

37. You can hear the sounds of 37 different birds, all chirping and singing to each other somewhere around you. The sound is melodic, almost hypnotic as it trills around you. The singing is beautiful, and with every note that you hear, you feel more and more at peace within yourself. Their song helps to create a beautiful melody within yourself that shields you from the anxiety that you feel.

You breathe in...

One... Two... Three... Four... Five...

And out...

One... Two... Three... Four... Five...

*I will sleep deeply as I fall asleep. Insomnia will not keep me awake today.*

36. The number 36 is round. You can see every single curve manifesting itself in your mind's eye. You can feel it within yourself. It is a square number. You see 36 apples, stacked

up 6 by 6 in front of you, precariously balanced upon each other. However, they are perfectly stable. They are just as stable and secure as you are in your own mind right this moment.

You breathe in...

One... Two... Three... Four... Five...

And out...

One... Two... Three... Four... Five...

*I can feel myself calmly drifting off to sleep as I count.*

35. You look up into the sky. There are 35 clouds floating above you. You can get to know each one. They all look completely different than the others. They each have their own aspects within them to consider, to revere, to respect. When you see these, you realize that you are in a position where you can succeed in relaxing yourself. As the clouds drift past you, they take away your anxiety, leaving behind nothing but peace.

You breathe in...

One... Two... Three... Four... Five...

And out...

One... Two... Three... Four... Five...

*Every night, I feel that sleeping is easier. It is more comfortable.*

34. You are starting to feel sleepier as you go through this count. Now, you feel as if you can do whatever you may need to do in this world. You can see it within yourself so that you can relax. You can feel it within yourself. 34 waves

of relaxation ripple across your body as you see the number in your mind.

You breathe in...

One... Two... Three... Four... Five...

And out...

One... Two... Three... Four... Five...

*I can hear myself becoming calmer.*

33. You are able to hear your calmness. It manifests in your breathing, slow and steady in your chest. You can hear the whispers of your breath into your nose and out of your mouth. You can hear it in your heart as it beats slower and calmer. You can feel the peace coming within you as 33 autumn leaves gently drift past you on a soft breeze.

You breathe in...

One... Two... Three... Four... Five...

And out...

One... Two... Three... Four... Five...

*I will naturally fall asleep as I count down.*

32. With the manifestation of 32 in your mind, you can notice your attention drifting. It wants to wander. Your thoughts want to slip away... And you pull it back to your counting. You focus your mind on your breathing.

You breathe in...

One... Two... Three... Four... Five...

And out...

One... Two... Three... Four... Five...

*I can feel myself calming down, and I will always calm down in the evening as bedtime comes closer*

31. You feel pleasantly calm in the moment. You are enjoying the stillness that reminds you that things can be calm. Things can be safe and comfortable. You can be at ease here, in your bed. You can see 31 small, soft white moths fluttering about around you, peacefully keeping themselves just barely aloft with their wings. They look beautiful, reflecting moonlight so brilliantly that they look like they might glow.

You breathe in...

One... Two... Three... Four... Five...

And out...

One... Two... Three... Four... Five...

*I am relaxed and at peace in the moment, and even if I am not asleep, I am relaxed.*

30. You can feel yourself feeling warm in your bed. You settle down deeper, nestling down into the perfect comfortable spot, and embrace it. This is the best you have felt in a long while... peacefully content with the world around you. You hear the sounds of 30 crickets quietly chirping outside of your room.

You breathe in...

One... Two... Three... Four... Five...

And out...

One… Two… Three… Four… Five…

*I deserve to be relaxed.*
29. You focus on the sensation of sleep. What is sleep? Sleep
is when you drift away. You focus on that hazy in-between
where you are not quite asleep but not quite awake, inviting
it to come into yourself to guide you off to sleep. You can do
it as you hear the soft rustling of your sheets underneath
you.

You breathe in…

One… Two… Three… Four… Five…

And out…

One… Two… Three… Four… Five…

*I deserve to get a full night of restful sleep.*

28. You allow yourself to drift in your mind. You tell
yourself that sleep is possible. You allow yourself to sort of
float on that halfway between conscious and unconscious.
You feel perfectly at ease.

You breathe in…

One… Two… Three… Four… Five…

And out…

One… Two… Three… Four… Five…

*I can sleep all night long and still wake up refreshed. I
deserve it.*

27. You feel pleasant where you are. You focus on the
numbers as you continue to count them. Just saying the
number is enough to invite another wave of inner peace to

you that you can use to help yourself find that point of sleep. The more that you do this, the closer to sleep you feel.

You breathe in...

One... Two... Three... Four... Five...

And out...

One... Two... Three... Four... Five...

*I release everything that happened today, and I am no longer worried about what I cannot change.*

26. You can hear your body relaxing. Your feet feel pleasantly heavy, sinking deeper into your bed. You cannot bear to move them as you sit there, enjoying the comfort that they bring. You stay there for yourself, focusing on what you can do to better comfort yourself.

You breathe in...

One... Two... Three... Four... Five...

And out...

One... Two... Three... Four... Five...

*I am thankful for what I did today.*

25. As you think about 25, you feel calm. You feel thankful for the day that you have and for every aspect of it. Every moment was valuable for you, and you genuinely appreciate it. Imagine the best part of your day for a moment, focusing immensely on it as you sit there in your mind. Relive that moment of calm quiet that you loved. Focus on how wonderful it was and how happy and grateful you are that you can move forward tomorrow as well, loved, happy, and well-rested.

You breathe in...

One... Two... Three... Four... Five...

And out...

One... Two... Three... Four... Five...

*Sleep is natural, and my body knows exactly how to get me to that point.*

24. You can see 24 stars above where you are. They are twinkling and glistening above you. They shimmer and shine. They dance and move. They are beautiful. You feel in awe of the and of the world that they exist in. You marvel at the wonders of the universe and feel so glad to be a part of it.

You breathe in...

One... Two... Three... Four... Five...
And out...

One... Two... Three... Four... Five...

*I am allowed to have a sleep that is restful and complete.*

23. You feel better now. Your body is entirely at ease. Now, you must help your mind find that inner peace as well, one step at a time. You hear your thoughts, one by one, dancing around you. They are getting louder and louder... Your doubts and fears... And one by one, you silence them. You let them drift away from you so that you can get back to your clarity and peace.

You breathe in...

One... Two... Three... Four... Five...

And out...

One... Two... Three... Four... Five...

*I can fall asleep whenever I am ready and whenever I choose to do so.*

22. You can feel that your body is ready to sleep, but your mind is still doubting. Gently, you remind your mind that everything that happened today happened for a reason, even if you do not understand it. You let go of the things that you don't understand, and you remind yourself that you can successfully get through your life, one night at a time.

You breathe in...

One... Two... Three... Four... Five...

And out...

One... Two... Three... Four... Five...

*My sleep and my dreams will be peaceful.*

21. Your mind is starting to slow down now... It still has some stirrings of doubt, of anxiety, of worry... But you know in your heart that things will be okay. You know that you can create the life that you want to live, and that begins with a night of good sleep.

You breathe in...

One... Two... Three... Four... Five...

And out...

One... Two... Three... Four... Five...

*I am in control of how I sleep.*

20. You remind yourself that you are what you attract. If you want restful sleep, you must project out that you are open to restful sleep, and you must genuinely open up your mind to it. When you open up your mind to the peace within yourself, you know that you can bring in that peaceful night's sleep.

You breathe in...

One... Two... Three... Four... Five...

And out...

One... Two... Three... Four... Five...

*I sleep soundly.*

19. The more that you focus on your sleep, the more inviting it becomes. You feel the need for sleep growing stronger... Heavier... More compelling. Your body is starting to feel far away as you continue to breathe and relax.

You breathe in...

One... Two... Three... Four... Five...

And out...

One... Two... Three... Four... Five...

*I can feel myself falling asleep.*

18. You are getting closer than ever to falling asleep, and you welcome and embrace it. You are happy to have that sleep coming your way, and all you must do is welcome it into your own life. If you want that peace and solitude, all you have to do is remind yourself that you can achieve it.

You breathe in...

One... Two... Three... Four... Five...

And out...

One... Two... Three... Four... Five...

*I can feel my muscles relaxing.*

17. Your whole body feels so far away that you feel like you are going to float away. You can see yourself in your mind's eye, resting comfortably and in total relaxation. You can see that there are no dangers here. You are in your own home, within your own walls, and able to get the rest that you are looking for.

You breathe in...

One... Two... Three... Four... Five...

And out...

One... Two... Three... Four... Five...

*I can feel my eyes getting heavy.*

16. You surround yourself in your mind with the peace and serenity you need. It slowly comes toward you, a peaceful, soft light that engulfs your whole body. You can see that you have a haze of light surrounding you, basking you in a faint silvery light. This light is your protection. It will help you to sleep.

You breathe in...

One... Two... Three... Four... Five...

And out...

One... Two... Three... Four... Five...

*I am happy to be here, ready for sleep.*

15. You tell yourself that the light around you is your barrier between the world and yourself. It will help you to keep the negative thoughts out of your mind, allowing only the positive thoughts into yourself so you can begin to relax and enjoy a night without worrying about burdening yourself or being unable to sleep. You focus on just how happy and content you are in the moment. You are perfectly relaxed, and you are happier than ever.

You breathe in...

One... Two... Three... Four... Five...

And out...

One... Two... Three... Four... Five...

*My dreams will be full of just as much serenity as I am right now, counting.*

14. You think about your most perfect dream. You can see it in your mind's eye, and you focus intently on it. You can bring it to fruition. The more you focus on it, the more likely that you are to sleep and dream it.

You breathe in...

One... Two... Three... Four... Five...

And out...

One... Two... Three... Four... Five...

*My head feels heavy as I rest it.*

13. You are so tired that you can barely stand it any longer. You can't keep up with fighting it off any longer. You can't keep yourself awake any longer in your current state, and

you know that... So you make the decision to let sleep overcome you.

You breathe in...

One... Two... Three... Four... Five...

And out...

One... Two... Three... Four... Five...

*My sleep will heal my body so I can feel better and ready to take on the day.*

12. You remind yourself of all of the wonderful benefits that you manifest when you are able to sleep at night. You know that your body will heal. You imagine there being great, big, healing waves flowing over your body, following your willingness to sleep.

You breathe in...

One... Two... Three... Four... Five...

And out...

One... Two... Three... Four... Five...

*I am a heavy sleeper, and I will be able to sleep, even if there is some noise.*

11. You imagine yourself sleeping all night long, waking up the next morning in total peace and comfort. You remind yourself that you can get yourself there. You just have to keep focusing and allow the sleep to take over.

You breathe in...

One... Two... Three... Four... Five...

And out…

One… Two… Three… Four… Five…

*I'm ready to let go of my anxiety and the insomnia that comes with it.*

10. You know that the sleep is going to take you over, and you are welcoming it.

You breathe in…

One… Two… Three… Four… Five…

And out…

One… Two… Three… Four… Five…


*I'm ready to fall asleep deeply.*

9. You can hear your breathing shifting again. It is even slower and deeper. It is peaceful. You are at peace.

You breathe in…

One… Two… Three… Four… Five…

And out…

One… Two… Three… Four… Five…


*My body is open to a complete, relaxing state where I can sleep.*

8. You can feel yourself getting so close to sleeping. The more that you focus on the sleep, the more that you want it. You can imagine yourself sleeping. You can see your cells

within your body healing themselves, becoming more capable of getting through to you. You can feel yourself relaxing more and more... And you are ready to embrace it.

You breathe in...

One... Two... Three... Four... Five...

And out...

One... Two... Three... Four... Five...

*I release the negativity and negative energy within myself.*

7. The negative thoughts that have bothered you all night long are rejected. There is no reason for your anxiety to rule you any longer. You should not allow those thoughts to hold you back or prevent you from success. You can do this. You just have to embrace it.

You breathe in...

One... Two... Three... Four... Five...

And out...

One... Two... Three... Four... Five...

*My bedroom is my sanctuary; my point of peace and relaxation. It is my place I can truly be at home.*

6. You take that silvery light that was shining around you, and you feel it expand around your entire bedroom. It shields you. It protects you. It prevents you from giving in to the negativity in the world while also shielding you from the negativity that exists out there as well. You can fend it off this way. You can thrive and survive.

You breathe in...

One... Two... Three... Four... Five...

And out...

One... Two... Three... Four... Five...

*I am worthy of that stress-free sleep that I will achieve.*

5. You remind yourself that you deserve sleep. Everyone deserves sleep just as much as everyone deserves food, warmth, and love. Sleep is essential, and you deserve to get a good, peaceful night's rest within yourself. You deserve to feel good, to feel content, and to feel in total love with yourself. You deserve to get that sleep, and you are the only one that can give it to yourself.

You breathe in...

One... Two... Three... Four... Five...

And out...

One... Two... Three... Four... Five...

*As I sleep, I will attract more success and peace tomorrow.*

4. You remind yourself that your sleep will help you. You have no reason to sacrifice it to try to force through other things. You deserve to rest. You need to rest. You will rest.

You breathe in...

One... Two... Three... Four... Five...

And out...

One... Two... Three... Four... Five...

*I know that my insomnia is interfering with my sleep, but I will reject it. I release it back into the world. I am ready and open to sleep.*

3. You are so close now... you can barely even think. You can barely even focus on your breathing within your chest. You are ready to give in completely. And you do.

You breathe in...

One... Two... Three... Four... Five...

And out...

One... Two... Three... Four... Five...

*My body is awake during the day, so it can sleep at night.*

2. You give in to the need to sleep, and you will thank yourself tomorrow for it.

You breathe in...

One... Two... Three... Four... Five...

And out...

One... Two... Three... Four... Five...

*I will wake up to my alarm clock, awake, and ready to go.*

1. You are ready. You are asleep. You are at total peace without an ounce of anxiety left in you.

You breathe in...

One... Two... Three... Four... Five...

And out...

One... Two... Three... Four... Five...

*I am now ready to sleep entirely. My body is perfectly relaxed and ready. My mind is at peace. My heart is happy. Good night, sleep well. Rest peacefully.*

# Description

*Bedtime stories aren't just for kids anymore...*

Do you find that you suffer from insomnia, no matter how hard you try to cope with it? Are you always exhausted even though you know that you shouldn't be? If you find that bedtime is impossible for you to cope with, then this book is for you!

As you read through this book, you will be introduced to the idea of using stories and mindfulness to help yourself drift off to sleep. There is a reason that bedtime stories are so recommended for getting children to sleep. After all— having time to enjoy a story allows your mind to relax and allows you to begin to focus more on the moment. As you listen to bedtime stories, or as you read them, you are able to feel at peace. You can allow your mind to focus on those details that you might not otherwise be able to. You will find that being able to enjoy a story will help your mind relax and grant you that ability to sleep.

In this book, you will first be introduced to the idea of mindful meditation so you can begin to understand just how powerful it can be. Then, you will be provided with several options for bedtime stories. Each story is designed to be a calming slice of life story about the various adventures (and sometimes misadventures) of Sophie Rogers, a young woman that lives in the Pacific Northwest with her German shepherd pal, Bella. Together, and sometimes separately, they get out and enjoy their lives, and the stories of her day to day life can help you to relax and soothe yourself into a state in which you will be able to relax. As you read, you should find yourself calming down and preparing for a night of sleep. Each of the options that are provided to you should be fun and engaging without keeping you up at night.

Finally, at the end of the book, you will be given two more traditional mindful meditations that are designed to trigger that state of mindfulness within yourself so you can then begin to relax and enjoy a restful night's sleep. When you learn to use these various techniques, you can work with yourself to ensure that you can calm yourself down when you need to, allowing yourself to get that relaxation that you need.

If you're ready to start sleeping better, then you are in the right spot. This book may be able to help you relax enough to fall asleep! As you read, you can expect to see:

- An adventure in which Sophie and Bella go hiking and get lost in the mountains
- A rush for Sophie and her best friend, Cara, to get to the airport in time for their vacation to Greece that teaches them a valuable lesson
- A tour through the Acropolis of Athens, the place of Sophie's dreams
- A trip through a beautiful mansion as Cara tries to buy a house in the area and tours some of the nicest areas that town has to offer
- A story in which Sophie runs into her old roommate from college and catches up with her
- A misadventure through the mall where Sophie tries something new and learns not to trust all of the different activities and ideas suggested on the internet
- Two guided meditations to help you fall asleep with ease

If you're ready to fall asleep, then don't let another day pass you buy. Enjoy these stories and see if sleep is more within your grasp than you realized!

# Bedtime Stories for Adults:

*Soothing Sleep Stories with Guided Meditation. Dive Into Deep Sleep Hypnosis to Prevent Anxiety and Panic Attacks. Let Go of Stress and Relax. Book 2*

# Table of Contents

# Introduction

Stress is something that we all carry within us. We have finances. We have relationships, romantic, personal, and platonic that can weigh on us. We have careers that we have to manage. We have families (possibly). We have responsibilities that force us to act within the world and those can be incredibly exhausting. We can find ourselves barely able to cope with ourselves in these times. In fact, roughly 33% of adults report that they struggle with sleep at any given point in time. They may find that they can't fall asleep. Others find that they can't stay asleep. No matter where you may fall on that spectrum, however, the consequences are real. You can't sleep and you feel *awful*. You feel like you can't successfully get through anything. You find yourself struggling with everything that you do and that is not fair to you. It is incredibly unfair that you find yourself feeling entirely bogged down by your inability to sleep, and all day long, you will struggle to perform up to standard. You won't be able to help yourself or succeed at anything that you need to do.

Sleep is essential to your day. It is imperative to your body and mind. You must be able to sleep at some point, and if you don't get it at night, your body will take it in other ways. Working heavy machinery when tired is dangerous. Driving while having not slept in the last 17 hours creates equivalent impairment to being legally drunk with a blood alcohol level of 0.05% due to the slowing responses that you will have. If you aren't careful, you can find yourself in a serious accident if you are not getting enough sleep to keep yourself well cared for.

Beyond just causing impairment, however, not getting enough sleep is going to make other problems come to light as well. You are going to find that you struggle with being able to function in all aspects of your life. Of course, struggling will only exacerbate those feelings of stress that you have, and that will in turn lead to you getting even less sleep in a constant feedback loop of your own personal struggles. If you want to avoid this problem, you need sleep. Of course, that is easier said than done when you are tired and stressed out! Insomnia tends to repeat itself and make itself worse over time. It can cause you to seriously struggle by no fault of your own, but you can learn to fix the problem.

This book is here to provide you with a handful of stories that you can enjoy that will help you to gently fall asleep. As you read though this book, you will be treated to two guided meditations and seven different stories that are designed to help you. Those first two meditations are not the traditional bedtime story that you may be accustomed to—these stories are guided meditations. They are meant to help you fall asleep by redirecting your focus. The remaining seven stories are there

If you have read the first book, you know that there were three meditative techniques that were introduced. In this book, you will be introduced to another meditative technique that will be used—this time, we will make use of progressive relaxation to slowly but surely let go of your anxiety and depression or stress that may be holding you back from getting your sleep. You can find that sleep that you are looking for—you just have to learn how to achieve it and this book will help you. You will also be focusing on the mindful concept of acceptance—of being in the moment and not resisting.

Progressive relaxation starts first with a body scan. You will work your way throughout the entire body, bit by bit. You will look at each part of your body to understand what may hurt or where your tension or anxiety is manifesting. Then, with progressive relaxation, you will slowly release it little by little. You will start with your head, feeling your scalp relax first, then your forehead and your other body parts as well. Over time, you will eventually make your way all the way down to your toes to help yourself relax. This involves working over your whole body to leave yourself relaxed and calm so that you can achieve anything that you may want.

Keep in mind that if you currently suffer from anxiety or depression, this book will not magically treat you. It will not make you suddenly un-depressed or un-anxious. This book is not the substitution for a doctor or anything else, either. It is something that you can use to help yourself to alleviate symptoms of anxiety and depression by teaching you how you can relax your body on your own time. You will be empowered to take control of your own body so you can successfully achieve the sleep you have been missing. However, if you find that these techniques do not help you, you may want to consider seeing your doctor for a more thorough checkup to ensure that you are not suffering from something else that is causing the problem.

Relaxation comes from within. If you want to be at peace with yourself, you have to be willing to accept yourself. You have to practice accepting the current moment without resistance. You must help yourself to stop trying to resist what you cannot control. You must sometimes be willing to accept that all there is for you to do is to be at peace. Sometimes, all you can do is remind yourself that you must simply relax and be one with yourself. Sometimes, your anxiety is about things that you cannot fix, and that is what will keep you awake at night. The easiest fix for that is to let go. It is to release that fear and anxiety within yourself so that you can do better. That is what these meditation stories are here to teach you—you will explore worlds and learn that sometimes, you must just focus. Sometimes, you must just go with the flow and see what happens. This is freeing— it will teach you that you don't have to waste your time worrying about things that you have no control over.

Now, if you are ready to get started, a full night's sleep is within your reach—you just have to get started. If you are ready, find your way to your bed, get yourself comfortable, and let's get started. Good night!

# Story 1: Beachside Bonanza

*Sophie completely forgot that she had agreed to go to the beach with all her friends, and when her good friend Cara shows up, demanding that she goes along with them anyway, even on short notice, Sophie realizes she has no choice! She has to fulfill the beach day promise, and even if she doesn't want to at first, she knows that she'll have a great day doing nothing at all—and it will be worth every moment of it thanks to doing nothing at the beach.*

"What do you mean you forgot?!" a young woman, perhaps 25, cried out in disbelief as she stared at Sophie, eyes wide. She had beautiful blue eyes, perfect blonde waves that cascaded down her shoulders, and a perfect fit body. She was the epitome of the beach babe as she sat there, staring at Sophie in shock as she waited for her best friend to explain herself. She was all ready to go already, dressed in a bikini with a thin, lace cover-up and a wrap skirt around her waist. Her sunglasses were perched carefully above her face, and her full lips were in a full pout. "Sophie! If we don't hurry up and leave, we won't get the best spots!"

Sophie grinned sheepishly. "I'm sorry, Cara, I forgot!" she looked around her house. She could probably be ready to go in about fifteen minutes, but she still felt bad. Traffic could get quite bad on those Saturday morning drives out to the beach, especially when the weather was forecasted to be hot. "I can hurry!"

"You better!" Cara frowned playfully at her friend before ushering her away with perfectly manicured hands. Cara was the kind of woman who had to be fashionable in all senses—but fashionably late. She was the kind of person that had to be perfectly punctual everywhere that they went, and if she wasn't 10 minutes early, she was late. Sophie, on the other hand... Now, Sophie was the queen of fashionably late. She was always running behind wherever she went, and whenever she left. She was constantly finding herself battling against the clock, and unfortunately for her, she typically was the loser.

Off Sophie ran, tossing together as many of her beach items as she could into her beach bag, silently thanking the universe that she had felt compelled to shave the night prior. At least that was one thing she didn't have to worry about. Into the bag went her sunscreen, a beach towel, a change in clothes, her favorite book, and a water bottle, and she rushed into her room to change into her swimsuit.

"I'm waiting!!" she could hear Cara cry from downstairs, and she grinned.

"I'm coming!!" she cried back just as loudly. She picked up the bag and barreled back down the stairs as quickly as she could go, but Sophie, ever the ungraceful one, managed to slip near the bottom, crashing down onto her butt and sliding down the final three stairs. "Oof!" she cried out, looking up at Cara. Her cheeks were tinged red with embarrassment and her eyes watered a bit from the pain.

"Shake it off, sweetie, we're going beach bumming!" Cara extended her hand and pulled Sophie up with a smile before she squealed in excitement. "Let's get going! Everyone else will be there soon!"

"I know, I know!" Sophie replied, rubbing her bottom with a sigh. It was just her luck to go to the beach with a bruised tailbone! She rushed out the door and headed toward the car, bag over her shoulder, phone and keys in hand, and ready to go.
An hour later and they were pulling up onto the beautiful white sand of the beach. They were lucky to live in such a diverse area—the mountains were an hour away from one direction, and the beach was the other way, and on that day, she was thrilled to be there. The weather was projected to be

100 degrees all day long, and at the very least, being by the beach would make it bearable if they chose to get into the water. More than anything, however, Sophie was glad to gather up with all of her friends. It had been a while since they had all gotten together, and she was thrilled to have the opportunity to do so for the first time in far too long.

"Oh, great!" Cara called out, raising one hand up as high as she could and waggling her fingers to wave at someone with a grin. "Looks like Lucian, Selah, and Declan are already there. They got a good spot, too! Look—close enough to the snacks, but far enough away that we're not going to be trampled. Good picking, guys!!" The last sentence came out as a squeal of delight as she tried to project her voice toward the other side of the beach. She grinned at everyone. "Aren't we so lucky?"

"Incredibly!" Sophie agreed with a grin. "Let's go!" As soon as their shoes touched the sand, they immediately came off. It was soft and so warm from the sun. Each step caused it to mold around their feet as they sank a little bit, but it was quite pleasant to walk atop. The sun wasn't overwhelmingly hot yet, and the cool ocean breeze brought the temperature just low enough to comfortable. Before long, they were setting up next to their friends, complete with beach umbrellas, plenty of beach towels, a cooler of drinks, and plenty fo excitement for the day.

"Hey, Sophie!" Declan called out with a grin. He was standing there with a grin on his face as he waved at her. He was topless, exposing his impeccably toned and tanned abs, wearing a pair of Hawaiian print swim trunks. Declan's warm, brown eyes met Sophie's gaze and he was genuinely happy to see her as he passed her a cold drink from the cooler. "So, how's the day going?"

"Smashing," Sophie replied with a grin and Cara groaned in mock annoyance at the pun, lightly swatting at Sophie's arm.

"Sophie here just had a bit of an accident this morning. No big deal," Cara chimed in. "Why don't you tell them about it?"

And suddenly, all eyes were on Sophie as she looked at her friends. They were eager to hear what she had to say, and she sighed. "It was no big deal—I slid down the bottom of my stairs, that's all."

Lucian winced in response, flashing a sympathetic smile. "You okay?"

"Yeah, fine!" Sophie replied. "So, what's the plan for the day?"

"Just this," Declan replied, stretching out on his towel. "Lots of R&R out here while we soak up some waves.

"We could go play volleyball!" chimed in Selah.

"Or... *you* could go play volleyball, and we'll cheer you on," Lucian replied, and everyone laughed. It was great to be there, relaxing and no one was quite ready to get out and get sweaty yet. They would much rather spend the time just enjoying the moment of peace.

Selah settled back down onto her towel. "What, Luce, too afraid I'll wipe the floor with you?"

"Something like that," he replied through a sip of his drink. His eyes glowed with laughter as he looked at her. Lucian and Selah had been dating for some time at that point, and they were a great couple together—lots of teasing, but Sophie could tell they genuinely cared for each other.

"Well, I don't know about you guys, but I think I'm interested in some sunbathing, and then maybe burying

Lucian in the deepest hole we can manage. Although, it'll be kind of hard to bury that level of ego!"

"Ooh, Sophie, I'm hurt!" he replied with a faux scandalized look on his face.

"Not as much as Sophie's butt!" Declan tossed in, and they all laughed for a moment. It sure was great to be back together, Sophie noted. She was thrilled that they got this opportunity together.

The group fell into a comfortable silence at that point. Sophie was sprawled across her towel, positioning it in the sun at the moment. She was lying, stomach down, simply watching the waves come in and out. Sometimes, it was just fun to people watch while sitting about, and she was thrilled to have that chance.

The ocean itself was shining a beautiful deep blue color, reflecting the sun off of the ripples and waves as it gently lapped up on the shore, rhythmically creating that heartbeat of the song of the beach. The water went on endlessly onto the horizon, meeting the deep blue sky along the way. There was not a cloud in the sky that day—just blue as far as the eye could see up until the sandy beach, covered in rainbow umbrellas, towels, and people wearing every color imaginable. Along with the sounds of waves, Sophie could hear the piercing cries of the seagulls, and the squeals of laughter of both adults and children alike. The sound of music could be heard in the distance and she could tell that the entire day was going to be great. A day at the beach was always a day of leisure, and even if she never moved from that spot, she knew that she would be satisfied with herself and the entire situation. She knew that the day would be a total win if she could sit there just a little bit longer.

As the sun warmed her back, she watched a group of children not too far from where she was sitting. They were happily building a sand castle where they stood, carefully scooping up wet sand into their buckets that they had brought with them. The sand, when wet, was almost the color of brown sugar, she noted, and stuck together about as much as well. She watched them as they worked to pack it in and then carefully place the lump of sand right into place. Their castle was quite intricate—it was clear that they had done this a few times. It had four big pillars, connected with carefully hand-sculpted walls. All around the castle was a great, big moat that they had filled with water, and they had even constructed a carefully built drawbridge with driftwood that they could push over and allow their small collection of action figures to cross at will. The castle was even decorated with all sorts of different items as well— there were seashell windows and a few sand dollars that were being used as decorations at the top as well, and a couple of seagull feathers as flags. All in all, it was quite creative.

Soon, Sophie found her attention drifting to the nearby volleyball game. They were sitting somewhat near a net, likely thanks to Selah's preferences and affinity for the game. She noticed that Selah was over there, too—Selah was petite with deep black hair, great curves, and bronzed skin, and she was fantastic at volleyball. She never ceased to remind everyone about her own experience playing in high school and college, and she continued to play at her local gym as much as she could as well. Sophie watched as Selah got a few great spikes in and wiped the floor with the opposing team, while Lucian was cheering for her from his position as well.

Sophie smiled as she heard him cheering for her—she was so glad to know that he liked her as much as he did. Lucian had always been the bachelor buddy—the one that they all bet would never get married or even settle down into a serious relationship. Seeing him do so was a breath of freshwater.

Her attention drifted again, back to the waves. There was a group of people playing in the waves, and further out at sea, she could see tiny fins, brightly colored. They were sails for boats, all far out at sea, probably fishing for something. There were also people jet skiing, surfing, and floating about. There were children splashing around, squealing happily, in the waves, and people who appeared to be completely uninterested in going in the water at all. It was always interesting to see the different people, Sophie told herself.

"Honey, you have to roll over, or you're going to be well done on your back!" Cara was peering down at her, over her shades. She raised a brow at her friend and used one hand to gesture for Sophie to roll over. "Well? What are you waiting for?" Sophie grinned and groaned and rolled to the front. It was nice to get her back out of the sun, but now, she realized, it was too bright to do anything at all but close her eyes.

So, Sophie shut them, basking in the sun. She allowed the sunlight's warmth to bask over her, covering her in the light that is produced. It was just comfortable, teetering on too hot and it was relaxing. She found herself growing more and more relaxed as she sat there, soaking up the rays, and she didn't really want to get up at all—she just wanted to keep enjoying the moment.

As she sat there, she listened to the sounds of the beach once more, slowly turning her attention to the sound of her breath coming in and out. It was gentle and slow as it came, and she could tell just from the sound of her breath alone that she was feeling highly relaxed. She was ready to enjoy her moment.

# Story 2: Wedding Bells Ring

*Who doesn't love love? Sophie is thrilled to go to her good friend's wedding, and she is so happy for the lovely couple. She spends her day rushing to get ready, thrilled to enjoy the moment and watch as two more people in the world declare their love for each other and decide that they are going to commit to a lifetime of togetherness. It's so beautiful!*

Sophie was up before her alarm for once. She found herself lying in bed, looking out the window. The sun was already up and shining in the sky, and there was not a cloud in sight. It was a perfect day for an outdoor wedding, and that was exactly what they were going to have that day. Sophie was heading out for the day for a local destination wedding—she and a dozen of her friends were all going to be out at an island only accessible by ferry for a beautiful wedding, followed by a day staying in a few of the local bed and breakfasts before everyone made it back to the mainland. They were only maybe an hour from home, but they were so separated by virtue of needing to take the ferry to get there that it felt like a far off destination wedding. It was going to be exciting and beautiful, and a real testament to their love. Sophie was thrilled to see it. She knew that it would be a fantastic wedding, complete with plenty of love and happiness. They didn't need to have some extravagant wedding far from home—just the small, cozy ceremony would be enough for them and it was perfection as far as Sophie was concerned. What was more intimate than enjoying the day with your closest friends and the family that you love?

Sophie was excited to see that testament to love. She was confident that it would be great—it would be just as perfect as she was imagining and she honestly couldn't wait. Though Sophie wasn't married herself and even though she hadn't come even close to finding her own special someone in her life, she knew that she would eventually and she

found great joy in watching other people around her get it.
She loved to see what people's lives were like after they
married and she was confident that she would have a
fantastic time listening to everyone else.

She pushed herself out of bed and went straight to the
shower. The wedding party would be getting ready to go at
the island, but she knew that she should at least be
presentable as possible on the ferry. After all, the ferry had a
nice café, and she figured that she and her friends would all
be stopping to get some coffee while they waited on the
thirty minutes that it would take to get there. So, shower, a
nice sundress, and makeup it was before she left for the
ferry.

It didn't take her long to be ready to go—she just had to
wash her hair, throw on a basic amount of makeup, and get
dressed to go. She spent maybe thirty minutes in all
preparing, putting on a pink dress. It had short sleeves, and
the material flowed all around her. There were small red
flowers printed across the fabric to accentuate it, and the
color went perfectly with her skin and hair. It made her look
warmer, more vibrant, and more alive than she had been,
and it looked great if she didn't say so herself.
The journey to the ferry terminal took all of thirty minutes,
and when she pulled into the line with her car, she was
ready to go. She pulled out a book that she had been
reading. It was a riveting tale of star-crossed lovers who
fought against the odds to be together. Though Sophie
wasn't much for romance in her day to day life, she couldn't
help it: She was a romantic at heart. She loved being able to
see these beautiful proclamations of love, and she loved
reading about the romanticized versions of life as well.

Eventually, the ferry was loaded up, and she got the
message from her friends—head inside the cabin for a quick
drink at the café. So, off Sophie went, leaving her book in
place and heading inside. All of her friends were there,
huddled around a table near a window that overlooked the

beautiful blue water that they were crossing. Sophie took a
seat next to Cara and Selah. Around the table, there was
also Lindsay, Freya, and Alyssa. They had all been friends
since college and stuck to being able to spend time together.
Lindsay was a pediatrician in a nearby city. She was married
with plans to adopt children in the near future. Freya was
happily single as well, with no intention of settling down.
She was enjoying the off-beat artist's life, painting and
selling her services and pieces of art to local cafes and
restaurants. She did quite well, and she figured that
children would only slow down her lifestyle. Alyssa was a
preschool teacher who loved children. She was the bride to
be, and she looked *amazing.*

Alyssa was fair-skinned—she looked as though she might
burn if she were out in the sun for longer than twenty
minutes. Her features were soft and almost ethereal as she
smiled serenely, light shining in from the window nearby.
She had soft blue eyes and pale blonde hair, and she was
quite dainty in appearance. Her eyes were shining with
excitement, and Sophie could tell that she was *thrilled* to be
heading to her wedding destination.

"Are you ready?" asked Cara, feigning concern. "After all, as
soon as the day is over, you're off the market. *Forever.*" She
laughed with a smile on her face, and Alyssa returned it. Of
their friends, Alyssa was by far the shyest of the group. She
was happy to be there with them all, but she was always
happiest watching everyone else enjoy themselves without
feeling the pressure to really engage with them too much.
She was there as added support, but she was definitely one
of the best listeners in the group. She was beloved for this
reason—she was like the group mother that always had
answers whenever they got stuck doing something that they
couldn't get through. She was greatly appreciated for her
work because of that, and none of the group could imagine
life without her.

"It'll be great!" Alyssa said, smiling shyly. "Thank you for coming. Really. It means a lot that you're all here with me. I couldn't imagine it any different than this."

"Of course, we're here. We love you!" Freya said, patting her on the shoulder. "You're one of our best friends!"

The others echoed the sentiment, nodding their heads emphatically. They were thrilled to see her there, and they were perfectly content being there.

Alyssa blushed and looked down in response. She hadn't really expected that from her friends, and that made her happy to hear. Sophie reached across the table to hold her hands. "We're happy for you."

The girls all chitchatted together as the ferry made its way across the water, and before they knew it, they were pulling into the dock and being instructed to get into their cars and drive off. They were planning on meeting at the local country club, one of the few places on the island that had something other than trails. The island itself was quite small, and there were only a few buildings there. There were only about 600 houses across the entire island, a single small one-stop-shop with one little gas pump, the restaurant, and the one country club for the island members that people are visiting could also rent.

It was a beautiful island, Sophie discovered as they drove off. The whole island was plush with growth, and it hardly felt like they were in a town at all. All of the island was said to be one small town, but to Sophie, it felt more like a forest paradise, separated from the hustle and bustle of the mainland while still be close and accessible if they needed to go to it. It was almost picturesque, feeling like it was more of a movie scene than anything else, and yet they were there.

The club was on the opposite end of the island—they drove across the whole thing, a whole six miles and without a single stop light, all the way to the club. There was a large marina that spanned across the entirety of the shore there, overlooking a beautiful scene of nothing but blue ocean. Puget Sound was technically part of the sea and connected all the way out to the ocean. Whales were known to go through the area that they were overlooking. While it didn't look like there were any whales at that moment in time, they also knew that there was a chance that there could be.

Inside the club was a big community room. It wasn't anything fancy, but it had plenty of space for a meal for all of them to enjoy, and it looked great. Inside the room, there were two long banquet tables, topped with white tablecloths and small bouquets of baby's breath and pale pink roses placed every few place settings. There were maybe 20 in all setup—enough for the guests and the bride and groom. It was definitely a small setup, but each white plate was beautiful ceramic, carefully etched, and molded to create a beautiful design of delicate flowers all along the rims. Each chair was carefully pushed in, with white tulle bows tied at the back. There were strings of lights in a soft white hanging above them, sparkling in the sunlight. Sophie was certain that when they were turned on later, they'd look fantastic, glimmering, and providing a gentle glow to the evening.

They were ushered around, with people who were planning and organizing getting everything going. Sophie found herself very quickly in a room in the back of the club that she was being done up in. Each of the women who were attending the wedding was in there, getting their hair done and their makeup put on. Sophie changed into her dress, a beautiful champagne colored mermaid style dress, hugging her waist and flaring out at the end. The top was lace and the fabric itself was a soft, silky material. It was comfortable, breathed well even in the summer heat, and she thought she looked great.

Sophie looked at herself in the mirror and smiled as she tied her hair up into a loose bun, and she perfected her makeup on her face as well. She was satisfied with how she looked and turned to see how everyone else was doing. Everyone looked great and so far, there was no drama at all. Everything was going perfectly so far and she was thrilled.

Before long, they were all gathering up and congregating at the location for the wedding ceremony. They were going to a point in the island that overlooked the water. They were surrounded by trees, beautifully verdant all around them. There was a wedding arch painted white, covered in flowers all around it. It was gorgeous and underneath it was space for the bride and groom. There were a handful of chairs all positioned in front of it, and quickly, they were all filled up. It didn't take long for everyone to get settled, and then the music started.

As soon as the wedding music began, heads turned. The groom, a man named Alex, walked down the aisle in his suit. He wore a fitted black jacket over his vest and white shirt. His slacks matched perfectly, and his tie was a beautiful maroon color. He had a white rose pinned to his lapel as well as he settled down on one end of the wedding arch. There was an officiant standing there in the center of the arch, waiting for them. Then, Alyssa came down the aisle. She stepped out, looking absolutely stunning. Her hair was allowed to cascade behind her, lightly waved, but free to flow. Her makeup was impeccable—she looked almost unworldly with how beautiful she looked. Her dress had a nice deep v neck plunge, curving to wrap around her breasts, and lace sleeves. The waist was tucked in, and the tulle and chiffon body of the dress shimmered in the sunlight as it wrapped around her, flowing in the gentle breeze. Her shoes were a light silver strapped sandal with small heels. In her hands was a beautiful bouquet, with white calla lilies and deep red roses, along with a few clusters of baby's breath. She held the bouquet up to her chest as she walked down the aisle shyly, the faintest hints of a blush staining her pale cheeks as she did. Her lips were parted ever so slightly as she gazed at her groom, smiling as they locked eyes.

Alex was almost dumbfounded as he saw his bride. His eyes widened, and his smile grew across his face. He couldn't take his eyes off of her as she approached him. Sophie could have sworn she saw tears spring to his eyes as he was finally able to see her for the first time. Sophie always loved watching the groom's reactions to seeing their soon-to-be wives—it was always so pure seeing the sudden rush of emotion in their faces, and she was always so excited to watch on.

As Alyssa made her way to her groom, everyone stared with wide smiles. They joined hands together, and Sophie could see Alex whisper something to Alyssa that she couldn't quite make out, but judging by her teary-eyed smile, she was happy to hear it.

The officiant smiled at the couple. He had a book in his hand, glanced at the paper, then back up at the crowd before he began to speak. "We are gathered here today to witness the union of Alex and Alyssa. Welcome, all! Today is the beginning of a lifelong journey for this couple, and you are here to witness it. Through their mutual love, trust, and respect, they have chosen to live their lives together, embarking on the next major chapter. We are here to celebrate the love and light that we can all see in their relationship, sending them off and wishing them well on such a joyous occasion."

The officiant looked back and forth once more. "So, if anyone would like to object to the forming of their new union, speak now, and forever hold your peace." He looked around the crowd expectantly as Alex and Alyssa tore their eyes away from each other to glance at their audience. The wedding attendants chuckled but remained silent, and both the bride and groom smiled. Sophie wasn't surprised at the lack of objections—they were like the perfect couple for each other, and she was so happy they were finally making it official.

The officiant nodded his head sagely in acceptance. "Perfect, then let's get started!" He looked to the couple once more. "Marriage is one of the most integral parts of our lives as people. As we stand here, we acknowledge that the vows that you are about to take are amongst the most important of your life. They are vows that we have honored throughout the generations, recognizing the real commitment that comes with the declaration of husband and wife. And today, we are here to witness this for Alex and Alyssa. We are here to recognize the choices that they have made to bind together, to enter this union of marriage, to share all aspects of themselves with each other. Today, we witness two individuals becoming one to each other. Now, let's hear from the couple as they recite their vows for each other." The officiant fell silent and nodded to Alex.

Alex looked nervous at first, but he turned his attention to Alyssa, and all of his fear melted away. "Alyssa, I love you with all my heart. You are a beautiful person, inside and out, and I love how you can bring out the best in me, even when I'm at my worst. I love just how loving you are, and how you're the kind of person to stop and help anyone that you see in need. You're that beacon of light that guides me home when I'm lost, and that soft space for me to land. You're everything I've ever dreamed of and more. I promise to you that I will love you, protect you, and cherish you to the best of my ability. You make me a better man, Alyssa, and I vow to help you become the best version of yourself that you can be as well." He smiled at her, and Sophie could see him squeeze her hands.

Alyssa was watching him with teary eyes, smiling. At the moment, all she was focused on was her partner, and the entire crowd was silent as they watched the tender moment.

The officiant nodded to Alyssa to get her to start her own vows.

"Alex, I promise to love you and honor you every day of my life. I promise to be your biggest cheerleader as you make your way through the world, and the one to help you when you're at your lowest. I promise to help you as much as I can and to raise you up. I will always do my best to help you and to cherish you. I promise to support you in any way I can." She blushed as she spoke, and Sophie could see the tears springing to both Alex and Alyssa's eyes as she did.

They fell silent and gazed into each other's eyes for a moment, smiling tearfully at each other.

The officiant smiled at them both. "Now, Alex, Alyssa. It's time to join hands." He waited for them to intertwine their fingers with each other. "Alex, in front of friends and family that have gathered here today, you are preparing to take Alyssa as your lawfully wedded wife. Are you ready?

"Yes."

"Alyssa, are you ready to accept Alex as your husband?" The Officiant turned to look at her.

"Yes," she replied quietly.

"Alex, do you take Alyssa as your lawfully wedded wife, to love and cherish from this day forward, to have and to hold in sickness and in health, for better or for worse, for richer or for poorer, until death do you part?"

"I do," Alex said, his voice barely above a whisper.

"And Alyssa, do you take Alex as your lawfully wedded husband, to love and cherish from this day forward, to have and to hold in sickness and in health, for better or for worse, for richer or for poorer, until death do you part?"

"I do," she replied softly.

The officiant nodded with a soft smile. "Wedding rings are a traditional symbol of the bond, the never-ending commitment, and the strength of the relationship of two soulmates. The bond is unbroken, continuous, and endless in a perpetual circle. By wearing these rings that represent your perfect union, you will always be reminded of the connection that you share, as well as the vows made out of love today." He passed one ring to Alex and one to Alyssa. He dropped his voice down lower and began to recite something that Alex began to copy.

"I, Alex, present to you, Alyssa, this ring as a symbol of our everlasting love and of the vows I have made to you. Let it never lose its luster, just as my love for you will never fade." He gently slid it onto Alyssa's finger with a smile on his face.

Alyssa then began to speak as well: "I, Alyssa, preset to you, Alex, this ring as a symbol of our everlasting love and of the vows that I have made to you. Let it never lose luster, just as my love for you will never fade." And with that said, she slid a ring onto Alex's finger as well.

The officiant smiled at the couple. "And with that, by the powers vested in me by the state, I now pronounce you husband and wife! You may now kiss the bride!"

Alex reached forward and pulled his new wife close, kissing her gently on the lips as her hands snaked behind his neck to embrace him. They lingered a moment as the audience cheered. Sophie clapped and cheered for the new happy couple as she watched them.

As they separated, smiling at each other happily, with Alyssa's cheeks blushing, the officiant said, "Ladies and gentlemen, I now present to you, Mr. and Mrs. Johnson!"

# Story 3: How Lucky

*Sophie meets someone new! Sparks are flying after Sophie runs into someone new while taking a walk with Bella through the park one fine autumn afternoon. She wasn't expecting it, but she couldn't deny the chemistry between them. She's happy to spend her day with him, though!*

An autumn chill clung to the breeze that flew by. It smelled of that musky, earthy, sweet scent of leaves as they started to fall, and the leaves all around in all of the trees were a warm yellow. The trees were lit up with color, glowing with red and orange hues that spread across the entire area. It was a beautiful sight to behold as Sophie walked down the park trail with Bella at her side. Sophie wore a beige jacket that fell down to her mid-thighs with black buttons along with it. She wore a loose white shirt, covered up with an oversized orange scarf. Her pants were so dark blue that they were practically black, and she wore a pair of grey tie-up boots as well.

Next to her, Bella was perfectly content to walk along. She was well behaved, walking right next to Sophie. She was happy to follow along without a problem—she wanted to enjoy her walk through the park. She just wanted to go about her day. The dog was really quite well trained, all things considered, and she loved to follow along obediently. She was content the most when she was able to enjoy a nice leisurely walk. She didn't even really enjoy being forced to run around.

At the very least, Sophie told herself, walking around in the autumn air meant that between warming herself up moving around and the air chilling her off, she was very comfortable as they wandered through the trails. They were walking along a nice urban park, filled up with plenty of greens, grass, trees, and sidewalks with the occasional bench that could be sat on. It was a beautiful park that was clean, safe, and enjoyable, and because it was the middle of a school day, it was quiet enough without children playing around. She loved that she was free to go about her day as if nothing was going on. The sheer pleasantries were enough for her to feel perfectly content.

Sophie wasn't expecting anything but an ordinary day. She certainly didn't know what was in store for her, and she certainly wasn't expecting what happened next.

Out of nowhere, Bella stopped, perked her head up, sniffed at the air, and bolted away, tearing the leash out of Sophie's gentle grasp. Bella *never* ran off like that—she never bothered to hold onto the leash very tightly because she had never felt the need to do so. She took off running as far away as she could with no indication of stopping. Sophie was shocked, to say the least. She was definitely not dressed for a jog through the park—she wasn't even sure that her boots would allow her to run! But, the desire to not lose her dog outweighed the discomfort of trying to run in such un-athletic clothing, and off she went as quickly as possible. She ran ad ran as fast as her legs would allow in such unsuitable clothing. However, Bella could not be deterred. She seemed determined to find something as she ran, and the faster that she went, the harder that Sophie felt she needed to run.

Sophie was panting and sweaty by the time that Bella finally stopped. She was sitting under a beautiful tree that was alight with color. The beautiful oranges and yellows across the branches were gorgeous. The pup was sitting there perfectly—she was looking up at Sophie as if she had done exactly what she had been commanded to do. She sat there with a doggy grin on her face, tail curled perfectly along her haunches as she waited for Sophie to catch up.

"Bella!!" Sophie gasped out as she stopped, resting her hands onto her legs. "What has gotten into you?" She looked down at the dog with an almost exasperated expression as she ran her hand through her hair. "You usually never run

136

away, girl. Why this time," Of course, she wasn't expecting an answer in return as Bella stared up at her with that self-satisfied, wolfish grin. Her tongue was lolling out to the side of her mouth, and she twitched an ear in response as if she knew exactly what she was doing. "At least I got my workout in for the day..." she murmured to herself as she picked up the leash from the ground. It was dirty and covered in little bits of leaf litter that stuck to the nylon length while Bella dragged it through the soil. At least it wasn't wet; she told herself as she picked it up delicately, wrinkling her brows at it as she did.

As Sophie stood up, she saw someone staring at her, and she froze. He was looking at her quizzically, one perfect eyebrow arched right over his warm, brown eyes. He was confused at her outburst, perhaps, or he simply found it fun to start at or accost women that were having a hard time. Sophie opened her mouth to speak up but found herself staring at the man instead. He really wasn't bad looking, and as soon as their gazes met, she felt her pulse quicken. She found herself wondering who this person was—she wanted to know everything.

And in that moment, Sophie had to wonder if there was such a thing as fate after all.

She could feel her heart thudding against her ribs so hard that she had to wonder if they were going to break. What should she do? What should she say? Would she need to change what she was doing? Should she say something at all, or would it be better if she waited for him to speak to her? It was hard to know what was right and what she should do when her mind felt so foggy she couldn't think.

Sophie wasn't usually like this—she was not one to be swayed by this idea of love, nor was she the kind of person who believed in love at first sight—but she was definitely feeling *something* in the moment. She opened her mouth to speak, breaking their eye contact as she glanced at the ground, but before she could say a word, she heard him speaking instead.

"Are you okay?"

She looked back up at him in surprise. Okay? She was fine! Yeah, she was a bit sweaty and disheveled from chasing after her partner in crime, but she was doing a lot better than she could have been. After all, she could have been hurt, or Bella could have been lost. "Do I look like I'm not okay?" she blurted out, immediately kicking herself for what she had to say in response as soon as the words left her mouth. *How embarrassing.*

She heard him chuckle in response. "No, no, it's not that. Just... You're looking a little tense is all." He smiled kindly at her. "I just figured I'd ask. You know, it's not every day you see people running down the park in that. You don't exactly look like you're dressed to jog."

He had a point there, and she nodded, running a hand through her hair in an attempt to tame it and smiling sheepishly. "Yeah... *Someone* decided it would be a good idea to take off on a marathon around the park."

Then, Sophie realized that he was standing there with his own dog. She had been so caught up in looking at his eyes and face that she hadn't even thought to look anywhere else yet. She looked down and saw a grey husky with the most vivid blue eyes that she had ever seen sitting next to him patiently. He was exceptionally well behaved for a husky, just sitting there without so much as moving, though he couldn't keep his eyes off of Bella. "Looks like you might understand my predicament a bit more than I thought, huh?" Sophie asked, laughing. "And what's this big fella's name?"

"This big man here is Koda," he said, patting the husky on the head. "He's surprisingly agreeable today, it looks like."

138

The man smiled affectionately at the dog, and Sophie felt her heart swell as she saw him. She felt her cheeks tinge pinkish as she looked at him, and she looked back down at the dog to look away from the handsome man in front of her. "And my name is Felix."

The man, apparently named Felix, looked at Sophie expectantly, and it took her a moment of looking back at him to figure out what he wanted. Her name! Of course, he was waiting for her to tell him her name as well. Right—that's what she was supposed to do when someone introduces themselves to you. *Get it together, Sophie,* she told herself.

"I'm Sophie, and this is Bella. It's really nice to meet you, Felix," She patted Bella's head in a very similar way. This was nice—she wasn't just saying it. Sophie was happy to have that interaction, but she still wasn't sure what she was supposed to do about the situation that she was in. It was weird to suddenly be in this position in which she had no idea what she was doing, or whether she needed to be able to run away, engage in a longer conversation, or anything else. She didn't know how to feel about this tall, dark, and handsome stranger in front of her.

Felix nodded his head thoughtfully, his gaze softening as he looked at Sophie for a moment. Sophie could have sworn she saw a hint of laughter hidden beneath their warm depths, but it was quickly forgotten when Bella licked her hand, shocking her back to the present.

"Do you normally walk around here?" he asked her, letting his hands slide into his pockets naturally as a cool breeze flew by. It was chilly outside, and she couldn't blame him for this. Though usually, hands in the pockets were a bad sign, she had to admit that she wanted to do the same thing. It was cold!

"Not really. I was just a bit bored and needed a change in scenery. It's quite pretty here. Much better than just staring at my home garden all day long. It's nice to get out and about sometimes. I work at home, and that gets really boring really quickly when I'm on my own at home without anyone around." She stopped speaking when she realized that she had opened up the floodgates, and the words were flying out. With her eyes widening, she glanced up at Felix shyly. "Sorry," she murmured, looking down. "Sometimes, I just start talking, and I can't get myself to shut up. It's so embarrassing—and I'm doing it again!!" She sighed. "I'm sorry!"

Felix shook his head, eyes shining with amusement. "No, it's fine. I asked, and you answered!" He seemed so incredibly patient as he looked at her, and Sophie felt her heart-melting. She didn't normally feel so attached to men—but she couldn't help it. She just wanted to get to know this guy in front of her. She wanted to know more.

Sophie looked down at the ground, steeling up her resolve. She was going to do it! She was going to ask him for his phone number so they could meet up again! She just had to build up the courage somehow. Her thoughts were racing a mile a minute as she sat there, looking at him.

"Hey, Sophie?" he asked with a kind look on his face.

"Hmm?" She looked up at him, her train of thought immediately cut off.

"I apologize that this is somewhat forward... But could I have your phone number, please?" She was *shocked*. She didn't think that he'd want it—but he did! She nodded her head almost numbly before she could say a word in return.

They exchanged phone numbers and spent some time together, chatting about anything and everything that came to mind. She was perfectly content, getting to know him, and working to understand who he was better. She loved hearing what he had to say and how he said it. His voice alone was like music to her ears, and the longer they chatted, the more she wanted to linger.

Even Bella and Koda got along well. They happily walked next to each other, tongues lolling out. Though both breeds were commonly considered aggressive, there was no way that such goofy faces could be seen as problems as they strolled through the park together. They talked about their jobs and about their goals. They spent time discussing where they grew up and what they did in college. Overall, it was incredibly pleasant, and Sophie was thrilled to finally have a deeper connection with someone. She hadn't planned for it, but the effect was undeniable. She liked him. She wasn't sure if she liked him as more than a friend, but she definitely felt that magnetic pull toward him that she couldn't ignore. She wanted to be around him.

Eventually, the sun was starting to set, and they realized that they had spent the entire day just walking through the park, chatting about life and everything that it has done for both of them. They spent time discussing all sorts of topics that she had never imagined that she would discuss with others, but she wasn't embarrassed. No, she was thrilled to have that closer connection to someone else, and she didn't want to lose it. When it became clear that they had to part ways, they still dragged their feet, but eventually, Sophie found herself walking home on her own.

As she walked home, she couldn't help but feel her mind focused on him. She couldn't help but feel like she was on cloud nine the whole time she went along her way. All she thought of was Felix. His warm, brown eyes were almost the color of honey. The look of joy he had when he went about everything he did. The kind smile... He was such a genuinely good guy, and Sophie wanted to get to know him sooner rather than later. She wanted to know that she could trust him, and she was pretty sure that she could.

The entire time she made her way home, she was desperate to hear her phone go off. She was hoping that it would ring in her pocket, that he would text her. She could imagine the whole conversation in her head.

*"How are you doing?" he would ask her over the phone. His voice would be gentle, curious, but that small note of longing was unmistakable. She knew that he was just as interested in her as she was of him, and she couldn't erase the feeling.*

*"I'm good, thanks. How are you doing?" she would ask him back, nervously twirling her hair. Was he thinking about how nervous she was? Was he nervous himself? Her own voice held that slight air of timidity, that fear of being rejected.*

*"I'm glad I got to hear your voice again," he'd practically purr into the phone line. "You're such a sweet person; you know that, Sophie? I couldn't wait until tomorrow to reach out... I just had to hear from you again." His voice was soft, almost urgent. She could almost feel his fervor in his voice, and she would find herself wishing that she was there...*

But, then, something shocked her out of her daydream—her phone was ringing.
She blinked in surprise as if she were just waking up, and she pulled her phone out of her pocket. She was hoping that she would hear him on the other line, but a glance at the name deflated the excitement that she felt within herself. It was just Cara, ready to hear about her day.

She told Cara all about the day. She told her about Felix, about how sweet he was, and about how much she couldn't wait to hear back from him. She was smitten before she even realized it. Cara laughed at her, telling her that it was definitely a crus and that she had to act upon it sooner rather than later. "He sounds like a good guy," Cara purred into the phone. "You should take him off the market before someone else does. He won't be single forever, it sounds like. You only live once! What are you waiting for, hon?"

When Sophie and Cara got off the phone, Sophie was shocked. Did she like him romantically? Her phone buzzed with a text message, and when she looked down at it, she saw:

*Hey, it's Felix, from the park earlier today.*

She felt her stomach fluttering in those butterflies that she had not felt since high school, and she realized it. She was totally smitten with him. But did he like her? She wasn't so sure, but she knew one thing: She would be genuinely upset if she couldn't get to speak to him again.

All night long, Sophie and Felix texted. She eventually fell asleep with her phone in her hand, a half-written message there for her to see in the morning, a testament to just how interested in him she was. They had a great conversation, and Sophie felt like they really hit it off. She just had to convince him that they could be wonderful together and give them a shot. The more that they spent time together, the more confident she was that they would enjoy their time together.

# Story 4: Breaking the Cycle

*Sophie is bored with her routine. Day in and day out, she does the same thing. She gets up, checks her email, does some work, heads out for lunch, comes home, works some more, then gets ready for her peaceful evening at home. It's easy and predictable... But also so drab. She's sick of it. She's ready to do anything that she can to break the cycle and do something new. Something exciting! Variety is the spice of life, and she's ready to find something to spice up her cycle. Join Sophie as she spends a day directly breaking her usual routine to find some excitement and pizzazz to bring back to her life.*

Sophie yawned as she poured her coffee. It went right into her usual cup, filled to the brim and steaming. The cup was her typical light, a baby blue mug with the quirky quote engraved on the side: It had a picture of a fox on it and said *'Zero foxes given'* and Sophie loved it. It usually made her smile as she pulled out her coffee mug, but that day, she just sighed. She looked down at the mug with a frown. Something *had* to give. She couldn't take it any longer! Something needed to be different before she lost her mind.

She slammed her coffee mug onto the counter with a clatter and dropped her hands into her face, feeling the frustration and fatigue of the same thing day in and day out wearing at her. She needed something to change, or she would have to *scream!* Something needed to be different! She couldn't take it any longer! She had to change it up before she blew up. "That's it!" she mumbled to herself, looking around her home. Of course, nothing was out of place, other than the tennis ball that Bella had left there for her. Something had to be different. Something needed to change!

She looked down at the counter and realized that some of the brown liquid had splashed out, pooling on the surface, and she sighed, pulling over a paper towel and wiping it up. There had to be something she could do for the day...

Anything at all... Into the trash went the paper towel and Sophie pulled out her phone, glancing over her calendar for the day. It was the same as it always was. Work until lunch, then spend some time working on another project after. It was exactly the same as it always was, and she was *sick of it*. With a frustrated eye roll and a sigh, she looked down at the ground. Maybe it was a day of spontaneity. She normally had to work, but she could take care of that the next day instead... she felt like what she needed the most was to go do something exciting and different!

Sophie ran upstairs to get dressed without so much as a plan in mind. She'd figure it out one way or another—she just had to do something. Anything would work that day. Her outfit for the day was simple but practical: She picked out a pair of nice, dark blue jeans that hugged her hips nicely and accentuated her legs. For a top, she pulled out a nice floral blouse that hung loosely around her, flowing as she moved. It was black with soft, pink designs as it hung off of her, and she finished the look with long, knee-height grey leather boots.

Off she went down the stairs after tossing her hair into a loose bun to keep it out of her face. She wasn't quite sure what to do during the day. She wasn't sure if she was going to go shopping, or if she was going to spend her day wandering, or if she would pick up some new books. Whatever she chose to do, however, she knew that it needed to be different. She picked up her purse, walked out the door, and hopped into her car. She sat there and sighed. "I don't know what to do..." she groaned to herself as she started the ignition.

As she drove off, she looked around the neighborhood. She saw a woman pushing a stroller with a dog trotting next to her. They were enjoying the afternoon sun as they walked down the road, and it brought a smile to Sophie's face. She loved being able to watch people happily going about their days. It was fun being able to see other people and imagine what is going on in their minds. She liked seeing what people did in their lives to see what they liked. She loved seeing it all.

The houses were all neatly cared for and the yards were immaculately groomed to be perfect as she drove by them all. The houses all looked quite similar as she went down—they were nice, two-story houses, lined up with big, white, two-car garages in the front and great big bay windows. Each house had a small tree in front of them—they were maple trees that, when fully grown and matured, would shade the sidewalks as people chose to walk through it. The houses were all in nice, warm colors, in tans and browns. They looked great with their perfect, white garages and white front doors, almost as if there was something requiring every house to be made up the same way. As Sophie went through them all, she found herself staring in awe. They were beautiful and the front lawns were immaculate. Each lawn was carefully cultivated, and there were small gardens underneath the front windows. The flowers were beautiful, in bushes with little white ones growing in small clusters. Some of them had great, big hydrangea plants growing, in all sorts of different colors as well. Some were more blue while others erred toward redder shades.

Though the houses all looked quite similar, they had marked differences as well. She could see some that had bigger windows than others. Some had big window walls, and others had rooms over garages. They had different kinds of porches and different kinds of paths leading to their doors. Seeing the cohesion between the houses made her happy as she went by them all. It was refreshing to see the different ways that the houses come together. It was great to see, especially when the families were outside the house and doing what they do.

Soon, she turned off the road she was on and made her way toward a park down the road. It was a great, big park with

146

trees bigger than any others in the area. The trees had massive canopies, branching out for feet and feet as they shaded the grass underneath them. Sophie loved that park—there was a big playground for kids, but there were also plenty of paths for walking, and lots of grass for sprawling out, for running in, and for having picnics. It was one of the parks that Sophie used to go to with Bella when she was younger—but lately, they had chosen out a different park a bit closer to home.

Briefly, Sophie debated stopping in there to see what it would be like. She looked over everything, only to shake her head. No—she wasn't going to stop in at the park. Today was a day for doing something new. A day for discovering a new sense of self. It was a day for figuring out what she wanted to do at the moment—for spontaneous decisions, and that was what she would do, and she would start it all off by trying out that new sushi restaurant at the mall that she had meant to go to.

The sushi restaurant wasn't too far away, and she knew that she could get there quickly—she just had to drive down a couple of miles, and she'd get there. She turned up the music, bopping her head along to the beat as she drove, a big grin on her face. She looked forward to that new sushi restaurant—all she had to do was drive a little bit further, and she'd get there. She had heard it was one of those fancy conveyer belt sushi places where you took half a roll at a time and got to mix and match your plate into exactly what you wanted. She always really liked those ones—you could try something and get only a couple of bites without having to worry about the cost when you tried something new. She loved picking out a new dish or a new type of fish every single time. The last time she had gone to a sushi restaurant, she tried the eel, and it had been surprisingly delicious. It had been a bit intimidating to go out of her way to try it, but she was certainly willing to give it a shot just to say she had. After all, trying something new every day was a great thing-- everyone always recommended it, after all.

Within a few minutes, she found herself pulling into the parking lot, and she grinned. She was *starving*. She stared at the sushi restaurant, aptly named "Sushi Belt" and on the sign, she could see a cute, cartoonized roll of sushi wearing a big belt across its waist, sitting on a plate on another belt. It was something adorably delicious to look at and just made her even hungrier as she walked off on her way.

The parking lot was surprisingly empty, but that wasn't too surprising. It was still early for lunch, and the restaurant was only just then opening. She went into the restaurant and took a seat at a single bar, plopping her purse next to her. A waitress quickly brought her a menu and handed her a glass of water before stepping away. She looked at everything in front of her, watching the little plates go by. Each plate had a different color around the rim, marking it as worth a different amount from the others. There were five colors in all, and each had different foods. The cheapest ones were covered in edamame, sautéed green beans, and egg rice balls. The most expensive ones touted shrimp, crab, and salmon. There were pieces that were simply raw fish on plates. There were other pieces that were rolled into nice pieces and cut carefully. Others still were lumped onto balls of sushi rice. The different options went by at a gentle pace, with the occasional plate of fresh fruit, seaweed salad, and miso soup passing by as well.

The restaurant smelled great, and Sophie looked over the menu. There was bound to be something interesting to try new that day—she just had to choose something out. As the food went by, she picked up a few of her favorites—she grabbed a seaweed salad with little sprigs of green onion and sesame seed sprinkled atop it, and a bowl of miso soup. She picked out a few regular plates of sushi as well— grabbing a California roll, a spider roll, and a plate of seared tuna.

The meal looked great, and as she broke her chopsticks, she considered what she would be doing next. She could go see a movie... or she could head over to the mall for some shopping. But, neither of those seemed all that exciting to her when she had so many other things to do as well. Well, she told herself as she picked up a piece of California roll and popped it into her mouth, enjoying the savory crab salad within it as she watched the lazily revolving sushi bar spin around and around in front of her, she could do just about anything that day. It didn't matter—she just needed to choose something.

Before long as she went along, she realized something: their octopus on the menu. She had never tried it before—the strange tentacle shape always put her off from the idea of even trying it, and she cringed to think of the suckers on them clinging to her lips as she tried to chew it up. She frowned as she debated it for a moment, but then something overcame her—she was going to do it. She *had* to do it. She wanted to reclaim her independence and reclaim her ability to do new things. It wouldn't be the worst thing she had ever done, after all—and she had to try something new.

When the waitress came by again, she strengthened her resolve. When she was asked if she wanted anything else, she nodded her head. "Yeah, actually... Could I try the octopus?" She smiled at the waitress, but she was certain her apprehension was received loud and clear from the woman, who smiled politely and nodded her head.

"Sure thing, hon." She walked off after filling up Sophie's water again and left Sophie to her meal.

The seaweed salad tasted great as she turned to that, enjoying each and every piece in front of her. She loved it: It tasted better here than at the other restaurants she had gone to as well. It was perfectly salty, delicate, and delicious. As she thoughtfully chewed it through, she wondered what the octopus would be like, hoping that it wouldn't be tough or anything. She didn't want to feel like she was chewing on a rubber or something. Next came a sip of her miso soup, which was warm and made perfectly.

As Sophie slowly and thoughtfully ate at her food, the waitress returned, placing it right next to her and leaving her to it. She looked at the octopus as it sat on the plate, apprehensive about what to do next. Obviously, she had to take a bite of it—but she was hesitant. She wasn't sure she really was ready for it. She wasn't sure that it would be worth it. The tentacles were curled slightly on their plate, and she could see the suckers. She was thankful the tentacles had been removed prior to the food being cooked. That was perfect for her—she wasn't sure she would have been able to stomach it if the octopus had been entirely whole when it was presented for her. She looked at it closely and studied the color. It was orange-ish with tiny white suckers alongside it. There were three tentacles left onto the plate for her, and she wasn't quite sure where to begin. Before she thought much more about it, however, she simply grabbed one tentacle with her chopsticks and popped it into her mouth. It was surprisingly tender as she chewed it up, and the taste wasn't too much, unlike lobster, she decided as she carefully chewed it up. It was surprisingly decent as she ate it. In fact, it was so decent that she decided to have a second bite as well. She even ate the third bite, too, finishing the plate. She was glad she had taken the chance and tried it—it was delicious.

As she finished eating her meal, someone popped into the chair next to her. She was another woman, all on her own, simply enjoying the moment, from what Sophie could tell. She smiled and waved at Sophie as she sat down. She was an older woman with salt-and-pepper hair and with a kind look to her face. There were wrinkles from smiling and laughing around her mouth, but it really just added to her kind look of authenticity, Sophie decided as she popped another piece of sushi into her mouth.

Just then, the waitress came by. "So, you liked the octopus, eh?" she asked as she peeked in to see if Sophie was done eating.

"Yeah, actually. It was surprisingly good!" she replied to the waitress with a smile. "I didn't expect to enjoy it so much, but it was great!" She was genuinely shocked that she liked it that much, but stranger things have happened, after all. As the waitress left, the woman sitting next to her looked at her.

"You tried the octopus?" she asked, sounding impressed.

Sophie nodded, feeling her cheeks flush a bit in embarrassment. "It was surprisingly good," she replied with a grin. She watched the woman see what her reaction was. "It tasted kinda like lobster," she told her. "I really enjoyed it. It could have been a lot worse than it was, that's for sure."

"What made you try it?"

"I figured I'd try something new. You know, do something new, or frightening once per day and all." She shrugged her shoulders. "I wasn't sure how I'd feel, but you'll never know how you feel about something until you try it, and that's what I did. It could have been much, much worse, that's for sure. But, you know what? Now I know I actually do like an octopus. I'm not sure I'd go out of my way to order it form a restaurant again in the future, but I know I wouldn't turn it down if I were offered it." Sophie felt a bit braver already just discussing it. She was proud of herself. That was definitely unexpected.

"Well, good for you! I'm glad you did it. Maybe I'll give it a shot, too," replied the old woman as she glanced through the menu. "I'm sure it's good if you talked it up, and if you're willing to try it, I should be too."

Sophie smiled back at her. "That's the spirit!" she replied. It really was good for them to try new things every now and then after all. Sophie pulled out her phone to glance at the time. It was already nearing noon, and she realized that she actually needed to get running. While it was great that she had enjoyed her morning and her lunch, she also knew that it would be a good idea for her to get started on her work as soon as possible if she wanted to do it all that day.

She finished up her meal quickly, enjoying every last succulent bite on her plates, and went out of her way to pay for everything. As she was collecting her receipt, she heard the woman next to her ask for the octopus and smiled to herself. She was glad that her adventure had not only helped her but the woman next to her as well. It would be good for her to get that new experience out of everything.

So, with her belly full, and feeling a bit better after having done something new for the first time in a while, being unpredictable, Sophie took in a deep breath and moved out of her way to get going. She picked up her purse and hopped into her car, feeling justified, invigorated, and happier for the day. It was the perfect way to head off on her own.

# Story 5: Road Trip!

*Road trip!! Sophie is bored with her time at home and wants to go somewhere new. She's ready to get out on her way and see the world—or at least, whatever of the world exists along the interstate within about ten hours of their location. Join Sophie, Cara, and Felix as they head off to enjoy a quick weekend camping trip.*

*Beep! Beep! Beep!*

The banging sound of Sophie's alarm clock made her groan to herself as she forced her eyes to open. She didn't want to be awake—but she was. It was the last thing she really wanted to be doing, but she knew that she didn't have a choice in the matter. They were set to get going for their camping trip that day, and she knew that if she didn't get going, Felix would be worried that they'd be too late to get there. They had to drive seven hours, then get themselves settled into their camping site before they did anything else. It was perfect—they'd get there, and they'd have plenty of time to unpack, set up shelter, and everything else.... And all they had to do to make it happen was get up at the ungodly hour of 2 am. She forced herself to roll herself out of bed and walked into the bathroom, blinking blearily as she tried to force her eyes to focus.

As she turned on the light, she felt her eyes burning as they struggled to adjust, and she lazily turned on the shower and began to brush her teeth. It wasn't her idea of fun—but she knew that Felix would be thrilled, and Cara was game to try it out too, even though she usually found herself happiest in luxury hotels. She was willing to make an exception for her best friend, and though Sophie wasn't quite sure what to expect as they went, she was also pretty sure that they would have a grand time doing anything that they set their mind to.

So, off she went into the shower to force herself to wake up a bit more. She knew that she'd be needing at least a few coffees before the day was over. She stepped into the shower to wake herself up, spending a few moments, enjoying the warmth as she made her way through her normal showering routine. It should be a good day, she told herself as she made her way through everything.

Before long, she was showered, dressed, and packed up, with her bag of packed goods all setup. She had plenty of dried foods that would not perish on the way, and she had a duffel bag full of her clothes next to an air mattress and a sleeping bag. Felix was bringing the rest of the stuff as far as she knew, and before long, she saw the lights flashing outside her house as Felix pulled into her driveway. With a yawn and a mug of coffee in hand, she stepped outside, holding the door open so Felix and Koda could come inside. They walked in together, and she smiled at him, giving him a quick peck on the cheek as he did. "Hey, honey," she told him.

"Hey!" he replied, looking far more awake than she was in the moment. "You ready?"

Sophie nodded, leaning against his chest, sleepily for a moment. She was thoroughly exhausted, but she wasn't going to let that stand in her way of having a good time that day. He smelled of sandalwood and clean laundry as she rested there, and she smiled against his chest. "Thanks for stopping by," she murmured against him.

"No, thank you for coming with me," he replied with a soft smile in return, putting a hand against her head. "We're still waiting for Cara, right?"

"Mhm. She should be here soon," replied Sophie through a big yawn.

"I hope so," Felix said, looking at his watch. They had to get going, or they'd be late. "Where's your stuff?"

"In the hallway." Sophie gestured over her shoulder to where the duffel bag, sleeping bag, and mattress were waiting. "Should I load it up now?"

"I'll do it," Felix insisted, planting a kiss against her forehead. "I've got a place for everything, and—"

"Everything is in its place?" Sophie finished for him, looking up with a sleepy, smug smile.

"Exactly! You understand me," Felix bantered back, winking as he made his way to go get the bags. Koda plopped himself on the floor, next to where Bella was sleeping. Neither of them seemed too keen to be up in the middle of the night when they had better things to do—like sleeping. But, of course, they needed to get on the road sooner rather than later so they'd have time to get through their unpacking, so they had no real choice. Drastic times call for drastic measures and all that.

While Felix was busy organizing the space in the back of his big SUV, Sophie saw Cara pull in. She had someone else sitting in her Prius, but Sophie couldn't quite make out the face. It was too hard to see through the car, and she couldn't help it—she had to stare. Of course, she'd find out in a moment.

Out hopped Cara and Alyssa was with her. Sophie was pleasantly surprised, but she glanced over to Felix to see what his reaction was. He didn't seem fazed at all to be going camping with two other women, apparently, so Sophie shrugged it off. It would be fine, she was sure. She smiled widely and went up to her friends to give them a quick hug. "Hey, Alyssa! I didn't know you were coming!"

"Mmm, Cara didn't want to go on his own. She didn't want to be the third wheel, after all." She smiled, but Cara seemed to blush. Even in the darkness, it was obvious that she was flustered by what she heard, and Sophie smiled. "don't worry, Cara, there's no harm in that!" Sophie nodded in agreement.

"I'm sure it'll be fine. Besides, the more, the merrier, right?" As long as they'd all fit in Felix's car, that was.

Felix walked over to them after finishing loading up Sophie's belongings and looked at the newcomers. "Hey, Cara, Alyssa," he nodded to each of them as he went by. He was totally fine with the fact that there were more people there, as far as Sophie could tell, and that was plenty for her. She was totally happy with that result. "Where are your guys' things so I can pack them away?"

Cara pointed to her car. "In the trunk. They should fit, I hope."

"I hope so too!" Felix said with a chuckle, heading over to get the last of the things out. Before long, they had packed everything into the car, piled the dogs into the back row of his SUV, popped Cara and Alyssa into the second-row captain's chairs, and Sophie sat next to Felix in the front. It was 3:32 when he finally turned on his car, and they set off, and they had ten hours to get to where they were going.

Sophie yawned as he pulled out of the parking spot. The house was all locked up, and Cara's car was safely parked in the garage, and off they went. It was still inhumanely dark outside—no sane people were up at that hour except for them, as far as Sophie could see, but she wasn't willing to let that stop her from having fun. She looked out her window with another yawn as they started driving.

Felix's car was surprisingly comfortable in the dark, Sophie found herself thinking as they dorve. She was comfortable where she sat, looking absently out the window. It had plenty of space for all of them and everything in the trunk as well, and she was thrilled about that. It was so great to have that space in there, and Felix had even turned on some soft music. It had a soft, pulsing beat to it, somewhere between electronica and synth. It was almost like video game music, Sophie thought, but the beat was enough to keep her awake, driving them forward as the moments ticked by. Little by little, she found herself staring out the window. Little by little, she found herself getting sleepier and sleepier...

The sky was already brightening by the time that Sophie woke up with a stiff crick in her neck. It hurt as she straightened herself out, looking around. Dawn was spreading across the sky and shining brightly as she looked to the sky and a glance at the clock said that it was already 5:30. She had slept for almost two hours.

"Welcome back," Felix said with a smile, reaching over and patting her hand. "Feel better?"

Sophie nodded, rubbing at her neck. "Yeah, but my neck is killing me." She looked over her shoulder and saw that both Cara and Alyssa had also fallen asleep, but they hadn't woken up yet. She smiled at her friends as she saw them, not thinking much about what they were doing at that point. "Man, we've still got a ways to go, huh?"

Looking out her window showed that there was nothing around them—they were driving through a huge field that looked like it could go on forever—there were no endings in sight as she looked around, and she was pleasantly surprised. It was nice to see that there were no people around, but it also made the road feel kind of strangely abandoned. Living in a big city, it wasn't often that Sophie noticed that there weren't other people sharing the road. But surely, no one was stupid enough to get out of bed at 2 am on a Saturday to go driving throughout the state to the middle of nowhere. It seemed like a fool's mission, and yet there they were, heading to do exactly that.

The grass around them was yellowed and billowing in the wind, and she could see the occasional cow grazing in the distance. They were in some sort of rural land with no signs of the modern city that she lived by. It was strange just how detached they were from their surroundings or just how different things could be without much change going on in return.

They continued on their way without much to say, simply listening to the music as it played. They didn't want to wake up any of their sleeping passengers, so they chose to keep quiet instead. Instead, Sophie chose to look around at all of the random things she could find out and about around her. She saw things like cars with strange bumper stickers, strange cars, out of state license plates, and even someone driving a strangely nondescript box truck, riding around with rainbow-colored hair and a clown nose on his face. That one, she was never quite able to figure out.

Eventually, however, they made it to where they were going. The plains turned into forest, and forest turned into a mountain, which eventually flattened into even more plains. After several rests stops, stops for food and coffee, and

simply getting lost a few times at strange turns, they
eventually made their way all the way to their campsite.

The site was remote—not like what Sophie had in mind. She
had been thinking that they would be staying in tents, but
no: They were at a strange cabin that she had never seen
before. Now, it was admittedly a nice cabin, but Sophie had
been under the impression that they were outside.

"Okay, now that's my kind of camping!" Cara announced
with a grin as she looked at the great, big cabin in front of
her. It was beautifully crafted and completely surrounded
by forest. There was a fire pit outside of the cabin, and a
small creek that ran past it.

Alyssa looked around with wide eyes. "Where are we?" she
asked. She pulled out her phone—but there was no service
where they were. There would be no way for her to get a
hold of anyone there. She frowned down at her phone. "And
what do we do in an emergency?"

"Oh, don't worry about it," Felix said with a smile. "This is
one of my parents' cabins. I camp here all the time. We have
a satellite phone inside that we can use if we want to. We're
pretty far out to get actual phone service here. But that's
okay, the whole point was to get away for the weekend,
wasn't it?"

Sophie nodded as she pulled the dogs out of the car. That
was certainly the point, but now that they were there, she
was feeling a bit intimidated. They were so far away from
everything, and she wasn't sure what to expect.

They all walked inside and were amazed. The cabin had a
massive open floorplan within it, with beautiful honey
hardwood flooring and an entire wall of masonry
surrounding a fireplace. There were leather sofas inside of
it, with a coffee table sitting atop an ornate rug, and a
massive television sat in the corner. There was an entire

wall of built-in hutch along with the other, and they could
see right into the kitchen as well, which was filled up with
stainless steel appliances and granite counters.

There was an upstairs area as well that was where,
presumably, the bedrooms were. Sophie was in awe of
everything around her—but she couldn't help but wonder
why they were told to pack camping stuff if they were just
going to stay in a cabin. She glanced over at Felix, and he
smiled at her as he let the dogs off their leashes inside of the
cabin. They both happily ran into the house to go explore,
and Alyssa and Cara ran upstairs into the rooms to start
unpacking their belongings.

"What do you think?" asked Felix. He was watching
Sophie's reaction intently as if he was genuinely curious
about it. His happy smile said that he was aiming to
impress, but Sophie wasn't quite sure that she'd be able to
protect it. She wasn't as happy as she could have been, and
she didn't know how she should tell him that.

"Well, I think that we could have a lot of fun here this
weekend," said Sophie finally after searching for a tactful
way to tell him exactly what she thought. She completely
skirted around the issue entirely—she didn't want to tell
him that his idea of camping was wrong. But, she had to
admit—this was more along the lines of what she would
have wanted anyway. She loved the comforts of the indoors,
and sleeping on a real bed instead of an air mattress would
definitely save her back—but it came at the cost of not doing
what she thought they would be. No matter what, however,
she knew that things would work out one way or another.

Felix's face fell. "You don't like it," he replied flatly.

"No, no, that's not it at all! It's lovely… It's just this wasn't
what I had in mind when I thought we were going camping,
that's all." Sophie smiled at him, reassuringly. "I'm totally

happy, though. This is perfectly fine with me. I'm not sure I'd have really loved the camping anyway, to be honest."

The response seemed to confuse him further. "If this isn't camping, then what is?" asked Felix.

"You know…Tents and sleeping bags. Outside stuff, not sleeping in a private cabin." Sophie smiled. "I love the cabin, though. So, what can we do here?"

"Well, there's a hiking, hunting, fishing, ATV riding. You know, outdoorsy stuff." He looked over Sophie. "We could do whatever you wanted to. Just let me know what sounds fun."

Sophie shrugged her shoulders. "I think that right now, what I need is a nap!" she replied. It had been a long drive there, and Sophie was more than ready to tuck herself in for a bit. She wanted to stretch her back and actually find some comfort.

Felix nodded. "I'll show you the bedroom." He took her hand and guided her up the stairs and to the second floor, where there were four rooms all lined up. "Those two are the smaller guest bedrooms, and it sounds like Cara and Alyssa already took those. Then, this is a bathroom, and this is the master bedroom." He opened the door to reveal a large bedroom, with a recliner in the corner and a king-sized sleigh bed, with the frame made out of beautiful cherry wood. There were dressers against the back wall and a television mounted on the wall, connected to a DVD player. "We don't get any cable or service here, but we have a ton of DVDs if you want a movie night."

Sophie looked around in awe. The room was beautiful. There were some nice floral paintings on the wall, and the big, bay window in the bedroom was stunning. She looked at it all and nodded her head. "Looks great."

"The bathroom is over there, too," he said, pointing to the bathroom that was connected to the bedroom. "There's a big soaking tub in there that you can use if you want to." Felix dropped off their bags inside the room. "I'll leave you to it, honey," he said with one last kiss on her head. "I've got some stuff to set up to make sure that we're good for the entire weekend, but I'll come up here to join you later, okay?"

Sophie nodded her head as she pulled off her shoes. She was too tired to protest, or even change out of her jeans that she had worn in the car. She climbed into bed and was immediately greeted by the softest, plushest mattress surface she had ever felt, and she was in *love*.

It barely took any time at all for her to fall asleep, wrapped up in a comfortable blanket. In fact, she was probably asleep before her head even hit the pillow. After all, long car rides like that were utterly exhausting, and she was ready to rest.

# Story 6: Happy Birthday!

*It's Cara's birthday!! Sophie is thrilled that her best friend is another year older and she is so ready to party! But, she must get everything set up, so her friend doesn't realize that everyone is gathering for a surprise birthday party. Wish Sophie luck as she does her best to remain unspotted as she sets everything up once and for all. Can she fly under the radar long enough to surprise Cara? Only time will tell!*

It was a special day. Not just because it was the second Friday of the month, or because Sophie's favorite sushi restaurant was giving off food for 50% off. No, that day was special because it was Cara's birthday, and Sophie was determined to make it as special as possible. She was ready to ensure that everything that Cara did was exciting, pleasing, and would leave Cara feeling loved and appreciated. After all, Cara was such a sweetheart—she deserved a good party!

Of course, that meant that Sophie needed to figure out how to outdo the parties that she was certain that Cara's family would throw for her. But, Sophie had the condolence of knowing that Cara disliked the fanfare and crazy efforts that would go into a big party. Cara wanted smaller, intimate gatherings with her closest friends—not parties that forced her to kindly go around and say hello to every single person she passed. Sophie wanted Cara to enjoy her party, not walk around like another prop that had to introduce herself to everyone. After all, what fun was it when you had to thank everyone for coming to a party that you didn't want to be in the first place?

Sophie looked down at her phone. She had a few messages from her friends saying that they would be there at the party. All they had to do was show up. All they had to do was figure out how they were going to hide everything from Cara.

Speaking of Cara, Sophie heard her phone start to go off and glancing at it, she could see that it was Cara who was calling her right that moment. Sophie's eyes widened, and she gasped a little bit, feeling that sudden shock—that concern that she had to make sure that she wasn't spotted. She had to make sure that she wasn't going to be found out somehow. So, Sophie answered the phone and put on her best fake happy voice. "Hey, Cara! What's up?" She was trying her hardest to pretend that everything was normal.

"Oh, nothing," Cara replied. "I was just wondering if you wanted to go out for lunch today. My treat!" Sophie could hear that her voice sounded unconvinced—she wasn't fully confident that Sophie would agree, and Sophie felt a pang of guilt. She'd have to lie to get out of it, or she wouldn't be able to finish up the birthday party.

"Oh, Cara," she said, using her best disappointed voice. "I'm so sorry! I've actually got a uh... Gynecologist appointment this afternoon." She chose out the most invasive routine appointment she could think of—and what would be more invasive than a pap smear? Hopefully, Cara wouldn't ask any more questions after that, she told herself as she looked over her shoulder to look at the time.

"Oh, dear..." Cara replied, sounding mildly concerned. "I'm sorry to hear that! But, thanks anyway. Maybe we can try for dinner?" Her voice sounded a bit more hopeful then.

"I'll try, but no promises... I've got some crazy deadlines I have to meet today," Sophie answered. "I'm sorry, honey. I don't like having to tell you no. Why? Is today special?"

Cara hesitated for a moment. "No, not at all. Good luck at your appointment and thanks anyway! Love you, talk to you soon!" And with that said, she hung up the phone.

Sophie sighed, putting her phone onto the table. She felt incredibly guilty telling Cara no, especially on her birthday, but hopefully, it would all be worth it by the time that they were done. She had high hopes that things would be perfect—they just needed the time to get through everything. Sophie was tasked with decorating her home while Alyssa picked up the birthday cake, and Felix said he would pick up some catering on his way. They should be able to get everything just right and hopefully would all be ready at exactly 1:30. That would give her plenty of time to contact Cara and tell her to hurry over as quickly as she could, and Sophie was hoping that she wouldn't feel too rejected and just skip when she called.

So, Sophie got to work, trying her best to get everything as organized as she could to ensure that everything looked perfect. She was wiping down counters and polishing the cabinets. When everything was clean, she moved on to decorations. All sorts of them went up around her—she put up balloons first, blowing them up on her own. They had chosen mint green and silver balloons for her birthday party decorations—colors that Sophie knew that Cara would love. She blew up at least a few dozen of each by herself, blowing directly into them so she could hang them up on the walls and counter corners. They were draped down from some streamers and attached to the ceiling in some places, too.

Another couple dozen balloons were blown up with a helium tank Sophie had picked up at the store, tying them up with matching ribbons and then securing them in clusters of three or four in various areas. There were a few in the center of the table, weighed down with a big, silver weight with streamers and tinsel coming out of it. It was just gaudy enough that Sophie was sure that Cara would love it. After all, Cara was one of those people who loved to do things backward from what her family expected of her. Though her family was incredibly wealthy, she wanted nothing to do with the idea that she was better than other people. No—Cara would be willing to give a gift, or even the very shirt off of her back if she needed to. She was totally happy doing things that the upper class might scoff at, such as going to theaters to watch a movie or going camping. Yeah, Sophie had to admit that her idea of average life was a bit out of touch sometimes, but Cara was such a good friend that she deserved to be showered with lavish attention. If anyone deserved to have that kind of wealth, Sophie often told herself, it was Cara thanks to her attitude.

Before long, Sophie had finished up all of the balloons, and it was time to start on with the streamers that she had bought. They had to be carefully twisted around each other before they were hung up so they would nicely combine. Sophie wasn't quite sure what she was doing, but she had seen it once on Pinterest and figured she could do it herself. Of course, Sophie also refused to admit the existence of the dreaded Pinterest fails as well… Which is exactly what he streamers eventually became.

Sophie frowned, looking at her tangle of tissue streamers, and shook her head with a sigh. It was harder than it looked. Again, her phone went off, and when she checked it, she saw a message from Alyssa. She was warning Sophie that Cara was asked to hang out that afternoon and that Cara never said a word about her birthday either. Sophie felt her brows furrow, and she shook her head. She had to hurry up before Cara got too impatient and just came over!

Instead of trying to add some pizzazz to the streamers, Sophie changed tactic—she just hung them up the normal way without trying to figure out how to put them up in any sort of fancy manner. It wouldn't matter, would it? There was no way it could matter that much; she told herself and simply shifted her efforts. Streamers went up. Balloons were blown and hung around. And, Sophie told herself that things were looking great.

Next, Alyssa arrived, carrying a box of cake. The box was quickly placed on the counter. "Can I do anything to help?" asked Alyssa kindly. She smiled up at her friend.

"You know, you could help me figure out how to put these streamers up. I'm really not doing a very good job!" Sophie smiled sheepishly. "Sorry," she told her friend.

"No, it looks fine over there! But I'm happy to help. No need to apologize! Just gotta get to work!" Alyssa happily began to put everything up and where it belonged. She was ready to take care of it all. "How about you get all of the space ready for the food while I do this?"

That sounded perfect. "You are a godsend, Alyssa; you know that?" Sophie told her friend with a relieved grin. "Thank you!!" So, off Sophie went, getting the tablecloth all set up and then lining everything up. Felix was bringing back a bunch of appetizers for them all to enjoy with some wine, so Sophie had a bit of an organization to do. She double-checked that the bottles of wine were in the fridge, that she knew where the bottle opener was, and she set up ten wine glasses that they could use to give everyone their drinks. It was perfect! They just had to wait for the food to get there.


And, as if on cue, in came Felix, holding several baking sheet half pans of food. They were all stacked upon each other carefully, with three piled together. "There's more in the car, hon, can you get them?"

Sophie nodded and ran out, gathering up some more of the boxes. She was eager to get them all to put away as soon as possible. The clock was ticking, and they'd need to hurry up if they wanted to do everything the right way!

They carefully unloaded all of the food, carefully keeping it in the foil to keep it warm. "Are you ready for me to call her over?" Sophie looked at the clock. Everyone else should be piling in within the next few minutes, and Cara lived twenty minutes away, so calling then seemed like a fair bet.

Alyssa nodded her agreement. "Yeah, good idea!" she told her as she looked to Felix, who simply shrugged his shoulder, munching on a carrot stick from one of the trays.

"Hey! Leave it for later!" Sophie told him playfully with a quick swat on the hand. "You shouldn't be eating that!"

"Sorry, sorry! It was my delivery fee!" Felix added quickly with a chuckle as Sophie dialed in Cara's number.

The phone barely rang before Cara answered. "Hey, what's up? Are you okay? How did your appointment with the lady doctor go?" Cara was talking a mile a minute—she was upset. Sophie could tell instantly. She felt forgotten.

"Oh, you know, I wanted to talk to you about that. Can you come over right now? I really need to see you." Sophie glanced over to the door, seeing out the window that there were a few more people walking up. They were all told to park down the street from Sophie's house so they wouldn't have their car give away the party.

"Yeah, I can do that. I'll be there in twenty." Cara sounded curious, but she didn't pry any deeper.

"Thanks, honey!" Sophie said. "See you soon!" She hung up the phone and glanced at their friends. It was time to get situated. "Okay, guys, she's on her way now. We're going to have to be careful if we want to surprise her. Where can we hide...?"

"Couldn't we just turn off all the lights and curtains and scream 'Surprise!!' when she walked in?" asked Felix. He had a point, too. Wasn't that what they normally did with surprise parties? Wasn't that how they always did it in the movies?

"Perfect. We've got a few minutes, and everyone else is on their way... This might actually work!" Sophie grinned at her friends. "Good job, team! Let's make this happen!" Sophie looked at her friends, who looked back at her with their own smiles in return.

"Will Cara like this?" asked Felix, looking around at the party. He was more than happy to help, but it seemed like something that she wouldn't necessarily care for.

Sophie nodded in return. "This is exactly what she needs," she replied. "She loves the simpler things in life, and this is right up her alley. She loves silly birthday parties. I remember that one year, she told me that she wished her family had done surprise parties. They always did weird gala things, and she's pretty done with them.

Felix nodded his head. "Yeah, the birthday galas aren't exactly all that fun..." he said as he trailed off, losing himself in his thoughts. Clearly, he was somewhere else, and Sophie wasn't about to interrupt him. As the last-minute stragglers started to arrive, Sophie worried that she had not actually done enough. She worried that Cara would not actually like what she had arranged. What if she hated the colors? Or the balloons?

Sophie's face betrayed her stress. Everyone around her could see it clear as day in her eyes. "You know, I bet she'll love it," said Felix with a quick nod of his head. He was totally convinced that this was exactly what she needed after hearing what Sophie had to say. "She'll be thrilled that you did all of this for her when she is used to all those galas. You've got this!"

Sophie smiled at him. "I sure hope you're right," she replied.

And, she couldn't dwell any longer—she saw Cara's Prius pull into the driveway. She knew that Cara would just walk right in—they didn't knock at each other's homes. "Quick, everyone, get in place!!"

Everyone ducked to hide somewhere that they could. Behind the bar—behind walls and more. And, as soon as Cara opened the door, she was greeted with a loud cry of "SURPRISE!!" from everyone in the room.

Cara stopped and stared in shock. She had not been expecting that at all—and now, there was everyone, standing in her way, staring at her. They were all watching her and waiting for her reaction. Her purse fell out of her hand and onto the floor. She looked from person to person in the group, and her eyes trailed all around the room, absorbing in the decorations and watching closely. She seemed entirely surprised to see the party there—she hadn't been expecting it, but that was exactly the point as far as Sophie was concerned.

"For me?" Cara asked, looking around. Her voice wavered. She looked like she was fighting back the tears, and Sophie felt guilty. She didn't want to make her friend cry—that had been an accident! She hadn't meant to make her friend lose it.

"For you," Sophie confirmed, looking closely for any sign of happiness. But, Cara's tears came almost immediately, and Sophie ran to her. "What's wrong? I thought you've always wanted a surprise birthday party?" She gazed deeply into Cara's eyes, looking for any sign of an answer.

"Yes, I have always wanted one of these… that's why I'm crying." She smiled at Sophie tearfully. "I'm sorry! I don't want to bring down the mood. I can see that you worked really hard on everything that is here, and I don't want it to go to waste. It's really beautiful, Sophie. You've really outdone yourself here!" She sniffled a bit and looked at everyone else there as well. "Thank you all. I'm so glad you all came out here today and that you all came over to support me. It's so sweet of you all to be here, and I cannot thank you enough for your love and kindness you've shown to me." She looked at everyone again. "You know, my family wanted me to sit at some sort of dinner to bring everyone together, but they don't throw parties. We all just sit, eat some food, make some small talk, and move on with our lives as nothing has happened. I'm sick of it... But you all? You're like family... And thank you." Cara was tearing up again, and Sophie smiled sympathetically.

"Thanks for coming so quickly when I called you, too," Sophie told her in return. "I know that I can count on you when I need you, and I wanted to give you that happiness in return. I wanted you to know that wherever you are and whatever you do, you can count on me to be there too! I want you to know that you can trust me to help you and to bring you that happiness and love in your life when you need it the most. Thanks for being such a good friend, Cara. You deserve the world!"

Felix clapped his hands, and as he did, everyone else started to clap as well. "Enough of the friendship mumbo jumbo... Let's all dig in! I'm starving!"

Everyone laughed at Felix as he said this. He started opening up all of the appetizer dishes that he had brought with him, and he lined up all of them for everyone to get their fill. Everyone started talking and enjoying themselves, getting plates of food and glasses of wine, and they all smiled at Cara, wishing her a happy birthday.

Sophie smiled and patted her friend on the back. "I'm glad you love your party," she told Cara. "I was terrified you'd hate it!"

"Hate it? Why?" Cara looked genuinely surprised—she hadn't expected that.

"I don't know...Maybe because it isn't very fancy or something. I've tried, though, and I wanted you to feel that love and appreciation the way that I do when I'm with you!" Sophie plopped her head on Cara's shoulder. "Happy birthday, friend."

"Thank you, Sophie," Cara replied, leaning her own head onto Sophie's. They sat there for a few moments.

"You know this means you're old now, right?" Sophie said after a few moments of silence.

Cara feigned offense. "Old? Me? Never!!" she cried back, shaking her head. "No, no, no. You've got me mixed up. I'm still young! See? No greys!"

They both laughed. Being that close to a best friend was always a perk, and she was thrilled to have her own best friend always around.

The party was a success. The food was enjoyed, all three bottles of wine were happily drunk, and the cake... Was less than perfect, but tasted delicious! The orders had accidentally been swapped, and by mistake, they wound up with a kid's birthday cake, with some superhero dogs riding in vehicles on it, but it tasted fantastic. The chocolate with strawberry filling really brought the night together, Sophie thought as she grinned, looking at her friends and family around her. It was a perfect day as far as she was concerned—she just had to trust that Car enjoyed her day too.

# Story 7: Novel Heights

*Sophie has always been terrified of heights. Going up mountains and looking over them? Terrifying. Going over bridges? Nerve-wracking! She hates going over cliffs or looking out the windows when she was up on the higher floors. So, when Cara begs her to go up to the Space Needle in Seattle, she's faced with two options: Turn it down because she can't handle the height, or go up anyway and force herself to face her fears. Join Sophie as she tries her hardest to head up and ends up enjoying the views, realizing that the heights aren't actually as bad as she thought and that they can actually be appreciated!*

"Okay, I'll see you at 4:30!" Sophie announced with a falsetto in her voice. She tried to sound excited for her friend on the phone as she hung up, looking down. She could see the picture of Cara from her social media account staring back up at her, and Sophie sighed. "Don't give me that look!" she demanded huffily as she stared at her friend's profile picture. "You know I hate heights, lady!" She shook her head and looked out the window. Surely, there was a way they could get out of going up to the Space Needle in Seattle. Surely, they'd be able to get out of having to ride that big, see-through elevator as they were taken up nearly 500 feet to the top. Surely she could get by without having to see the city from such a high view. Sure, some people loved it, but Sophie? Nope. Keep her away from anything even remotely resembling heights—she hated them all. It was one of those things from childhood that she never outgrew after she fell off a bunk bed in elementary school and broke her arm. Ever since the idea of heights defined loosely as anything more than maybe four feet off the ground was appalling.

Sure, her room was on the second floor of a house. Sure, she had to climb the stairs every night. But, that didn't mean that she had to look down the stairs or even out her window regularly. She could live in utter denial of her fear of heights without repercussions most of the time. Of course, Cara was there to completely and utterly demolish that idea. Of *course,* Cara would choose the one thing that would instill fear into Sophie without meaning to, and of *course*, Sophie would feel compelled to follow through with it anyway. Sophie had no real recourse. She had no real way to tell her friend no when there wasn't a reasonable reason to say no in the first place. She had no choice—she would have to go or tell her friend the truth.

"Just suck it up, Sophie," she told herself. Bella looked up at her, confused, but Sophie didn't budge. "You can do this. The heights aren't that scary, and the elevator isn't going to fail on you. You're not going to fall. You don't even have to look down at the ground. You can look up at the sky instead. Or, you can look at Cara, or at your reflection, or even close your eyes... You can do this. You don't have to be so worried!" Just suck it up and make it happen so you can be happy. You've got this!!" Sophie, despite her pep-talking, wasn't convinced, however. She was certain that she was going to be utterly miserable, cry at some point, and maybe even completely embarrass herself somehow. She wasn't convinced that she could keep it together long enough to get to the top of the Space Needle and actually look at the whole city of Seattle without fear. She was too terrified to do that. She was horrified.

The what-ifs raced through her mind. What if there was an earthquake while they were going there? What if there was lightning striking it? What if there was a problem with the elevator? What if all of the people on the elevator were too heavy to get it up to the top? What if the attendant had a death wish and decided to open up the door somehow halfway up so the wind could blow them out? What if the whole building collapsed? Or if there was a fire? She shook her head back and forth, desperately trying to clear her mind.

Of course, the Space Needle would be a safe place to go—it was designed the way that it was for a reason. It was designed to be safe and durable. It was meant to be somewhere that they would be able to stay safe and to be somewhere that they'd be able to enjoy. It was meant to withstand earthquakes and the wind because that is something that happened regularly in the area. While massive earthquakes weren't unheard of, they weren't common, and the building had managed to survive through many different windstorms. It couldn't be that bad if it could do all of that, right? It couldn't be something impossible to rely on if it was capable of being so dependable and reliable? It couldn't possibly be doomed for failure if thousands of people daily go through it.

Sophie sighed. She took in a deep breath. "Get a grip, Sophie," she told herself. "You're letting your stress get the best of you again." She breathed in... And out... And she tried her hardest to relax a bit more. There was no reason to be so terrified, she reminded herself. It would be fun, she insisted. She didn't have to be so afraid, she told herself, and she took another deep breath. They didn't live in Seattle, but they were near it. She knew that they'd have to get over there sooner rather than later, and she was sure she'd find a way to get over it.

They were going for an evening viewing of the Space Needle in hopes of seeing the sunset and the nighttime view. Sure, it was bound to be beautiful, but it was also going to be intimidating as far as Sophie was concerned. After all, they'd still be high up.

4:30 came quicker than Sophie had hoped, and soon, they were hopped into Cara's car and on their way to Seattle. They lived about an hour south of the Emerald City, and it was a straight shot to get there on the interstate. Off they went, with Cara happily babbling about everything that they were going to do, see, and enjoy. She was thrilled to get the opportunity and Sophie… Was hesitant. She wasn't quite convinced this was what she wanted, but she was accepting that it was what they were doing. All she had to do was smile and nod… Smile and nod…

"You know what I'm looking forward to, though?" asked Cara with a grin, glancing at her friend in the driver's seat.

"What?" asked Sophie, feeling her stomach drop. She had a feeling that she was not going to like the answer that she got. "The glass floors. Can you believe it? Glass *floors!!*"

That sounded absolutely terrifying. Not fun at all. Nope—all of the alarm bells were ringing in Sophie's mind. Avoiding looking down on the glass elevator was one thing, but having to avoid looking down the entire time? What if she had to look at her phone? Or go tie her shoe? Or dig her wallet out of her purse? There were a million little reasons she would have to look at her phone with all of them being reasonable, and yet doing so would be horrifying. She wasn't sure how well she could cope with that, to be frank, but she knew she had to try.

"Sophie?" Cara called out, trying to snap Sophie out of her stress-induced reverie. "What's up? You seem distracted."

Sophie shook her head. "No, no, it's nothing! I'm fine!" She smiled. "I just need a coffee, that's all."

Cara looked unconvinced. "If you say so…" She replied, quirking a perfectly sculpted brow at her friend. "Well, you know what they say. There's plenty of coffee in Seattle!" They were almost there at that point—they had maybe another twenty minutes to go before they'd be parked— assuming they found parking, which in Seattle, was a hot commodity. "I heard there's a café in the Space Needle, too,

so you can pick up a coffee as soon as we get there. How's
that sound?"

"Perfect!" Sophie announced with another fake smile,
turning to look out the window again. She was running out
of time to build up her resolve enough to get up to the Space
Needle, and she had no idea how she would do so or how
she could possibly get out of this predicament that she had
somehow gotten herself tangled up in. She was stuck.
Stucker than stuck—she had no choice but to just *do it*.

And, before she knew it, she had no other choice. They were
standing in front of the Space Needle, and she looked up. It
was so tall that, from the bottom, she had to crane her neck
all the way back to see it. The line was mostly filled with
college students wearing purple sweatshirts with the letters
*UW* emblazoned across them, courtesy of the local state
university, and they all looked thrilled to be there. They
were all chatting excitedly, and Sophie watched them all,
baby-faced, happily get into the elevator without a single
complaint, and here Sophie was, whining about how scared
she was.

"... Sophie?"

Sophie blinked her eyes and turned to look at Cara. She
looked concerned, and Sophie wasn't sure why.

"You're not doing okay, are you?" Cara looked over Sophie
once more.

"I'm fine. Why?"

"No, you're not. You're shaking, and I don't understand why
you keep lying to me," Cara replied. She shook her head
with a sigh. "You don't have to hide things from me, you
know."

"I know, I... Honestly? It's embarrassing." Sophie looked at the next group of people, watching as they all piled into the elevator without a single hesitation. "I'm afraid of heights."

Cara stared at her in disbelief. "Afraid of heights?"

"Yup."

"How?" Cara seemed shocked at the idea. "I mean… I thought the Acropolis was your favorite thing we saw in Greece, and that was so high up." She frowned as they moved up in line. "Do you want to head home?"

"It was my favorite! I… Just don't do well with heights. They scare me. But I loved being there. It was a childhood dream of mine, and so that kinda helped me get over the fear, I guess? But, I was terrified, in a good way." Sophie trailed off, looking around. "No, I don't want to leave, but uh… Could I maybe hold your hand when we go up?" She looked up at Cara, almost embarrassed that she had even asked.

Cara smiled. "Of course," she said. And, before she could say another word, they were ushered into the elevator for their own turn. "As soon as that door closes, you're stuck, you know," she reiterated to Sophie, who nodded.

Sophie was well aware of what she was getting herself into, and for Cara, she was happy to do so. She just had to suck it up and make it happen. She just had to close her eyes, hold Cara's hand, and pretend that they were at home like nothing was happening…

Cara reached out to take Sophie's hand and gave her a reassuring squeeze as the doors closed. Then, the elevator began moving up, little by little. It made its way up, floor by floor, and the ground underneath them vanished. Sophie squeezed Cara's hand back and tried her hardest to stare up at the sky instead. It was an uncharacteristically clear day for a Seattle autumn evening. The sky was a perfect shade of blue, connecting in the distance to the hilly horizon. She watched a few birds fly by, as the crowd around her exclaimed their own awe at what they were doing. The entire elevator ride wasn't terrible, but Sophie had also refused to look down at that point. She could feel her heart pounding away in her chest. She was terrified at what she might see if she looked at the ground as it disappeared.

*Breathe... Just breathe... In... And out... In... And out...*

Sophie tried her hardest to just focus on her breath, but it was hard for her. It was hard for her to act like there wasn't a single problem as she made her way up the needle. But, holding Cara's hand helped a lot. Being there with her friend, who knew that she was afraid and was willing to comfort her, meant a lot to her, and she was glad that she was lucky enough to have that courtesy.

The elevator stopped, and they were all ushered into the building. There was plenty to see there, and thankfully, not the entire floor was glass. There were parts of the floor that were solid as well, and Sophie did her best to focus on those. But, it was impossible for her to avoid looking out at the heights—the entire building was one long, windowed corridor. Everything was windowed—the walls were made of massive panels of glass, and the flooring was also glass across much of it. It was strange being so high up, and she had no idea how to really feel about it. She was up that high, but as she looked out, she realized it wasn't so bad. It was more like looking at a postcard scene.

She stopped and looked out the window. She could see a big cluster of skyscrapers that made up much of downtown Seattle, and directly to the right, she could see a massive body of water, with treed land in the far distance on the other side. It was strange being that high up—but it was also beautiful. The sun was very rapidly setting, too, and the sky was starting to tinge with pinks and oranges.

"Sophie?"

Cara's voice shocked her out of her reverie, and Sophie turned to look at her. "Hmm?"

"Are you doing okay?" Cara looked concerned, watching her friend closely. She had a look that almost said that she thought that Sophie would explode if they weren't careful, and that wasn't okay with her. Her own feelings were her own to manage—not Cara's.

Sophie nodded her head. "You know, this view is actually pretty great, as long as I don't look down at the ground." Sophie chuckled. "You know, it's a beautiful view, and I have to admit—it is something that I would never have done on my own. I'm glad you convinced me to go."

"Convinced you? I just asked you!" Cara looked at her with surprise. "You didn't sound like you were terrified of heights when I asked you to go. You sounded excited. Why?" Cara watched her closely, waiting to see if she would lie about anything.

"Oh, well, you know, I just wanted to be a good friend. I wanted to support you in what you were doing and what you wanted to do, and if that meant that I had to go up this giant building, even if I'm afraid, I wanted to be there with you. And you know what the weird thing is? I'm not so afraid any more—I'm not so terrified because you're here with me, and that makes all the difference. How could I possibly be afraid of such a good friend right here with me? What could I possibly have to be afraid of if you are here right by my side? This is because of you." Sophie smiled softly and squeezed her friend's hand. "You've always made me a better person, Cara, and I can't tell you how much I appreciate it."

Cara's cheeks tinged red in embarrassment. "No way, Soph. This is your victory. Don't try pinning it on me this time! Just own it—accept that you're a great person, and let's move on. We can do that, right?" Cara laughed, and so did Sophie.

"Well, it wouldn't hurt to watch the view. The sun's setting now—isn't it supposed to be stunning up here in the nighttime?" Sophie grinned at Cara. She had seen the postcards before—the picture of the buildings all lit up nicely, and the city streets all brightly lit with cars. It was a gorgeous sight to behold, and she was honestly looking forward to it now that she had gotten past that bit of fear. It would be better than she had imagined as far as she could tell, and she was ready for it.

So, together, Sophie and Cara sat at one of the benches of the Space Needle, enjoying the sights as the entire building slowly and lazily rotated. Their view of the surrounding area was constantly shifting with the moving floor, and though it was a bit strange at first, Sophie also found it strangely comforting. It was nice to know that she didn't have to walk across the surface of the glass, and it would move for her to get a full panoramic view of everything.

One by one, the lights came on, and as the sky continued to darken, Sophie realized that her fears were entirely unfounded. She hadn't needed to be afraid at all, and honestly, from being up there, she was happier. She was enjoying the view enough to even consider going back again in the future. So, Sophie and Cara chatted together, waiting for the sky to completely darken as they watched the city lights around them. When the lights finally did turn off all the way, it was amazing to see the city in the dark. The streets were illuminated to glow almost golden colors, and the sparkling lights from the city looked like millions of stars all over the city. It was gorgeous, and there was no other word to describe it. It was a fantastic view, and she was thrilled she didn't have to miss it.

As they were heading out of the Space Needle, Sophie squeezed Cara's hand. "Thank you. I mean it."

"Don't mention it," Cara said. "Thanks for coming with me. That view was stellar!"

"It was!" replied Sophie. "We'll have to come back again sometime in the future. I'd love to see it again!"

Cara laughed. "Really? You'd be willing to come back there? Did I cure your fear of height?"

Sophie laughed back as they walked to Cara's car. "Something like that. But hey, it worked! We should do it again in the future, okay? It'll be my treat next time."

"Oh, in that case, of course! We'll have to go again. Maybe we can check out that new restaurant that they have in there... Did you know there's a revolving restaurant up there? Isn't that cool?" Cara unlocked their car and headed inside with a grin as she started it up.

"Oh, is there?" Sophie replied as she jumped in as well. "We'll definitely have to check it out then!"

They both grinned at each other and made their way home, happily chatting about all of their adventure that day. It had been a busy one, but it was one that Sophie would love to repeat again in the future.

# Guided Meditation 1: Exploring Time and Space

*In this guided meditation, you will be encouraged to explore the world and the universe around you, discovering that while you may think that something is big and unbearable in the moment, you can let it go and let it fade away with ease if you simply distance yourself away from it. Even the biggest problems will not seem so bad in the grand scheme of things if you are able to take a new perspective, one that is far from the perspective that you have taken. Through traveling through space and time, you will put yourself in a position where even galaxies can seem so far away that they are insignificantly small. You learn to focus on your acceptance of the situation at hand so you can prevent yourself from letting your stress from overwhelming you. As you do this, you become able to envision your home, your room, and your bed as your safe space, distanced away from all of the stressors and anxieties of the day so you can get a restful, quiet sleep.*

Close your eyes and take in a big, deep breath. Feel the air flowing through your nose. Notice how it feels. Focus in the temperature and the smells. Feel it filling up your lungs, with your lungs swelling up within you like great, big balloons in your chest until you feel like they can't swell up any more. Feel the air warming in your chest and exhale slowly, feeling the air pass your lips gently and slowly. Is it warm? With each breath that you take, you feel yourself calming down.

You breathe in... And out...

Now, feel yourself. Focus on your center, the point just above your belly button. How does it feel? Is it tense? Tight? Stressed? Focus on this point as you inhale in. One... Two... Three... Four... Five... and out... One... Two... three... Four... Five... Focus on that spot for another breath or two...

Now, feel the tension in your body. Become aware of any tension you are holding in your head and face. As you breathe in, imagine that you are pushing the tension down to the center above your belly button. Let it gather there. Now, feel the tension in your shoulders. Focus on that stress and tension and as you breathe in, feel it moving down to your center. Let it gather there, imagining your tension and stress all becoming balled up in the center. Feel the tension in your arms and hands gathering and flowing in to your center. Feel that center growing with the tension and allow it to build up. Then, take the tension from your chest and upper back, and flow it down toward your center.

Then, go down to your toes and feet, identifying the tension that is there. Push it up, feeling it flowing up your legs, through your pelvis and belly, and noting it as it arrives in the belly. Focus on it as it grows within you and allow it to flow.

Feel all of the tension in your body and imagine it turning into a flame within you. Imagine it flickering and burning within your belly, but as it burns, it is released into the world. You burn the tension more and more, helping it to release itself out of you. You reject the tension that was within you and push it to your inner core so you can allow it all to dissipate. You want to be relaxed and with every moment of burning within yourself, you find yourself relaxing more and more. Your head starts to relax and you feel your stress fading away. Your shoulders and your arms begin to relax and the fire in your belly comfortably burns it away. Your tension in your chest fades and you feel incredibly warm and comfortable. Finally, the tension from the other side begins to burn off as well, leaving your entire body entirely at ease and completely relaxed. You have released all of your tension and are left with a small, bright flame in your stomach, flickering along with your heart. With every beat, it crackles within you, helping you to stay relaxed.

With every exhale, you breathe out what was left of your tension. It gathers in your lungs with your used air. It all gathers up into one place for simple burning and you will be able to help yourself to stay relaxed. You can draw on this flame whenever you find yourself stressed with tension. Whenever you feel the need to alleviate the stress within you, you can focus on the tension and burn it within yourself, imagining as it all toasts up and burns away.

You now have space within yourself to welcome relaxation and positivity.

Breathe in... One... Two... Three... Four... Five... And out... One... Two... Three... Four... Five... As you breathe in, imagine the feeling of relaxation flowing within you, emanating from your inner fire throughout your body. Feel it in your head. Breathe in... and out... Feel the relaxation pulsating in your shoulders and arms... Feel it spreading throughout your chest. Feel it spread down to your legs and feet. It fills your whole body, bringing you utter peace and relaxation. Your mind feels incredibly open and ready to go on a peaceful, relaxing adventure. Your body is ready to fall deeper and deeper into your relaxation so you can become more and more relaxed. Your body embraces the relaxation and does not resist. It is happy to enjoy the warmth and peace within itself. It is ready to be taken on a journey.

As you become as relaxed as you can be, you are able to stop and focus on the world within you. You reflect inwardly, sinking into your mind and relax. You pull yourself into your mind, feeling more and more at peace as you do. You are ready.

You are but a speck in a field of blackness. You are surrounded by nothingness, so vast that you cannot comprehend just how wide it is. You are a drifter, but a speck in the world. You are a single point in the vastness of eternity around you. You are surrounded by everything and nothing all at the same time. As you focus around yourself, you realize that you are actually floating, unable to feel anything above or below you. You cannot feel anything touching you at all, and you can only see darkness about you. You are drifting aimlessly in the wide expanse of nothing. You cannot see anything but darkness. You do not hear anything but silence. But, you are at peace. You know that you are right where you are supposed to be. You are a single little speck, floating...

You float further and further away from your starting point without resistance. You don't know how or why you are drifting, but you are willing to accept it. You are willing to be that little speck, carried by forces that you are unsure of. You are willing to be a part of that, of being carried about, and you are content in your place. Every breath that you take pulls you further away. Every moment you end up drifting more and more, but it doesn't matter because there is nowhere to go.

You take a deep breath in...

One... Two... Three... Four... Five...

And out...

One... Two... Three... Four... Five...

As you do this, you feel yourself relaxing. You feel that little spark inside of you start to light up. It flickers into existence. Now, you are just a little bit bigger. You look around and you are surrounded by lots of tiny little specks. You can't see much—they are just little dots in the space around you, floating and drifting just as aimlessly as you are. Sometimes, they bump into you, but it doesn't matter to you. You just keep on moving within space.

You take a deep breath in...

One... Two... Three... Four... Five...

And out...

One... Two... Three... Four... Five...

You relax a little bit more. You surrender yourself to the feeling of being utterly at peace within yourself. You feel perfectly content as you float aimlessly. You grow a little bit bigger than you were before and you realize something. You are now able to do a little bit more. Now, you can move around yourself a little bit. You can sort of will yourself wherever you want and you slowly find yourself gravitating in that direction. It is incredibly freeing and you love every moment of it. You find yourself drifting about aimlessly at first, and then you start to experiment. You can move up... and you can move down... and to the sides...

You notice that you can stop running into all of the little particles floating around you... and many of them look different. There are smaller particles around you now, and some that are much larger than you, too. You realize that you're simply drifting among the particles in this great, big, vast nothingness, and you *accept it*. You are calm. You are not hurting. You are able to relax. Soon, you start moving more. You move quicker, easier. You grow larger. And as you grow, you realize something. You are floating through space and you are finally large enough to make it out.

You can see endless darkness, and the particles have disappeared around you. You are able to see stars all around you. You see something in the distance—a nebulous haze, filled with the vaguest hints of colors within them. You can see it, a sort of amalgamation of purples and blues. It all circulated around a central point. The one point in the center is entirely bright—you can't seem to make it out, but around it, the haze reaches outward, tendrils of the hazy galaxy stretching out across space. It looks so small from where you are standing... So distant, and yet you know that it is far vaster than anything you could imagine—so big, in fact, that it houses whole solar systems.

You take in a deep breath and you feel yourself moving away from the great, big galaxy. You are not ready to approach it yet. You are not yet ready to see just how vast and expansive it is. You move away from the galaxy, and see another one in the distance, and another one and another one. There are galaxies spread throughout space, some of them looking like tiny dots, barely visible while others appear much larger, with a glowing mass surrounded by spinning haze just like the last one.

All of the galaxies around you are beautiful, shimmering, and mysterious. You feel drawn to them, but you cannot help it—you want to stay back. You don't want to approach them yet. And yet, as you try to stay away, you find yourself naturally gravitating toward one. As soon as you see it, you are in awe with how beautiful it is. There is a single light point in its center, golden in color, and it stretches outward, as if several arms of nebulous haze reached out from one central point, spiraling around it. You are looking at the Milky Way galaxy. From your perspective, it swirls around that central glowing point. It wraps around, almost like a shell, and it sparkles. Each of the arms of the spiral is full of so many stars. You see them all in front of you, but you have no way to count them. You get closer and closer over time, breathing in and out as you go closer.

You breathe in...

One... Two... Three... Four...

And out...

One... Two... Three... Four...

As you continue breathing, the arms of the spiral get bigger and bigger... They get more and more white. You see that they are full of stars and spots around the stars. They are planets, rotating around the sun, more and more. They look so small as you view them. You see the planets rotating around the stars and the moons around the planets. They move faster and faster, and you can see them rotating as you breathe. The galaxy spins around that central light, all of the arms spinning. Within the arms, you can see that each one is made up of many different solar systems, each one rotating around a star. Each solar system is filled up with planets, with moons, with asteroids and more. Each one is bright and unique in its own ways. And all of them are connected together.

You breathe in...

One... Two... Three... Four...

And out...

One... Two... Three... Four...

You choose to approach one of the solar systems. The solar system's star is not very big compared to the rest. It still shines rightly right where it is, yellow-orange. Around it there are eight planets, all rotating around. You move closer through the stars, approaching that one solar system in the one part of the galaxy. You get closer and closer... You see the first planet get closer to you. it is massive and you can see just how large it is as you approach it. You can see its beautiful blue form, spinning about, with streaks of other colors within it. It is Neptune, at the edge of the solar system. You get closer and closer to it, breathing deeply as you move.
You breathe in...

One... Two... Three... Four...

And out...

One... Two... Three... Four...

You breathe in...

One... Two... Three... Four...

And out...

One... Two... Three... Four...

Breathing deeply, you can see the surface of Neptune, spinning round and round. You can see it spinning there, brightly shining in the sun's light. It is so far from the sun, and yet you can see it clearly. You can see the color perfectly reflected in the light, even from a distance.

You move past Neptune, and soon, you approach a big planet that is a beautiful blue-green color. It has an icy ring wrapped about it, and you can see it there, shimmering about. You pass it quickly, and move toward Saturn with the next breath.

You breathe in...

One... Two... Three... Four...

And out...

One... Two... Three... Four...

Soon, you're past Jupiter, and the asteroid belt, and with another breath, you pass Mars.

You breathe in...

One... Two... Three... Four...

And out...

One... Two... Three... Four...

Then, you approach Earth, getting closer and closer to see the bright blue water, and the green land, but you're careful not to get too close. You recognize the home there, but you choose not to get too close. You pass by and take a big, deep breath again.
You breathe in...

One... Two... Three... Four...

And out...

One... Two... Three... Four...

Soon, you pass Venus, and Mercury too, and you go all the way past the sun as well, and before long, you have left the solar system. Just like that, you're leaving it behind. You're growing. You're getting bigger and bigger. You're going further and further from your home, and soon, you are away from all things familiar. You lost, but you are not afraid. You are exploring the universe all around you and you are loving every moment of it. You feel like you do not have a care in the world.

You are a star. You are brightly burning as your inner flame grows larger and larger. You feel it spreading out, engulfing you, and granting you that endless peace within yourself. It protects you. It burns away your troubles, and as you burn, you realize that there are very few troubles that a star can have. You are safe. You are able to embrace yourself.

You feel at peace. As you leave behind the home that you know, you feel yourself growing bigger and bigger. You leave behind your troubles with the solar system, and the further you get away from them, the more you see that they are smaller and less significant than you thought. You have left behind all of the trouble. You have left behind all of the pain and the stress. The further you flow into the universe,

the more at peace you feel. You have left them all behind, all
of your stressors and you feel your body beginning to relax
more and more.

You breathe in...

One... Two... Three... Four...

And out...

One... Two... Three... Four...

You grow bigger and bigger as you go further away. You see
a comet in the air. It leaves a trail of icy dust in its path. You
can see it sparkling. You can see it glowing. You can see it
flying through the universe. Slowly at first. You can see it
flowing slowly. It's so slow that it looks like it isn't moving
at first, but the trail of ice it leaves shows that even it is not
stagnant. It is moving about. It is flowing through space and
time, just like you are.

You are made of the same cosmic dust as the comet right in
front of you. You are just as profound, just as unique, and
just as wondrous as comet is. You are connected to the stars
as a part of the same universe and when you look at the
grand scheme of the universe, those problems of your day
suddenly aren't so big after all. You can find peace in this
sort of revelation and any time you need to, you can return
to this inner cosmic world for yourself. it will help you.

You breathe in...

One... Two... Three... Four...

And out...

One... Two... Three... Four...

You breathe in...

One... Two... Three... Four...

And out...

One... Two... Three... Four...

Just as you grew into the great, big cosmic body, you find yourself shrinking back down again. You find yourself back in your usual human self. You find yourself floating there, in that great, big nothingness. You see yourself there, drifting comfortably through the space. You are at peace with yourself.

You know that you can leave behind your problems. You know that the problems might seem big when you're in the moment, but they can be left behind. You become aware of yourself in the moment in your bed. You are perfectly comfortable and content. You visualize that everything around your bed, in your room, is far, far from the outside world, and you feel at peace.

Your room is your special refuge, away from the outside world and the outside troubles. You can protect yourself when you are within your room and it is the perfect environment for sleep. Where you are is perfect to help you get a nice, full night, and you know it.

You feel yourself getting sleepier now as you drift on your bed. You are there, floating and waiting. You are there, relaxing and enjoying the moment. You are there and you can forget your stressors as you rest. You can allow yourself to get further and further away from Earth and from your problems, just by looking within yourself.

You breathe in...

One... Two... Three... Four...

And out...

One... Two... Three... Four...

You are feeling too sleepy to resist now. You can feel yourself getting heavy. You do not float about as much anymore, and you can feel yourself sinking into your bed, deeper and deeper. You feel yourself comfortable and ready to sleep. You can feel yourself forgive yourself for any problems form the day. You can feel yourself let go of your worries. You can feel yourself distance yourself further and further from them, welcoming only peace and love within yourself.

Your eyes feel heavy and your mind feels slow.

You breathe in...

One... Two... Three... Four...

And out...

One... Two... Three... Four...

You feel ready to sleep once and for all and you welcome it. You open your mind and your boy to the rest that awaits you. You welcome the peace and joy it will bring you.

You breathe in...

One... Two... Three... Four...

And out...

One... Two... Three... Four...

You breathe in...

One... Two... Three... Four...

And out...

One... Two... Three... Four...

*You are at peace and you are finally falling asleep. Good night and rest well.*

# Guided Meditation 2: Peaceful Paradise

*In this guided meditation, you will be transported to a world far from home, where you are able to find total serenity. Surrounded by ivory sand and cerulean water, with the crystal clear sky and a verdant green rainforest, you will be invited to explore your surroundings, to let your anxiety and stress melt away under the tropical sun and the blanket of the forest canopy, and allow yourself a moment to breathe in total relaxation to help you gently fall asleep before you know it.*

Close your eyes and take in a big, deep breath. Feel the air flowing through your nose. Notice how it feels. Focus in the temperature and the smells. Feel it filling up your lungs, with your lungs swelling up within you like great, big balloons in your chest until you feel like they can't swell up any more. Feel the air warming in your chest and exhale slowly, feeling the air pass your lips gently and slowly. Is it warm? With each breath that you take, you feel yourself calming down.

You breathe in... And out...

Now, feel yourself. Focus on your center, the point just above your belly button. How does it feel? Is it tense? Tight? Stressed? Focus on this point as you inhale in. One... Two... Three... Four... Five... and out... One... Two... three... Four... Five... Focus on that spot for another breath or two...

Now, feel the tension in your body. Become aware of any tension you are holding in your head and face. As you breathe in, imagine that you are pushing the tension down to the center above your belly button. Let it gather there. Now, feel the tension in your shoulders. Focus on that stress and tension and as you breathe in, feel it moving down to your center. Let it gather there, imagining your tension and stress all becoming balled up in the center. Feel the tension in your arms and hands gathering and flowing in to your center. Feel that center growing with the tension and allow it to build up. Then, take the tension from your chest and upper back, and flow it down toward your center.

Then, go down to your toes and feet, identifying the tension that is there. Push it up, feeling it flowing up your legs, through your pelvis and belly, and noting it as it arrives in the belly. Focus on it as it grows within you and allow it to flow.

Feel all of the tension in your body and imagine it turning into a flame within you. Imagine it flickering and burning within your belly, but as it burns, it is released into the world. You burn the tension more and more, helping it to release itself out of you. You reject the tension that was within you and push it to your inner core so you can allow it all to dissipate. You want to be relaxed and with every moment of burning within yourself, you find yourself relaxing more and more. Your head starts to relax and you feel your stress fading away. Your shoulders and your arms begin to relax and the fire in your belly comfortably burns it away. Your tension in your chest fades and you feel incredibly warm and comfortable. Finally, the tension from the other side begins to burn off as well, leaving your entire body entirely at ease and completely relaxed. You have released all of your tension and are left with a small, bright flame in your stomach, flickering along with your heart. With every beat, it crackles within you, helping you to stay relaxed.

With every exhale, you breathe out what was left of your tension. It gathers in your lungs with your used air. It all gathers up into one place for simple burning and you will be able to help yourself to stay relaxed. You can draw on this flame whenever you find yourself stressed with tension. Whenever you feel the need to alleviate the stress within you, you can focus on the tension and burn it within yourself, imagining as it all toasts up and burns away.

You now have space within yourself to welcome relaxation and positivity.

Breathe in… One… Two… Three… Four… Five… And out… One… Two… Three… Four… Five… As you breathe in, imagine the feeling of relaxation flowing within you, emanating from your inner fire throughout your body. Feel it in your head. Breathe in… and out… Feel the relaxation pulsating in your shoulders and arms… Feel it spreading throughout your chest. Feel it spread down to your legs and feet. It fills your whole body, bringing you utter peace and relaxation. Your mind feels incredibly open and ready to go on a peaceful, relaxing adventure. Your body is ready to fall deeper and deeper into your relaxation so you can become more and more relaxed.

As you relax, you realize that your feet have sunk into sand. It is warm, yet soft and smooth. The sand is wonderful underneath you—you love every step that you take within it. When you look down, you see that the sand is a beautiful ivory color and it spreads out in front of you for what seems like forever. It glistens in the noonday sunlight, shimmering and sparkling as the light catches the sides of the crystals.

You look to the right and see the brightest, clearest, bluest water you have ever seen, cerulean in color. The top is rippling with white reflections of light as the water shifts about. It is nearly still, save for mild rippling. The gentle waves lapped at the sand, leaving lines of wetness, darkening the sand as they pulled back toward the sea. It was an endless dance—the water comes in, spraying at the sand, and the water pulls back out, receding. It goes back and forth and you watch it calmly, breathing gently.

You breathe in…

One… Two… Three… Four…

And out…

One… Two… Three… Four…

Above you, the sky is nearly as deep a blue as the ocean. It is perfectly clear with just a few stray wisps of clouds drifting about. It is the perfect day for a beachside adventure and you are free to enjoy it however you would like to do. You are free to settle down and nap in the sun, enjoying the warmth, or you can choose to walk and explore. You could swim, or you could rest. What you do with yourself is up to you.

You breathe in…

One… Two… Three… Four…

And out…

One… Two… Three… Four…

You hear the distant cries of seagulls warbling in the ocean air. They sound shrill and high as they circle above the water. They are perfectly content to keep on circling above. You watch them lazily glide along the breeze that brings with it the scent of salt and kelp with a hint of fishiness included. It is a beautiful day to relax and you intend to do so. As you bask in the sunlight, you feel yourself radiating calmness.

Listen to your mind for a moment. Let yourself focus inwardly on it and experience where it stands. Do you feel any anxiety in the moment? Are you worried about something that you need to do in the next few days? Are you stressing out about something that is going to be less than fun?

You breathe in…

One... Two... Three... Four...

And out...

One... Two... Three... Four...

As you exhale, you feel your worries starting to fade away. They are starting to melt out of your body as you breathe. The more that you breathe, the more capable of calming yourself down you become. You feel empowered. You feel in control. You know that as you continue to breathe, you'll feel even better than before.

You breathe in...

One... Two... Three... Four...

And out...

One... Two... Three... Four...

You can see the line between the sand and the soil, where the plants start growing on the island. You can see the vivid, brightly colored foliage sprouting from the trees. Fronds of palm and coconut sway gently in the breeze, rustling together and creating an air of serenity about you. You can hear them creating a gentle, rhythmic sound as they rub together, and all around you, you can hear the sounds of hundreds of birds, all singing together. There are trilling birds and there are more loud screeching birds. There are birds that sound so faint that you can barely hear them, and there are birds that sound like they are right above you— because they are.

When you look up, you see a flurry of birds, fluttering from branch to branch, from tree to tree. They are beautiful and in every color imaginable. There are some that are so black, they look like they are impossible to see. There are some that are blue and green. There are big birds and small. They are each unique in their own ways. They all have their own specific look, but each one is worthy of your attention.

You decide to walk toward the birds, feeling the sand underneath your feet slowly change. Step by step, you approach that point of foliage on the island and soon, you are there, standing on the edge between where the beach meet the trees. You can see them all lined out there, creating a sort of wall. You can feel that the air is cooler there—it is still just as humid, but it is noticeably lower with the shade of the trees. You look back over your shoulder, seeing that there is the whole expanse of beach to explore, and you turn to keep going deeper. You walk further into the wooded area. You can see that there is a rich, fertile soil underfoot, perhaps from the volcano that once brought this island into existence. You can see it, dark and lush. You can feel how soft the soil is underfoot as well as you step, one by one. Despite the shade, it is warm underneath your feet.

You breathe in...

One... Two... Three... Four...

And out...

One... Two... Three... Four...

Look around yourself for a moment. You can see the bright green leaves just about everywhere around you. They come in ferns and in leaves. They come large and sall. Some have vines draped between them, dangling as long tendrils that weave in and out between the leaves, almost creating a tapestry between them. They are covered in leaves, and even the occasional frog that you can spot if you look closely.

You continue to walk through the small forest, looking around yourself and absorbing it all it. It is gorgeous, peaceful, and so compelling to walk through. You find yourself in awe with the beauty. You find yourself shocked at just how diverse the area is. You can see butterflies hovering and fluttering their way across the forest. They come in every color, but one catches your eye.

The butterfly is massive—easily the size of your hand if you were to outstretch all of your fingers. It is almost brown in color as it sits there on the plant. It has what looks like spotted eyes amongst its wingspan, and there are areas that are darker and almost barred. The color is reminiscent of a tiger's own stripes and there are a wide array of different shades present among the butterfly's wings.

You breathe in...

One... Two... Three... Four...

And out...

One... Two... Three... Four

You look closer at the butterfly, leaning in, and you can suddenly see its six long legs clinging to the length of a vine. You can see the great, big black eyes that stare back up at you, almost beadily. The antennae atop the butterfly's head quiver, picking up signals about the world that you will never understand.

The butterfly opens up its wings and suddenly, you are treated with a view of the bright sunset-colored wings that were hidden when they were folded up on its back. They shimmer in a ray of sunlight that falls through the canopy. The centermost part of the butterfly, closest to its body, is a beautiful white color, fading into yellow, then golden, and orange, with the bottommost wings a deep black. It was a beautiful butterfly—a sunset morpho butterfly, and with its wings spread out as much as they could be, you realize that it is much larger than your hand when you outstretch it. Its wings fold up and down slowly.

You realize that the butterfly there is not alone—there are many more of them, all sitting atop the vines. There are some in different colors. Your eyes find one that, when it opens up its wings to reveal the outsides of them, is the most brilliant blue that you have ever seen. The wings appeared black and soft before they were opened—with eye spots of black, yellow, and violet along their surfaces, but as soon as the wings are unfurled, you see them for what they are—that azure color that rivals that of the ocean that you have just seen. You see the blue appear to shimmer almost iridescently in the filtered light, and then, suddenly and unexpectedly, all of the butterflies take flight.

There are hundreds of them flying past you, in every color that you can see. They are wonderful as they flutter by, and you can feel yourself, your heart, growing lighter as they leave. One by one, they take away that negativity, that anxiety, and your apprehensions about the world. They leave you feeling more comfortable, calmer, and more willing to see the world as a kind, friendly place. They take away your fear as they fly by and as you watch them, slowly disappearing into your surroundings, you feel at peace. You feel at ease. You feel ready to commit to your own peace of mind and you embrace it.

You breathe in...

One... Two... Three... Four...

And out...

One... Two... Three... Four

You feel your peace and clarity within yourself and as you do, you realize that the clarity is freeing. You feel free within yourself. You are free from the troubles that you have. You are free from the struggles of your world and you are at peace. You are comfortable and relaxed. You are right where you should be in the moment.

You keep heading through the tropical forest. In the distance, you can hear what sounds like monkeys in the distance. Their voices are shrill, and yet jubilant all at the same time. They are happy in their cheers and they sound like they are heading toward you. You head toward them as well, curious about what made up the sound. You want to know why they are all squealing the way that they are and you head toward them, searching for the source of the sound. You keep your eyes up above you, scanning about the canopy in hopes of finding the source of the sound. You know that there must be monkeys running about somewhere. You know that they are probably having a grand time, swinging from branch to branch, so carefree and happy. You can have that same carefree nature, simply learning to trust yourself.

Soon, you hear the sounds get louder and louder, and when you look up, you realize that there is a tree full of little, black monkeys. They swing from tree to tree, clinging to the branches with their long, curling tails. They you will be able to see you as they swing about and they are watching you. Their cries slow down as they notice you, and one of them gets closer. It swings down, branch to branch, until it reaches a thick vine, and it slides down to look at you. It gets into your face and leans in closely.

The monkey is not very big—it is furry and black with a hairless face with big eyes. The eyes look up at you. The monkey is hanging upside down as it watches you, holding on to the tree with its long tail. Its hands look remarkably human as it watches you, eyes unfathomable. You look back into its eyes and feel calm. You feel content. You understand it as you both gaze into each other's eyes. You sense that the monkey wants you to follow it as it watches you, and you are happy to do so. You feel compelled to go with it, and without having to say a word, the monkey seems to understand.

The monkey leaves you, climbing back up the tree effortlessly. It flies up with ease, climbing as if it were easier than anything it had ever done before. It waits at the top, turning back to meet your gaze, and you understand. You must follow the monkey to see where it wants to take you. Just as suddenly, the monkey begins to move, swinging from branch to branch. It is slower now than it was earlier, and you know that it is moving slower for you. You slowly make your way to follow them, never letting your eyes off of them as you walk along the ground.

You have to dodge trees and climb over roots as you go, but you do it anyway. You don't think about how hard it will be for you to do so—your mind is simply focused on what you are going to do. You are going to follow those monkeys and see where they go. They must know the best places to go, you tell yourself. They know where to go and what to do. This is their home, and you are eager to see what it looks like.

You dodge vines and slip underneath ferns. You ignore the butterflies. You ignore the birds that sing their songs around you. All you focus on is the monkeys in front of you and your breath as you go. Your breathing is a bit quicker, but not strained as you go. As the monkeys pick up their speed, you pick up your own as well. You keep going for what feels like an eternity.

Breathe in…

One… Two… Three… Four…

And out…

One… Two… Three… Four.

Suddenly, the monkeys stop. And, when you look around, you realize that they have taken you deeply into the rainforest. You can barely see through the canopy and it is much darker where you are. The monkeys are quiet and when you look up at them, you realize that all eyes are on you, watching you as you sit there in their home. They want to know what you are going to do next.

You breathe in...

One... Two... Three... Four...

And out...

One... Two... Three... Four.

You realize that you can hear the dull roar of water where you are. You can hear it babbling as it flows from somewhere... And when you look around, you realize where it was coming from. It was coming from a small waterfall, babbling over a cliff into a small stream. The rocks are black and craggy where they are and the water seems to fall from them in a million different directions, spraying little drops of water everywhere. The water is shallow as it falls down the rocks, cascading gently. You are in awe of the water—it is crystal clear and you can see right down to the bottom. There are little frogs and tadpoles swimming about in the shallowest parts, away from the currents created by the waterfall.

You look back at the monkeys and they are still watching you, waiting for your response. It feels almost surreal as you sit there, listening to the water washing over the rocks. You feel at peace where you are looking and you are content. You enjoy the sound and you breathe.

You watch the water for a while. You watch it flowing, and you allow yourself and you feel at peace. You feel like you are able to enjoy the moment. You sit there, looking at the ripples as the water flows. You watch the bubbly froth where it arises at the base of the waterfall, and you feel peaceful. You feel as if your stress and tension fades away. You feel as

fluid and free and as light as the water that flows in front of
you. you settle down to sit in place for a while. You sit
yourself there so that you can enjoy the moment.

The monkeys around you are still quiet, and one by one,
they curl up in the trees. You see them cuddling, babies with
their mothers, and sometimes a few adults cuddled together
peacefully. You see them all, watching the water peacefully
and at ease. They watch it flow, listening to the cadence.
You are aware of the sound of a bird somewhere in the
distance—it is a single bird, trilling and tweeting in the
distance. You are aware of it singing happily. You listen
closely to it as it does and you feel utterly relaxed.

As you sit there, you are able to free yourself from the stress
and anxiety. You tell yourself to stop worrying about the
world. You focus inwardly on your breathing now, letting
the sound of the water fade to the back of your mind. You
feel fully present in the moment.

You tell yourself that you will be just fine. You tell yourself
that you are at peace. You are happy.

As you sit there, you become aware of that inner fire within
yourself. You focus on what you are doing. You feel how you
feel, perfectly at peace. You remind yourself that you are
within your perfect moment of peace. You feel good. You
feel calm. You take a deep breath.

You breathe in...

One... Two... Three... Four...

And out...

One... Two... Three... Four.

You are at ease. You are content. You can feel yourself
growing calmer and at peace as you sit. You feel your body

relaxing as you feel at peace. You feel yourself sinking. Your head feels heavy. Your body feels like it is sinking into the ground underneath you. You can feel the waves of sleepiness falling and crashing over you as you sit there. You feel like you are the rocks that the water is washing over.

You breathe in…

One… Two… Three… Four…

And out…

One… Two… Three… Four.

The longer that you sit there, the sleepier you become. The heavier your body feels as you feel ready to drift to sleep. You feel yourself become sleepier and sleepier as you sit there. Listen to the sounds of the forest as you relax more and more. Allow yourself to relax to yourself. Let yourself sink deeper and deeper into relaxation. You have released your anxiety. You have released your tension. Focus inwardly as you listen to the water flowing and the birds singing. Feel your inner fire burning to bring you relaxation. Feel your fire spreading throughout your body, providing you with protection. Your inner fire burns brightly to protect yourself and shields your entire body. It protects you, repelling the stress.

On your perfect paradise, you know that you are shielded. You are far from the stressors of life. You don't have to worry here—life is simpler here. It is relaxing where you stand. You feel your body growing warmer and heavier. Your eyes can barely stay open. You can barely keep yourself awake. You focus on your breathing again.

You breathe in…

One… Two… Three… Four…

And out...

One... Two... Three... Four.

You are getting so close to falling asleep. You stop fighting it. You welcome the peace and quiet. You welcome the peace and quiet that you have in your life. You feel perfectly content. You are at ease. Your sleepiness washes over you and you are willing to accept it. You embrace it and you drift off to sleep, peacefully, to the lullaby of the world around you.

You breathe in...

One... Two... Three... Four...

And out...

One... Two... Three... Four.

Good night, sleep tight and rest well.

# Bedtime Stories for Adults

*Depression and Anxiety. Have a Peaceful, Relaxing Sleep and Wake up Fresh, Happy, & Without Worries. Calm Your Mind NOW*
*Book 3*

# Table of Contents

# Introduction

If you've found yourself lying in bed often without being able to fall asleep, or you find yourself struggling to stay asleep, you may suffer from insomnia. Insomnia is one of those problems that could be isolated on its own, or it could be something that is indicative that you have other problems that need to be addressed. If you find that it is hard for you to fall asleep, stay asleep, or get back to sleep, you may need to address this sleep disorder, especially if it starts to impact your own personal quality of life. It can harm your energy level or your mood, as well as your efficiency and health. While we all need slightly different amounts of sleep, most adults require between seven and eight hours nightly, and if you are not getting at least that, you may be struggling with insomnia.

If you are, you are not alone by any means—most adults suffer from what is known as an acute episode of insomnia, where for a few days or weeks, there is a struggle sleeping, typically tied to trauma or stress. However, some people have longer-lasting chronic insomnia that can last for months at a time. If your sleep is suffering, know that you don't have to put up with it. You can make some very simple changes to your life to fix the problem.

In this book, we are going to be addressing two common causes of insomnia—anxiety and depression. Both of these can lead to major problems with feelings of insomnia, but you can learn to cope with them. Through learning how to navigate your own life and how you choose to interact with yourself, you can start to alleviate that anxiety and depression, and as those symptoms alleviate, your sleep should improve dramatically. This is because anxiety and depression are both known to negatively impact sleep one way or another.

You cannot "cure" depression or anxiety through meditative techniques—the anxiety and depression will still be there, but you will also be able to approach the situation better as well. You are learning to cope with the negative feelings that otherwise would have controlled you and prevented you from allowing the anxiety and depression to keep your mind reeling all night long. When you have the ability to cope with the negative thoughts that will typically get in your way, you realize that you are far more capable of succeeding at coping with your feelings than you were before. As a result, you should see some alleviation of insomnia.

This book is designed to help you to cope with your anxiety and depression through mindful bedtime stories. These are stories that require you to quietly focus on what is written, listening, and surrendering yourself to what you want to hear. As a result, you will be able to cope better. In this book, it is assumed that you have some degree of mindfulness background. This book is the third in a series of meditative stories meant to aid in the alleviation of anxiety and depression to aid in sleeping better, and it will use techniques that have been taught throughout the previous two as well.

The first book introduced you to the concept of mindfulness—it worked to teach you gentle mindful meditation through the use of mindful breathing, body scans, and affirmations. Each of these three techniques worked to help alleviate those stressors to allow for sleep to occur.

The second book expanded upon those basic techniques, introducing progressive relaxation. Progressive relaxation builds upon body scans, allowing you to begin to work better to help yourself with consciously relaxing several parts of your body little by little until you are done. If you can do this, you will realize that you actually do have the power to calm yourself down over time, something that is highly beneficial to just about anyone.

Finally, this book will introduce you to the use of passive thought observation without judgment for the moment that you are in. As you go through the use of passive thought observation, you learn how to keep yourself at the moment, aware of what is happening within your mind, but you do not engage with the thoughts that you have. You simply let them pass as they are without complaint and without judgment. This helps you to learn where your mind stands so you can be certain that you know what is causing the feelings that you have. Usually, the feelings are caused by certain types of thoughts that then trigger them.

When you can find the cause of the feelings, you can then address them in your life. If through passive observation, you realize that your biggest problem is with the fact that ultimately you are caught up in your emotion, you can then address the cause of the emotions to prevent them in the first place. This is where passive thought observation comes into play.

## Passive Thought Observation

Passive thought observation works to allow yourself to simply focus on the moment. When you use it, you find yourself simply sitting and becoming aware of your thoughts. You let them pass you, one by one, so that you can begin to see what is going on in your mind. Your thoughts are constantly at work within yourself. They are able to be tracked, one by one, as they pass in your mind. You can see them filling your mind, then drifting away. In doing this, you quietly listen to yourself and watch what happens.

This meditative technique makes you a visitor to your own mind—a quiet observer that is simply watching as the thoughts pass you by. If you want to do this, you must learn to focus your mind, listening to yourself, and then forcing yourself to avoid responding. It builds self-discipline and helps you to ensure that, ultimately, you don't simply become reflexively responsive. Ideally, you would ensure that you are able to respond accordingly and in a way that is beneficial rather than lashing out.

If this is something that you want to practice, the best starting point is with mindful breathing and a body scan to relax, at which point you can shift your focus away so that you can better influence yourself. When you are able to get to that point of mindful awareness, your next step is to make sure that you let your thoughts start to drift, and simply follow them. You may be surprised to see where they take you.

Each story is designed to be a calming slice of life story about the various adventures (and sometimes misadventures) of Sophie Rogers, a young woman that lives in the Pacific Northwest with her German shepherd pal Bella. Together, and sometimes separately, they get out and enjoy their lives, and the stories of her day to day life can help you to relax and soothe yourself into a state in which you will be able to relax. As you read, you should find yourself calming down and preparing for a night of sleep. Each of the options that are provided to you should be fun and engaging without keeping you up at night. They are designed to provide yourself with something that you can focus on so that you can relax as well. They will gently guide you through a wide range of techniques that are meant to slow down your mind and provide a peaceful clarity to yourself. If you listen closely to the meditations, following along with the instructions, you should find yourself beginning to relax while exploring beautiful scenes and discovering techniques that can help you to defeat the anxiety that you feel.

Hopefully, by following along with these stories, you find yourself starting to relax more and more. It is the hope that as you do read, the story will feel immersive enough that you will be able to pay closer attention to what is on the pages in front of you. It is my hope that as you read over this, you will discover that you are actually quite interested in hearing about Sophie and her friends and that the more that you listen to her and with her, the easier it becomes to sleep. Her stories are not meant to keep you awake, nor are they designed to bother you or make you want to go out and do something. They are here so you can properly focus and begin to sleep, little by little. As you use these guided meditations and stories for yourself, hopefully, you start to feel sleepier and sleepier—hopefully, you find yourself desiring time to sleep, and you are actually able to make it happen.

So, are you ready to get started? Are you ready to start exploring the world of meditation and everything that it has to offer you? Let's dive in!

# Story 1: Garden of Rainbows

*Sophie has always enjoyed gardening as a child, but in her adulthood, she found that she never bothered to do much with it. She didn't have the time or energy, but she has finally committed to designing a beautiful garden. Armed with her trusty gardening tools and plenty of space in need of utilizing, she is ready to turn her back yard into her own personal paradise once and for all, blooming with flowers and buzzing with life.*

Sophie yawned as she sipped at her morning coffee with her laptop sitting in front of her. She sat at her dining table, next to the window looking out over her yard. It was a nice-looking little yard but was rather plain. She ran a hand through her dark hair and frowned to herself as she looked out. There wasn't much to catch her eye—the yard was mostly just an expanse of grass for her German shepherd, Bella, to run throughout, and she knew that. It wasn't meant to be glamorous or perfect—it just had to offer her pup a chance to frolic around when Sophie wasn't really feeling walk time. The entire yard was gently sloped downward, and for her, that had always been a bit of a negative. Sure, Bella could run up and down the yard, and sure, she could always get those extra steps in herself as well, but she wasn't particularly fond of the yard. It was boring and bland, and she wished that there was a bit more pizzaz to it. Where were the colors? The nice, eye-catching details? The flowers that would attract hummingbirds and honeybees? She felt her yard was sorely lacking, and it was a point of contention for poor Sophie. She didn't know what to do, but she knew that she needed to do something quickly. She glanced away from her yard to look around.

Her neighbors' yards were filled with either children's toys and the happy squeals of kids running amok or with immaculate landscaping that was so well kept that she was honestly a bit in awe. How did they get their plants to look so perfectly groomed, or to make their flowers as brightly colored? It was amazing to her—she had no idea how they did it, and she wasn't sure that she had the green thumb to make that work for her either. For Sophie, she wanted something easy to look at but also low-maintenance. She just had to figure out what that would be. With a sigh, Sophie turned her attention back to her computer to type away at her work. She was working on an article about the summer push for hydroponic gardening and how great it was, especially when the plants were stacked to make use of the vertical space available to the gardener.

"That's it!" Sophie cried out loud as the sudden revelation hit her—what if *she* were to make it a point to build her own garden? What if *she* were the one going out of her way to tier the garden to enjoy the slopes while still making the most out of the situation? She could transform just one half of the garden into some nice, tiered beds while leaving the other half of the yard free for Bella to enjoy. It seemed like the perfect opportunity and the best of both worlds. Besides, being able to enjoy the garden and the sights and smells it would bring with it sounded plenty worth it to her at the moment.

Of course, what good is deciding to plan without having something that she could utilize for herself? What good is trying to figure out what she could do if she didn't know the first thing about different plants anyway? Sophie spent the rest of the day typing away at her computer, doing research, taking notes, and planning. When she set her mind to something, it was rare that she actually got sidetracked. She was very much a one-track mind kind of person, and now that she had set her sights on being able to put in a garden herself, she was determined to make it happen. All she had to do was make it a point to go shopping to pick up all the supplies sooner rather than later, and the sooner that she did so, the sooner she would be able to get to work.

She didn't waste any time, either—once her preliminary planning was done, she decided that it was time to go shopping immediately. She already had basic gardening tools present in her yard—rakes, shovels, and the like were all present without her needing to buy new ones. But, what she was lacking was the materials to start building tiered garden walls. She needed concrete, lots of rocks, and the patience to bring it all home on her own. She also needed plenty of flowers and soil as well. With that in mind, she began her shopping trip. It was ambitious, but she was confident that she could make it work on her own. She knew that she had the dive that she would need to ensure that the garden all came together nicely. She just had to set out and make it happen.

Shopping was the easy part, and before she knew it, Sophie was back at home, staring at the giant bags of stone and concrete that she would need to bring in. All she would need to do is make it a point to find a way to get everything in. If she could do that, she knew that she would be just fine. But, everything was far heavier than she had accounted for—she had asked for help when loading up in her car, and now, it was all on her to drag it out, bring it to the back, and get to work.

Rather than worrying about that immediately, Sophie chose to tackle the planning of the space first. She chose to make time to dig out the different spaces that she would be utilizing first. With a hoe in hand, she started marking out along her sod, where she wanted to put in the walls and started tearing down the soil that she would need to move. Clearing the area out was definitely one of the hardest parts of the whole job. She had to clear out some of the space and dig along the tiers that she wanted. Each of her tiers was going to be roughly 2 feet tall with about two feet of gardening space at each tier. She dug carefully, creating three distinct tiers that she would be using for her garden. It would be perfect, she told herself—the garden space was open enough that she could get a wide variety of flowers while also not taking over the whole yard. She was glad to have something breaking up the monotony of it all while still enjoying the space that she had.

The task of digging out the dirt, one shovelful at a time, was far more exhausting than she had expected. She could feel the hot sun beating on her neck, and she could feel the sweat starting to run down her face as well. It was almost overwhelming how hot it felt as she was actively working the land, but with a few well-timed iced tea breaks and plenty of water and perseverance, she was able to finish up digging with just a sore body as the cost.

From there came the time to dig out the concrete. It was time to make sure that the wall would sustain itself. She knew that building the wall up was important—but it also had to be secure. She had been told to choose pre-mixed concrete to use for her wall to make sure that it would be strong enough. Dumping the concrete mixture into a big bucket and mixing it with water, she was ready to start assembling the wall. She had to dump it straight into each footing of her tier to create a nice layer there for support, with rebar pushed in every foot or so along the way. From there, it was time to let everything dry, and Sophie was incredibly grateful for the chance to take a break and relax. She knew that she would need that time to herself and that peace of mind, so she gladly took it.

The next morning, Sophie awoke, tired, grumpy, and sore, but determined to ensure that she had finished everything up. She was determined to ensure that her garden would be finished, however, so she pushed through the discomfort with a groan and a desire to see her final product. After breakfast, a coffee, and a bit of relaxation time, she was right back out there to build up her wall.

Next came combining the mortar and using it so she could begin to build the wall up as well. The wall was relatively simple to put together, and she found that it was incredibly easy to simply slather the mortar between the stones that she was placing into position. This part went rapidly, and before she knew it, she had a beautiful wall in light, warm colors. It looked great, she told herself as she looked at the three curved tiers that built up half of her yard. She loved how they looked as they grew across everything.

Another day passed with everything firming up, and finally, it was time to get to business. Her favorite part of the process was the part where she got to plant all of her flowers right into the space that she had designed, and now that everything was dry, she was eager to get started. "You ready, Bells?" she asked her dog as she got ready that third morning to get started. It was going to be hard work to fill up those beds, she told herself, but it would be worth it—the view would be great.

The first step of the day was ensuring that she had plenty of soil all ready to go and tucked into each of the tiers. With that done, it was time to start on everything else, slowly and carefully filling up the plots of land with flowers. Sophie wanted to be strategic about things—she wanted to have a beautiful garden where the colors felt almost like a rainbow as they bloomed. She was thrilled to realize that she had plenty of space to do so. Being able to set up all of the flowers in such a nice order would be perfect for her—and all she had to do was get started on building it all up.

Sophie had picked up all sorts of different flowers for her garden. The first tier, she told herself, would have to be red and orange flowers. This gave her plenty of options, and when she had spent the time weighing her options, she settled on red roses and amaryllis flowers right along with that top row, with a few bushels of small, delicate peonies as well. They all played well together, she thought—they were beautiful shades of red and all different heights, which meant that she would have some very real variety in her garden space if she wanted it.

Next came a need for orange flowers to grow in her garden. Orange had actually been somewhat tricky for her to find as she was shopping, she had realized, but ultimately, a few well-picked zinnias did the job, and she scattered them through that first tier near the divider between the first and second. It was beautiful.

Then came yellow flowers, and for that, there was nearly no shortage. Yellow, it turned out, was a pretty popular flower color. Yellow also offered a stunning flash of color to the garden, she had come to realize. Yellow lilies were planted throughout the space, along with a few yellow tulips and rose bushes as well. Altogether, they would create a marvelous splash of yellow across the garden that she would be unable to deny would be beautiful.
From there came a bush of blue hydrangeas all spattered across the garden as well. They would grow into larger flowers, she knew, but they would also create a wondrous effect while they transitioned colors. It would be a wonderful addition to the garden as well, and they were easy to find as well.

Finally, Sophie needed a layer of purple flowers right along the bottom to complete her vision of her beautiful, rainbow layered garden. Violets made the most obvious choice there in that bottom row, and so they were added with ease. They all melded together to create that nice rainbow effect, and Sophie was *in love.*

With the garden all completed and watered, Sophie collapsed against her house, panting and aching. It had been hard work, but it was absolutely essential to ensuring that looking out with morning coffee wasn't miserable. She was looking forward to seeing just how her garden would turn out as it all had the chance to grow into place. And, she couldn't deny it either—she was *proud* of herself. It was not easy to build such a nice garden, nor was it something that she felt she could do on her own. She had to put her own sweat equity into creating that beautiful look, and she was ready to own it. She was certain that she could get plenty of likes and shares if she posted it on social media, and to be frank, she was too excited to wait for too long.

Of course, that would have to wait until after she had a chance to shower and soak in a bathtub to relieve her aching muscles. The prior three days had been exhausting, and while Sophie was happy to do the work, she was also thoroughly drained after having gone through it all. She had no idea just how exhausting it all would be to build it all up, little by little, all as just one person. Everything from moving the items from one place to another to digging the pits and holes and everything else was thoroughly draining.

But, as exhausting as it was, it was also incredibly satisfying as well. It was perhaps one of the most satisfying things that she had done in a long while—being able to say that she had constructed her own tiered garden all by herself was incredibly fulfilling. After all, she proved that she had the skill and the fortitude to do so.

Sophie's bath was perhaps the most enjoyable one that she had had in a very long time. She was thrilled to just soak in the warmth, enjoying every moment of it as long as she could. Every muscle in her body was so grateful for the chance to unwind and to soak up the comfort of the water, and she loved it. She soaked for as long as she could stand— long past her fingers pruning up to and all the way until her water finally lost its heat. When the temperature was no longer pleasant, she hopped out, feeling rejuvenated after her chance to unwind, and she decided to enjoy her first real day of being able to admire her yard at her spot from the coffee table.

It didn't take long until she was right back at her dining table with her laptop and a cup of coffee. She stared out into the yard and smiled to herself, feeling that sense of self-satisfaction as she did so. It was absolutely gorgeous to look out over everything. The flowers, though they had room to bush up and grow more vibrant, looked great where they were. They were all placed carefully between the different tiers, lining up nicely and growing together well. The colors worked well as they faded throughout the rainbow, and she loved the diversity in different types of flowers, all assembled carefully.

Taking a sip of coffee, Sophie had to congratulate herself on a job very well done. She had lacked the confidence she had needed at first, but now that it was done, she had to admit that she had outdone herself. It was gorgeous. And even better, it didn't take up all of the space in her yard either, which was the best part of all. She still had plenty of room for Bella to run around and plenty of room just to enjoy the scenery. As she sat there, looking over everything, she felt at peace and satisfied with herself. She felt proud of the efforts she put into everything and ready to move on in her life. She was ready to tackle the next big project that she would be pursuing, whatever that may have been—so long as it was not another DIY building a structure.

Maybe a tree, she told herself absently as she turned her computer on and took another sip of coffee. A tree wouldn't be nearly as difficult to plant and get started as a big tiered garden... Right?

# Story 2: Gone Fishing

*It's fishing time! Sophie has never been a big fan of fishing, but her new boyfriend, Felix, has insisted that she gives it a shot with him at least once. Reluctantly willing, she has gone with him to the lake for the day for a nice bonding event. Boats, fishing poles, and a long day alone together... What could go wrong?*

Sophie was never much one for hunting or fishing. She didn't like the idea of pulling out an animal and killing them to eat. Sure, she enjoyed eating meat—she could never give up bacon or steak to go the vegetarian route—but that didn't mean that she needed to see where her food came from first-handed! She didn't need to be the one to kill it if she wanted to eat it! She was firmly in the don't ask, don't tell camp when it came to where her food came from, and while some people found that meant she was either weak or hypocritical because she didn't want to see that animals suffered to feed her, she did it because she didn't want to feel bad for the animals. She *knew* that when she was eating a nice steak, it came from a cow, but she tried to distance the two in her mind. Eating fish that she or her family had caught? That, on the other hand, had always been difficult for her. The cow that she was eating was already dead—there was no undoing that. If she didn't buy it, it could end up going to waste. But, with an animal that she would have to harvest herself? That didn't seem as justifiable in her book. She had seen it alive—she couldn't justify ending its life just for herself. But, despite her protests that she gave Felix, he gave her that pouty puppy look that he seemed to master, and she found herself giving in before she knew what was happening. She couldn't tell him no when she saw those pleading, warm brown eyes.

Felix had met Sophie only a month or so prior to their fishing trip. It was going to be one of the last—the weather was already starting to get chillier, and the sun was setting earlier and earlier every day. But, Felix was determined to show her the wonders of fishing, so she decided to give him that one win. "Because you're too cute to let down," she told him fondly when she agreed to give it a shot. She meant it, too. He was *gorgeous*. He was conventionally attractive, and though she was not one that would have turned down a genuinely good guy, she definitely enjoyed the eye candy when she could get it. So, between his good looks, his charm, and her fondness for him, she agreed.

Felix had told her that they needed to get up early—they had to be up before the sun rose up so they could get on the road. The best local place to go fishing, Felix had insisted, was not too far away—but it would take a few hours to get there. It was worth it, though, he had made it a point to tell her. He loved fishing, and he wasn't about to just let the season end without going one last time. Sure, they could go fishing all winter long if they wanted to, but Felix was quick to let her know that he preferred going when he could still feel his fingers after being outside for an hour or two.

Sophie was up first thing in the morning, just as she had agreed to be. She was not very happy about it—but she was. She got up, out of bed, and forced herself to muster up some sort of enthusiasm over everything. Of course, that enthusiasm was kind of hard to manage when she was so tired. The first order of business was definitely making coffee, she told herself, and off she went, down the stairs and to the kitchen, so she could make her drink. She brewed the magical, warm liquid as she meandered around the kitchen, still almost half asleep, with just the light above her stovetop on.

The number on the microwave glowed dimly in the darkness, the neon green lines creating the time: 4:27, according to the steady blinking, and Sophie yawned to herself. She was ready to get back into bed at such an ungodly hour, but she couldn't let Felix down. So, she went about her morning as normally as she could.

Felix was there promptly at 5:13, and Sophie found herself climbing into his pickup truck. It was an older one—one that he wouldn't care so much about if it got muddy or damaged during off-roading, he told her. He normally drove something that was much more fuel-efficient, but if they were going into the mountains, he had told her, they needed to have something that could get through anything, and that beast of a truck could.

The back was loaded up with a bunch of fishing equipment that Sophie couldn't name, she had noted as she climbed up. She had chosen to wear the most outdoorsy clothes she had, hoping she wouldn't find herself running something that she would miss. Eventually, she had settled on a plain black long sleeve shirt with a turtleneck, with a vest over it. She also brought a thick fleece jacket with her for the coldest parts of their trip, and a pair of gloves that she had hoped she wouldn't need. There was also a bag of clothes that she could use if she got wet somehow, and she wore a pair of waterproof hiking boots on her head, with a wool hat pulled over her head. She let her hair hang loosely at the moment, not worried so much about whether it got dirty. It could be washed easily, at least.

"Good morning, beautiful," Felix purred, planting a kiss on her cheek as she buckled herself in.

"Mmm..." she began, only to yawn sleepily, pulling her arms tightly around her. The crisp fall chill still hung in the air, leaving her shivering. She was surprised that it was so cold in the mornings—she was almost never outside at that time. If she was awake at all, she was letting Bella run out to relieve herself. Then it was right back into the warm embrace of her comfortable bed.

"Coffee?" he asked, glancing over at her as he pulled out of her driveway to start their journey. He seemed perfectly fine being awake at such an hour, and Sophie sleepily marveled at the way that he seemed totally fine. She simply nodded her head in response, and he chuckled. "That, I can do."

They stopped into a drive-thru café to pick up a few drinks before heading on their way. They drove in comfortable silence, sipping at coffee as they went. Sophie watched as the city gave way to suburbs, and suburbs eventually gave way to the wilderness. They lived relatively close to mountains, and before long, they were surrounded by thick, green forest. Most of the trees were evergreens, so despite the autumn chill and the occasional blazing orange trees in the mountains, they were still green. It wasn't called the Evergreen State for anything, Sophie mused absently as she watched the trees.

It was dusky outside—the sky was threatening to light up, but the sun had not yet managed to rise high enough to be seen over the mountains. Soon, however, they could see the golden rays of dawn piercing through the darkness, and the sky grew brighter. They pulled off of the main road through the mountain to turn into a small path that Sophie would have never seen before. In fact, though she had gone through those mountains before, she had never actually noticed that it was there in the first place. They drove deeper into the wooded area, and Sophie found herself feeling grateful that, at the very least, they had sunlight to lighten up space. The woods were dense and wild and seemed like the perfect scene for a wild bear or cougar to walk right past them. At the very least, in the sunlight, they would be able to see everything before it approached them.

That made her feel a little bit better, even though she was totally out of her element.

They continued along that little mountain road for a long while, surrounded by trees that created almost a tunnel effect over them. The branches grew so densely that they may as well have been completely intertwined. They were beautiful, but also somewhat eerie as they shaded the area as much as they did. It was awe-inspiring—even though they all needed sunlight to thrive, they found a way to live comfortably for who knew how long that tunnel had been there. She knew that it was definitely something that had been there a while, though, or they wouldn't have tangled up so much. Though most of the light was blocked out, she could still see plenty as the sun continued to rise. Soon, the green trees began to fade into golden ones as more and more deciduous trees presented themselves. It was a beautiful mix between the greens and the yellows and reds, and Sophie found herself marveling at the look.

Before long, they parked, and Sophie felt confused. She didn't see anything in front of her. But, Felix must not have made a mistake because he stepped out of the car and opened the door for her to come out as well. He picked up the cooler and the fishing rods and tackle box and waited for her to get situated. As Sophie shut the door, she noticed Felix gazing softly at her. Their eyes met, sending a lightning bolt of energy through her body, and she grinned at him.

"Ready? Let's get going," he said, leading the way. Had his hands not been full, she knew he would have taken hers as they went.

"Where are we?" asked Sophie, looking around. She didn't see or hear any water—how were they supposed to catch fish without water?

"This is my family's favorite fishing place," he said, glancing over at her and then smiling his crooked smile. "Actually, it's my family's fishing place. We own the land."

Sophie was surprised, but that made sense—why else would they have driven along on that private road for so long? "Is there a lake here?"

"A small one," he replied, nodding his head. "It's a great place to go fishing, though. Since we're the only ones who ever fish there, it's always fully stocked."

It sounded perfect to her. And there was something comfortingly private about being able to go fishing on their own without anyone around. They had only been on a few dates, and they had visited each other's homes a few times, but it was nice going on their own private, secret trip where no one else would be with them. It was so comfortably private, and she was thrilled to get that chance.

Before long, the trees gave way to a small lake that was nestled into a clearing. The sun was finally starting to shine on the surface of the water, and it was gorgeous—it was shimmering back the reflection, and as she stared at it, she wondered what it was like to live so far out. There was a small cabin there, next to that lake, with a big window overlooking it. It was gorgeous. Everything was so picturesque that Sophie could hardly believe that she had been protesting going *there* of all places.

Felix laughed. "Like it?" he asked, setting down the supplies.

Sophie nodded her head, at a loss for words at the beauty. From there, they could see the sky above them that had been blocked out all along the private road. She never knew that she could see something so beautiful, and she found herself marveling at it. "It's beautiful," she told him breathlessly.

He smiled at her. "I agree," he murmured, taking her hand. "Come with me." He pulled her along with him, moving toward the cabin.

"Are we going inside?" Sophie asked.

"Yeah, we need to get some chairs. Unless you'd prefer to sit in the mud?" He quirked a brow at her, and she shook her head, grinning.

The inside of the cabin was almost as unbelievable as the lake. It was a warm wooden color inside that gave it the appearance of being brightly cheerful, and she loved it. It had an open concept, with a few rooms at the end of it. However, the living room and kitchen space were open and together, met with dining space in the center and a huge, wooden table with plenty of spaces to sit at. There was even a second floor of what Sophie assumed were more bedrooms upstairs.

"Wow," she breathed as she looked around. "This place is great. Did you come here often as a kid?"

"Yeah, I did," he replied. "I loved being able to enjoy the space. We ran around a lot and got to explore everything. But, lately, we're all too busy. Mom's remarried, and her new husband has no interest in going to the property that she and Dad built together, and Dad died last year. My brothers and sister all married and moved out of the area, so it's mostly just my space now." He was gazing at the ceiling with a faraway look in his eye, and Sophie squeezed his hand in support. That was enough to snap his attention back to what he was doing, and he looked at her. "But, you know what? I love the privacy. The chairs are over here." He gestured to a closet near the front door, and they went over to pick them up. He carried both folding chairs all the way back to the lake, and they got set up.

Before long, they were both sitting right next to each other, fishing poles in hand, staring out at the water together in peaceful silence. Sophie felt a bit bad for him after hearing his story, but she didn't want to tell him that. She wanted to enjoy the rest of their day. Her thumb ran over the smooth reel, feeling the individual lines of nylon, all wound up around it and looking at it. She was unsure of what she should do next.

"So, uh... Felix?" she mumbled, glancing at him almost sheepishly.

"Hmm?" She had snapped him out of whatever reverie he had lost himself in and turned his attention to her. Though he smiled politely at her, she could see the sadness underneath it. She briefly wondered if he really wanted to come out here at all.

She hesitated for a split second.

"What is it, Sophie?" he urged softly.

"So, don't get mad, but..." She looked at the ground.

"Out with it, woman!" he replied with a grin on his face, nudging her playfully. He wasn't actually mad—but he had a penchant for a bit of dramatic flair, and this was one of the times to make use of it. But, his eyes were on her and he was all ears, so she knew that it was time to speak. So, after a long moment of silence, she stared at him and finally opened her mouth.

"How do I know when I have a fish on the line?" She really hoped she wouldn't have one at all—when it was time to put the bait on her hook, she had chosen to do so in a way that was loose, so she didn't have to actually catch anything at all. That was fine with her! If she didn't have to see a fish suffer, she'd be perfectly content.

"You'll feel a tug on the line, and you'll notice that the reel will start to unravel as the fish swims away. But, the first sign is seeing just a little twitch at the tip of the fishing pole. That tells you that there's a fish nibbling at it and that you need to be ready." He looked over at Sophie, almost surprised that she knew so little about how to fish. "Didn't you write that one article on the top ten places to fish near the city?" he asked with a teasing grin.

"Shh! Yeah, but that doesn't mean that I fished at them all! I just went to see them and take a few pictures. I don't fish ever. Like at all. ... So, what do I do when there's a fish on the line?" Sophie looked away from him, sighing and running her hand through her hair. How silly she had been to think that she could get along fishing even for the day!

He chuckled to himself at her protests, and that just embarrassed her more. "Shush!" she squealed, patting his shoulder playfully as she giggled and leaned in for a hug.

Felix kissed her forehead again and smiled at her. "You tug it back—" He paused mid-sentence and stared out at the water. He was unmoving for a moment, and Sophie watched with bated breath. What was he doing? Was that something she had to do too? Would staring out to the water make a fish magically manifest itself onto her hook so she could pull it in for him to deal with? "Oh, I've got something. Watch me." And with that said, he went to work. Sophie had to admit—there was a beautiful craft to his work. His movements were gentle but strong and firm as he began.

The fishing pole twitched, and then the reel started unraveling. She watched as he suddenly held the line tightly to stop allowing it to go any further, and the tip of his rod was flailing about. He was watching the water intently, in his own little world as he worked to drag the fish in. He simply sat there, not moving, with the rod shaking. Sophie wondered if he was supposed to do something or if he needed to wait for something special. But then, as soon as the rod stopped flailing, she noticed that he started reeling again. "I'm waiting for the fish to stop pulling, and when it stops, I pull it back toward me. Every time it stops trying to get away, I pull it back."

It took what seemed like forever—he would pull it back, winding it as much as he could, and then just as suddenly, he'd stop doing anything at all, just holding the reel steady. "It's pulling now," he told her, nodding to the tip of the rod that was shaking. Sophie could see the muscles tightening in his arms as he tried to prevent it from pulling away. It was a clear testament to his strength as he sat there, holding it and stopping any more line from escaping. "It's a big one."

But, then, the fish stopped pulling again, and Felix pulled the pole up, so it pointed toward the sky. The tip of the rod was bent so much that Sophie was convinced that it would snap soon. Then, again, as the fish let up, he started reeling again.

This went on for quite some time, back and forth, and back and forth. Probably five minutes later, Sophie watched in awe as the splashing on the surface of the water grew stronger and stronger as Felix pulled it closer. His arms looked incredibly tense, but the expression on his face was sheer focus. He didn't seem concerned with what he was

236

doing, and he certainly didn't seem intimidated by the weight of the fish.

Soon, it was pulled close enough that Felix could reach in and pull it out. It was surprisingly large for a lake fish—it had to have been almost three feet long, judging by the length as Felix tried desperately to hold it up. It was silvery with mottled skin, and there was a long, pink stripe across the middle. Its gills were flushed with a bright red color.

"What is it?" asked Sophie as she stared. She was uncomfortable as she watched it.

"Rainbow trout," he replied, glancing over to Sophie. "If you're squeamish, I recommend turning away." He waited for a moment for Sophie to turn around and took care of everything that he had to do with the fish. "It'll taste great, though. Rainbow trout tastes a lot like salmon. It's delicious, and if you've never had it fresh out of the water, you've been missing out!"

Sophie felt herself shudder a bit at the thought, but nodded her head. Everything was taken care of within minutes, and he was suddenly cleaning out the fish, preparing it. "Let's enjoy it for lunch, shall we?" asked Felix.

"Sure!" Sophie replied, feigning excitement. She was a bit less than enthusiastic, but she knew she would, at the very least, give it a shot if he wanted her to. She'd just have to be brave about it.

Soon, he had a fire going and was preparing the fish. Sophie couldn't lie—it smelled amazing. He had brought lemon, garlic, and parsley with him and was cooking it in a pocket of aluminum foil over the fire that he had prepared, and the smell was mouthwatering. Maybe it wouldn't be so bad to try it after all. The fish was already gone, and if she didn't, then it would be going to waste.

Sophie was pleasantly surprised when it was time to eat it. She tried a bite and realized that it was amazing. It was so tender and sweet, and the garlic was great at adding to the flavor profile.

"What do you think?" asked Felix.

"It's delicious!" She was so happy he knew how to cook—she felt like a lot of the time, the guys that she had met always thought of cooking as "women's work" or thought that she needed to take care of it all. But, Felix? Not at all—he dove right in to enjoy the whole process. It was almost perfect— he seemed driven to not only find the food but to make it as well. That was certainly impressive, she had to admit as she sat there, enjoying the food. "Thank you!"

They enjoyed the rest of their day together, eating fresh fish, and simply enjoying each other's company. It was fun to talk together. It was great to be able to spend that time just getting to know each other better than they did before. It was so satisfying to find enjoyment in each other's presence. Sophie smiled at Felix. She was amazed at just how much he was coming to enjoy him around, but she couldn't ignore it. He was almost perfect.

# Story 3: Winter Paradise

*It's wintertime! Sophie is thrilled that she gets to enjoy the moment together with those that she loves. The winter season is filled up with feelings of enjoyment, of warmth, and of celebrating love. Though she doesn't get much snow near her home, her boyfriend Felix has asked her to join her for a trip to a nearby town in the mountains for a date night, and she is thrilled to go.*

Sophie's entire house smelled like pumpkin spice. She knew it was what the kids these days were called "basic," but she couldn't help it—it was just so enjoyable. She loved baking everything pumpkin during that time of the year, and she was one of those people who would load up on all the Christmas lights and festivities as soon as November rolled around. She was thrilled to have everything all laid out for her—she wanted to be able to enjoy the moment. She wanted to be able to enjoy the holidays for as long as she could. She loved just how pleasant they were.

That year was no exception. She was currently pulling pumpkin bread out of the oven to set on the counter to cool off to enjoy. It was the fourth round of pumpkin baked goods she had pulled out that week—she had already left pumpkin cookies for all of her neighbors, dropped off pumpkin muffins and scones for Cara and her family for their fancy-schmancy holiday party that Sophie always declined to go to. She loved her friend Cara, but she found that sometimes, Cara's family was a bit... Smothering, to say the least. She had even left a bunch of muffins for Felix to take to work as well.

She hummed to herself as the smell of pumpkin filled the air. She looked outside her window, unsurprised when she saw the rain falling. It was the Pacific Northwest, after all—rain during the winter months was just a fact of life. But, she was still just as happy to be there—she didn't have to deal with driving through the winter snow, and that was a major plus for her.

As she watched the drizzling rain fall from the sky, her phone buzzed, and she picked it up. It was Felix, calling her, and she quickly answered. "Hey, hon, how are you doing?" she asked him, barely able to contain the grin on her face.

"Great! I was wondering if you're doing anything tonight," he replied. He seemed excited about something.

"Not really, why?" Sophie replied.

"I have something that I want to show you," he replied. Sophie found her smile widening in response. She was excited to see what he had in mind. It had to have been great, whatever it was. After all, whenever he had a surprise, it usually ended up being fantastic.

"Sounds great!" Sophie replied. "What time will you be here?"

"I'll be there at 1. Make sure you pack an overnight bag, okay? We can drop Bella off at my place. I have a dog sitter coming to take care of Koda for the night. She can watch Bella, too." Sophie could hear the excitement practically buzzing on his voice. He couldn't contain it—he just wanted to show her whatever it was that he had in mind, and she found that his own excitement was far too contagious to forget about.

Sophie hung up the phone and ran around, getting ready. She packed a bag and froze. She had never spent the night with Felix before. They had spent plenty of time together, but it was time that was always spent separating when they went their own ways for the night. What was she supposed to wear? What should she bring? She couldn't believe that she would be staying overnight with him!

Before long, she was ready to go, pumpkin bread packed for the road, and everything that Bella needed in another bag to be taken to Felix's home. He wouldn't say no to another baked good... Would he? Of course not, she eventually reasoned with herself—what kind of man refuses baked goods from his girlfriend when they are homemade and fresh? It would be crazy for him to think that.

Not much later, Felix pulled up in a nice SUV, black in color. It was a newer one, and Sophie knew that there was a reason for it. They had to be going into the mountains—he normally drove his more fuel-efficient car around when they were staying in urban areas. But she didn't mind. Wherever they were going would be great.

"Hope you're hungry!" Sophie announced as she stuck Bella into the back seat as Felix helped her load up the bags. "I made pumpkin bread!"

"More pumpkin? Honey!" Felix feigned exasperation. "How much weight do you want me to gain? I can't keep eating this way!" He looked at her with a grin as he patted on his stomach dramatically, waggling his eyebrows. "I just can't help myself. Your food is too good!"

Sophie laughed. "Don't be silly. But, I was making pumpkin bread. I can't help it. The baked goods always smell so good! I just have to keep making them!"

"Well, thanks, hon. I bet it tastes great." He pressed the button to close the trunk and turned to walk into the driver's seat as Sophie closed up the back door to where Bella was sitting and hopped into the passenger seat. She handed him a generous slice of the pumpkin bread and watched him with bated breath to see what he would think about it. She was hopeful that he would love it as much as she did.

He took the bite, keeping his face stoic and his eyes straight ahead as he chewed, almost exaggerating the thoughtfulness as he deliberated the taste of the bread. "Hmm…" he murmured through another bite.

Sophie could barely stand the anticipation, and he finally nodded his head. "It's passable," he told her with a smirk and a playful wink. She grinned back at him as she wrapped up the bag.

"Well, that's a relief! I was almost afraid that I'd have to bother you to eat it all. Good thing you like it—I have a whole loaf."

"Why so much?" Felix replied.

"Well, everyone knows that the way to a man's heart is through his stomach!" she replied with a sage nod. "I have to keep you around somehow."

Felix laughed at her. "With pumpkin bread?"

"With pumpkin bread!" she affirmed with a grin. "Is it working?"

"Mmm, I think it is." Felix put the car in drive and off they went.

They set off, dropping Bella off and then driving through the mountains to the east, and Sophie wondered where they were going. Every time Sophie asked, he declined to respond seriously. They were clearly going to the eastern half of the state, but Sophie wasn't sure what was over there. There were maybe two cities on the east that were a decent size, but beyond that, everything was small and rural. It was certainly going to be cold, though, and Sophie was relieved that she had packed a whole bunch of warm clothes. She turned the heater on a bit warmer as she looked out the window. The further they drove, the snowier it became.

Soon, they were pulling into a sleepy little town. The sun wasn't set yet, but it was going to soon. They pulled into a parking lot, and Sophie looked around. She wasn't quite sure where they were, but she had to admit it looked great. It was snowy, and all of the buildings that they were around had a Bavarian theme—they were all built with the wooden lattices cross the white buildings. It looked great—kitschy, but nice to look at. And, with all of the snow lining the roads, and the crowds of people all dressed up and bundled in their winter gear, Sophie got the feeling that there was something more to what they were doing.

"*Wilkommen* to Leavenworth*!!*" One person called out to them, his German oddly lacking. Sophie turned to see a man dressed as a Christmas elf—he had a loose green hat and all green clothes. "I hope you're here for a good day!"

Sophie looked around in confusion. She had no idea where they were, but it looked fun anyway. "What are we here for, Felix?" she asked. She was smiling as she looked around, but she was still pretty lost wherever they were. She wanted to find out what the point of the day was and what they were doing in such a small town. It was cool—but it was jam-packed with tourists, and honestly, she was starting to feel a little claustrophobic in the crowds. But, then, Felix squeezed her hand, and she felt a bit better.

"I'll tell you later," he promised, planting a kiss on her hand. "Come over here." They spent the day wandering about the small town. It didn't seem like many people lived there—but a lot of people certainly came from out of town. There were groups of tourists speaking different languages and people who looked around like they had never been there before, much like how Sophie was looking around. There were people who had never seen as much as they could find all around them. And honestly, Sophie is related to them.

There were so many different stores that they were able to dip into. There was a beautiful wine store that they went through, loaded up with all sorts of bottles all around them. There were bottles in just about every color, filled with a different kind of wine for every kind of drinker out there. Felix picked up a bottle for later as they walked through the snow, holding each other's hands as they looked around.

Before long, they found a store that was filled up with all sorts of hats in every kind. There were hats that were silly, serious, and fashionable. There were cute hats and hats so garishly unflattering that Sophie would never so much as put them on her head. However, as she walked around throughout the store, she realized that there was a lot to see. There were all sorts of different styles.

"Hey, Sophie," Felix called to her. Sophie turned around to look at him just in time for him to plop a hat that was shaped like a big cheeseburger on her head. She looked at him oddly but then smiled at him. He laughed back, watching her. But, then, a glance at his phone seemed to remind him about something, and he nodded his head to himself. "Let's go! I want to show you something."

Sophie watched him curiously for a moment before nodding her head and allowing him to take the lead. She had no idea where he was going, but it was probably somewhere fun.

It was just getting dark as they walked outside, and strangely, there was a massive crowd gathering in the park right across the street from all of the cute shops that they were passing. Sophie looked at them all curiously. She didn't have to wait long, however, because suddenly, all of the buildings, in their neat little rows, started turning on a bunch of Christmas lights. They were brightly lit and designed to look like beautiful Christmas houses, lined brightly. Some were golden, others were brightly colored, and others still flashed and shone. They all sparkled and twinkled as they turned on across the entire street. One by one, they shone, and they looked fantastic.

Sophie stared in shock—she wasn't sure what she was expecting, but it was not that. She wore a dumbfounded smile as she looked at it all, soaking it all in. Somewhere down the road, there was Christmas music playing, and she could see lots of people cheering, enjoying the moment. She was happy to be there, and she felt Felix's hand wrap around her waist.

"What do you think about it?" he asked her softly as he looked at her. Despite all of the lights that were shining and the beautiful sights, he was looking right at her.

"It's amazing," she told him.

"So are you," he told her. "I've got one more surprise for you, and we have to head out now. Are you ready?"

She nodded her head, wondering what could possibly one-up what they saw at the moment. She was already plenty surprised, and she wasn't sure just how much more she could take. What could she possibly see that would be better than this? What could possibly be more entrancing than what they were seeing? She wasn't convinced that he could live it up, but he certainly was determined to try. He was certainly interested in impressing her, and she was greatly appreciative of it. She didn't even think that he had to impress her—she liked him plenty the way he was, but he always appreciated the attempts.

So, off they went together, with Felix holding her hand and leading her off. Sophie wasn't sure where they were going, but she knew that wherever it was, it would be good. It didn't take long before they were standing in front of one great, big horse. It had white books and a long, white stripe across its head. It was set up so it could pull a wagon that was brightly lit behind them. The wagon was wrapped up with Christmas lights, too, and it looked almost as stunning as everything else they had seen so far.

Sophie stared at it for a moment. "Isn't that cool?" she said softly. "I bet it'd be great fun to ride on that. I bet they're booked full though! There's no way they're not."

"We are booked full, ma'am. Sorry about that. We often are at this time of the year. You'll need to set up a reservation at least a couple weeks in advance." The driver looked at them apologetically. "I'm waiting for my next ride right now."

Sophie deflated a bit. "Oh, okay," she told him with a sigh. That was disappointing—but understanding. She glanced over to Felix, who was busy fumbling with his phone.

"You're in luck, honey, because this is what I came to show you." He showed the screen to the driver, who glanced, nodded his head and waited. "I bought us tickets to ride the carriage. Would you like to go with me?

Sophie gasped in shock. That was not what she was expecting. "Yes!!" she said happily, clapping her hands. "That sounds fantastic!!" She smiled at him, ready to get going. She could barely contain her joy as she looked at him in admiration. She had never known someone to spend so much time trying to make sure she was that comfortable. No one ever really made her feel like Felix had.

Felix smiled at her as he held out a hand to help her climb up into the carriage. She took his hand and stepped in, scooting along the cushioned bench to allow him space as well, and he quickly filled the seat next to her. He huddled up against her, wrapping his hand around hers and intertwining their fingers with a quick squeeze. Then, he looked down at her with a smile.

Sophie rested her head against his shoulder and took in all of the sights. There was a lot to see—all of the lights all around the city. The graceful gait of the horse in front of the carriage as its powerful legs pulled them along. The people were walking around, making space for the carriage, and looking at Sophie and Felix with smiles on their faces as they looked them.

Sophie felt proud as they went through the city together on the carriage. They looked through the main road, and around the next few blocks as well, gently following the trails. The people naturally made space, and the horse was perfectly content to continue about its way, every step causing jingle bells to ring amidst the clip-clop of its hoof steps. It was chilly as they went along the roads, and they could see their breath in big puffs in front of their faces, but that wasn't enough to remove the smile from either of their faces as they watched around.

They went past several ice sculptures too. There was a whole slew of them, all lined up nicely on the side of the road that had long since been closed off to general traffic. Only foot traffic was allowed, and there were hundreds of people walking along and looking at everything with awestruck faces. They were gorgeous—and she had to admit, she was just as in awe of them as they were. It had to be difficult to carve out such perfect lines. It seemed like it would be so easy to destroy them, but they were able to create such intricate designs as if they were molding clay. Somehow, the designs were there, and as they slowly trotted past them, Sophie looked.

Before they knew it, their entire ride around the town within the carriage was over, and it was time to get off. They thanked the driver, and Felix climbed down first, then offering his hand out to let Sophie down as well. Off they went hand in hand, down the road. "Ready to head in for the night? That wine isn't going to drink itself," Felix told her as she wrapped her arm around his.

Sophie nodded her head in agreement. After a long day of driving, then a few hours wandering around such a beautiful mountain town in the middle of winter, Sophie was ready to tuck n for the day. She wanted to take a nice, warm shower and get away from the chilliness for a while. Off they went, arm and arm. Felix had a plan and a place to take her, and who was she to deny him? So far, everything he had done had been perfect. She had a good reason to believe that the hotel would be just as great, too.
It turned out he had actually rented a nice cabin for the night. It was much smaller than his own cabin but was equally as comfortable. Their night went well, and they settled in happily, enjoying that bottle of wine with each other. Sophie was thrilled. She had been afraid that she was going to be nervous on her date with Felix, but they wound up enjoying every moment. It was peacefully perfect, and she was so glad that they got that chance that winter. She couldn't have imagined a better date for them to enjoy.

# Story 4: Caribbean Comforts

*Sophie's on vacation! She's gone off with her good friend, Cara, for another summer vacation. This time, she went off on a Caribbean cruise, and one of their stops was a beautiful island where they could scuba dive, and of course, they had to take that option for themselves! It was a wonderful chance for them to have some fun and unwind.*

Sophie awoke that fine morning to the sound of waves lapping against the side of the biggest cruise ship she had ever been on. Now, she hadn't been on many cruises in the past, but the few she had been on had never been as extravagant as that one. She woke up slowly and comfortably. On that ship, there was no reason for her to rush awake. There was no work to be done, and Bella was at home being cared for by her neighbor back home. That meant that she didn't have to worry about anything but enjoying her moment there on a bed that was almost unbelievably soft. It was softer than anything she had ever felt before, and she was so happy to be there. She deserved this, she told herself, as she stretched herself out across the bed, spreading her arms widely.

She smiled to herself as she rested there, not quite ready to do anything but sit there. She was enjoying the moment too much and felt like she could have fallen back asleep listening to the sound of the ocean through her window. Cara had, of course, splurged and insisted on the rooms with balconies and windows, so they were able to enjoy the sights, and Sophie had to admit—she was glad that they did. She loved every moment of the gentle sounds of the sea.

That was until she found herself interrupted.

"Hello?" she heard Cara call out, and the door opened up. Whether she wanted to sleep or not, that choice had officially ben taken away. Sophie opened up her eyes, peering over to see Cara peeking her head through their shared door. They had gotten conjoining rooms, as they usually did when they went on vacation together, and Sophie smiled at her.

"Good morning," Sophie said with a lazy wave of her hand as she yawned and stretched out across the bed before pushing herself up to sitting. "So, what's on the agenda today?"

"I'm so glad you asked!" Cara replied, bouncing up and down enthusiastically. She seemed almost uncharacteristically giddy at the moment as Sophie looked at her, and she had to chuckle. "We're going *scuba diving!*" she squealed out with joy. "We're going to be docking soon! Get out of bed so we can get off the ship!"

Sophie had never been scuba diving before, but she was certain that it couldn't be too terribly difficult. After all, she was, at the very least, a great swimmer, and she was confident that she would be just fine if she worked hard enough. All she had to do was make sure that she kept on swimming and that she learned how to use the equipment. It couldn't be terribly difficult. So, without protesting Cara's demands, she pushed herself out of bed and dragged herself to the shower to get ready. At the very least, the fact that they would be in the water all day meant that she didn't have to worry about makeup or to do her hair—she just needed sunscreen and her bikini, with a sundress put on over it. Easy-peasy.

It didn't take long for Sophie to throw everything together, and as soon as she stepped out of her shower, she saw Cara standing outside on the balcony overlooking the ocean. She was watching the water rush past them with a dreamy smile on her face. "Don't you just love cruises?" she asked Sophie with a wide grin. Sophie nodded in response as she looked out the window. She could see land on the horizon and knew that they'd be docking soon.

They made their way all the way downstairs, rushing as quickly as they could. Their cabins were on the top of the ship, and they had to go down a set of stairs to get to the place to check-in for porting. They knew that they would have to go there if they wanted to get off the boat. The tours were already gathering up. Some people were gathered for fishing, jet skis, general tourism, and of course, the one that is there for scuba diving. The various lines and groups were all lined up—they were all ready to go, and Sophie could tell exactly what each and every one of them was going to be doing just by how they were all dressed up. The people going to tour the island they were docking on were mostly wearing khaki shorts and lightly colored shirts. Those who were going to go scuba diving, Sophie found herself realizing they were all wearing swimsuits underneath clothing. Many of the women had themselves wrapped up in sundresses with the bikini straps obviously visible from underneath them.

"There's our group!" Cara announced happily, grabbing Sophie's arm and leading her away. She was thrilled to be there with her, and she made it sure that Sophie knew exactly that. Cara had talked all about how she was ready to go scuba diving the entire time that they were walking to their group. She talked about how she knew what she was doing and how she had been out scuba diving before on several other vacations. She talked about how she got to go diving in all sorts of different reefs, swimming and watching the fish go by. She mentioned getting to go all over the place. She enjoyed being able to watch the fish swim by and actually seeing them dart around her. She talked about seeing the fish like the ones in the movie where they had to go across the ocean.

When it was their turn to go scuba diving, then, they were thrilled. It might not have been Sophie's favorite thing to do, but they had agreed that after their last vacation to Greece, it was Cara's turn to choose out something that they would enjoy together. It was her turn to make concessions and allow Cara that chance to enjoy herself and choose out their main events. So, Sophie sucked it up and was willing to learn how to scuba dive.

Off they embarked from the cruise ship and Sophie looked around. It was strange being around all of those people that looked completely different. They were clearly happy there—so many people were wandering about with a look of comfort on their faces. Their relaxation was practically palpable as they wandered bout, and Sophie could tell that they were happy there. They were calm and at ease. They looked like they had been able to enjoy their time without worrying so much, and Sophie found herself feeling jealous. She found herself wishing that she could also enjoy the world that they were living in.

Sure, there were tourists everywhere, and wow were there a lot of them. The tourists were obvious in their clothes—they were wearing all sorts of touristy clothes and looking around in just as much awe as Sophie felt as she walked through the area. It wasn't until Cara squeezed her arm happily that Sophie blinked and looked at her friend. "Let's go!" Cara said.

Before long, they were suited up, ready, and heading to their destination for scuba diving. They were all meeting up in a relatively small bungalow on the beach—they were all brought inside with just a bit more space for themselves. They didn't have much room in there, but it was enough for them and a couple of instructors and all of the equipment that they would need for the day. The bungalow was painted a creamy white color with a thatched roof. It was picturesque there where it was, with the cerulean blue ocean behind it and a perfectly clear morning sky.

Each person was given their equipment—a wetsuit and plenty of other equipment. They had masks, goggles, breathing equipment, fins for swimming, gloves, and more. Everything that they could have needed was all lined up right there for them to use, and there was a lineup of tanks for breathing along the back wall. There was a tank for each of them, plus a few extras just in case they were needed.

The guides gave everyone a basic list of instructions, telling them everything that they would need to know and walked them through being able to practice everything they were doing, and before long, they were getting ready to go into the water for the first time. Sophie was thrilled as she carried her tank out to the beach. They were barely a three minute's walk from the shore, and Sophie grinned over at Cara. Sophie was bubbling with excitement, her steps bouncy, and her eyes shining in excitement. Cara was the picture of perfect grace and poise as she walked over, smiling as she made her way over. She somehow managed to make the tank look weightless, and the wetsuit look like it had been made specifically for her. She couldn't quite believe the inner beauty that Cara managed to exude to match the outer, but she had to admit that it was admirable that she could look as beautiful as she did while still having a heart of gold.

Before long, they were in the water, and Sophie found herself glad that they had the wetsuits to keep themselves from being soaked in the water. Yeah, they were in the Caribbean, and yeah, the sun was shining on the water all day long, but they still wanted the protection from the cool water. They were all masked up as they moved deeper and deeper into the water, dipping down underneath it. They sank deeper as they kept going into the water, and soon, they were swimming away from the shore.

Sophie took a deep breath out of habit before dipping her head underneath the water for the first time. The entire surrounding was blue. It was so strange going from above the water to suddenly see everything swimming underneath the water. All she could see was the blueness shimmering all around them. She looked around in awe. She was surprised at what there was around her. The ground underneath them was rocky and bumpy, and at first, Sophie didn't really see anything stand out. It all looked almost monochromatic until she realized that there were fish swimming about. She breathed out a big breath that bubbled around her as she swam, kicking her feet slowly. She made her way down to look at the rocky surface. It was almost reddish-brown in color—they weren't yet at the reef. But, there was still a surprising amount to see. As she got closer to the rocks on the bottom, she realized that they weren't just solid red— they were covered in little plants, organisms, and shells across the bottom. There were tiny crabs crawling about the bottom, one by one, inching their way around them. They were tiny crabs, but they still managed to move around rapidly as Sophie looked at them.

The crabs were maybe the size of her thumb tip as they scuttled around. They were red and white as they crawled around, barely noticeable. As Sophie got closer to them, they'd disappear too, scuttling away to hide in cracks and crevasses. They disappeared almost as quickly as Sophie was able to see them. They were so cute! Sophie leaned in as close as she could to try to see them scuttling around, and realized that she was actually looking at something else. There was a brownish-red sea cucumber there, barely moving. If she looked closely, she could see it undulating in front of her at a slow pace. It was barely moving there for her, but she realized that it was there. She realized she could see it there, shifting about. Where was it going, she wondered as she watched it barely moving.

Sophie felt a tap on her shoulder and when she looked over it, she saw Cara there, staring at her. She pointed further, and Sophie thought she understood—the tour group was going further away. They were going to reach the reef soon, she was pretty sure. They were heading closer to it. Before long, they were there. The reef was gorgeous compared to the reddish-brown ground they had passed up until that point. It was brightly colored and active as they approached. They could see the larger fish swimming about as they got closer. The fish was covered in all sorts of different colors. Red, blue, green, yellow, purple, magenta, and more, all just darted around in the water. There were anemone and coral growing in just about every color imaginable around them. They looked great, and Sophie felt her eyes widen as she looked over everything. The coral reef was alive with all sorts of movement, and everywhere she looked, there were new details to take in. She saw a small school of magenta fish swimming about. They were narrow, and about the size of her hand with a split-back fin. They swam about together slowly, darting from place to place without really doing much. They must have been eating, Sophie told herself, because why else would they circle around the same place over and over without really doing much? She watched as a blue tang fish, deep, vibrant blue with a yellow tail, swam past a coral, dipping behind an anemone.

There was even a small fish that swam about with its tailfin held stiffly behind it, and upon closer look, it was a shark, swimming past. The shark was small—maybe the size of Sophie's arm. Maybe it was a young shark, Sophie found herself thinking as she marveled at the way that the water's rippling waves cast shadows across its silvery skin. It had a little black tip on its dorsal fin on its back, and it moved lithely as it swam across the area. It was slow and deliberate as it moved across, and Sophie thought it was a wonderful thing to see as it moved across. It was wonderful to watch, and Sophie wanted to be able to enjoy the moment as she saw it off, circling lazily around the outside of the reef.

Before long, the shark began to swim away as well, leaving the reef just as silently as it had arrived. The fish seemed to sense that the shark was gone because the entire reef suddenly exploded with life far more vibrant than Sophie had been expecting. She could see the little schools of silvery fish swimming about, and she was convinced that they had to be happy.

Soon, there was a strange-looking fish that poked its head out from behind a piece of the reef. It was bright yellow with a strange looking nose that stretched out. Its tailfin was on a long, narrow stretch of the body that looked almost like a trumpet's bell. The aptly named trumpetfish stopped and looked at Sophie for a moment, or she thought it looked at her, and it stared, simply hovering there in place in the water, unmoving. If it weren't for the gills that slowly opened and closed, she would have doubted that it was okay there. Then, just as quickly as she had seen it for the first time, she watched as it pulled away, disappearing among the various coral reefs that could be seen.

Sophie thought it looked strange, but at the same time, she enjoyed the chance to see a new world. She thought that the different fish were worth traveling so far and learning to scuba dive. There was a small school of red and yellow fish darting about, almost like a fire flickering underneath them. There were yellow fish swimming about as well, and there were some pink ones, too. Sophie watched as there was anemone wiggling along the bottom of the reef, and saw some little shrimp crawling about on the ground as well.

Before long, they were off on their way back to shore, and as they approached, Sophie felt herself feeling a newfound love and respect for the wildlife there. She felt better seeing the different fish learning to live their lives in the wild without much protection at all. They learned to navigate the ocean, not out of choice, but out of necessity, but Sophie still had to respect their commendable spirit and resolve. As she surfaced up for air, she removed the mouthpiece and took a big gulp of air. It was nice to be out in the open air again, and she genuinely appreciated the opportunity.

They made their way back to the bungalow, the entire time, Cara chatting off Sophie's ear. Cara was just as excited as she was and chatted about the little spotted octopus she watched crawling across the reef. They had both seen some interesting things squirming around, and Sophie was so grateful for the chance she had to go see everything during her scuba diving expedition.

The rest of the cruise went well, but little seemed to compare to seeing that entirely new world underneath the water. Sophie thought it was the best thing she had seen in the day. She thought it was fantastic—she thought that she had seen a lot of interesting things that she never thought possible.

# Story 5: Girls' Night Out

*It's Friday night!! And that means that it's Girls' Night Out! Join Sophie and her best friends as they spend a night enjoying everything that the world around them has to offer. There's a lot to see out there! That fine summer night, they were heading off to a nice restaurant for dinner and wine before heading over to watch a show in the theater. It was a special night for a special occasion!*

"You mean, you got the house?" squealed Sophie into the phone.

"Yes!!" exclaimed Cara on the other line. Cara had been house hunting for some time, but most of the homes that her family encouraged her to purchase were far too big, too fancy, or too overwhelming. Cara came from wealth, and her family wanted her to live like it. But, Cara rarely ever wanted to flaunt it. She was quite practical, all things considered. She drove a new Prius because she wanted a higher fuel economy. She went on lavish vacations, but that was because she would rather pay for experiences than things, and she was totally happy to take all of her friends off on her adventures with her. She took an adventure to Greece and to the Caribbean with Sophie in the past year, and now, she was getting ready to settle into what would hopefully be her forever home. Cara and Sophie had gone looking at a wide range of houses, from multi-million dollar properties on the waterfront, to which Cara complained that they were too big or too lavish. *"Why would I need two kitchens when I don't even like to cook?"* she had asked after one of the houses was just too big. They had looked at beautiful mountain properties with fantastic views of the world around them. *"Why would I want to live so far away from everyone?"* she had asked herself.

She had eventually settled down for a nice house that was a bit on the smaller side, but she'd never complain about it.

She loved it—it was perfectly graceful without requiring her to walk half a mile to get from point A to point B, and that was something that Cara appreciated. She had chosen a small home near where Sophie lived—the home was beautiful, but nothing like what her family wanted for her. She didn't feel the need to have a house that was so big that it could house ten families when she herself was a single woman without a family. Even then, if she wanted to have children of her own, she wouldn't need a mansion. It would just be more hassle than it was worth to her, and she wasn't interested in dealing with it. She wanted to make sure that she dealt with things differently than she had grown up— there was no need for those great, big halls or rooms the size of a modern apartment. She just wanted to have enough space that she could be comfortable and enjoy herself. Too much space became nothing but a hassle that she didn't want to deal with.

"Congratulations!!" Sophie squealed into the phone happily. "We've gotta celebrate! Where do you want to go?" she asked Cara.

"I've got a plan in mind... Meet me at the restaurant at 6!" Cara's voice was ecstatic, and Sophie could imagine her jumping up and down for joy. Yeah, Cara usually kept it together, but she was also going to be highly excited. Sophie couldn't blame her! Getting a new home was thrilling! When she bought her home, she had been so happy to finally be a homeowner. She was so glad to finally have that space to herself where she could enjoy what she wanted. She loved being able to paint the walls whatever color she wanted—not that she ever did actually paint, but just having the option was enough for her. She loved that if she wanted to paint, she could.

Sophie grinned to herself as she went through the kitchen to make her coffee. It was warm and enjoyable, and Sophie had a great time sipping at it. She wanted to make sure that she would be ready for what would surely be a great party.

She was confident that they'd also be inviting a few other friends out to celebrate and knowing that Cara was involved, she was certain that whatever it was would be enjoyable.

By the time that 5:40 rolled around and Sophie needed to leave to meet up, she was wearing a knee-length dress in a nice teal color. It had white flowers printed across it, and the dress itself was flowy—it tucked in at the waist but then flared out in pleats that practically bounced about her when she walked by. She loved that dress. It had spaghetti straps with a nice V-neck cut to it that revealed her defined collarbone and a small white gold pendant that sat right above it. Her makeup was done with a sultry smoky look to it—the eyeliner was accentuated by grey eyeshadows with a hint of green to draw out her brown eyes. She wore deep red lipstick as well, and her face was carefully made up. She had to look great for such an occasion! Her hair was carefully done up so that she was showing off her slender neck, tied up in a loose bun.

When she arrived at the restaurant, Cara was already there, parked in her car. She was watching out for their friends to show up, and one by one, they did. One by one, they gathered. Cara had invited a few people—Sophie was there. They also had a few other close friends. Alyssa, a newlywed, had shown up, her soft features alight with joy for her friend. Their friend, Olivia, walked up as well. Olivia wore a cute black dress. She had a plumper face, and her skin was a warm tan color. Her long, thick black hair hung around her shoulders, and her bangs framed her face perfectly. She wore dark makeup in the cat's eye style with smoky eyeshadow, and her lips were a bright red color. Olivia was a great friend of Cara's—they had both taken the same major in college and spent a lot of time together.

Olivia, Alyssa, Cara, and Sophie all walked toward their favorite restaurant. It was known around town as being a great place to get some wine with a nice seafood dinner, and it was absolutely delicious. The interior of the restaurant was a bit eclectic, but it did its job well. The tables were a nice granite, and the booths had warm, brown and red cushions that were among the most comfortable that they had ever enjoyed. The floor was a bright blue carpet, the color of the deep sea, and there were pendant lights hanging above every single table there. There was a big sculpture of a sperm whale hanging from the ceiling, mouth widely opened as if it were about to take a bite of something. There was a bar on the far end of the restaurant, and the women all looked at each other. Should they go all the way over there to the bar? Or should they choose to sit at a booth?

Cara made a choice for them—a nice booth that overlooked the Puget Sound. They could see a dock of all sorts of lavish, white sailboats that shone in the evening sun, and there were all sorts of people out on the water enjoying it. They could even see kayakers and people on canoes enjoying the summer warmth. They all settled down into the booth with space for everyone. Cara sat next to Sophie, and across from them was Alyssa and Olivia. Their waitress quickly brought them a stack of menus and a bottle of wine along with four wine glasses for everyone to enjoy before dipping away. The waitress seemed to understand the difference between knowing just how much to stick around and when it is a good idea to gracefully dip away. That was a good trait for a waitress—it was good for them to make sure that they were around just enough to be helpful but not enough to disturb the meal.

"So, Cara," Olivia said, placing her head on her hand and leaning in closer. "Tell us about the new place?" Olivia had a smile on her face, ready to hear all of the interesting details of the house, and Sophie grinned back. The house, from what Sophie had seen, was great, but she was also pretty sure that she was the only one that was allowed around it. She looked at Cara, waiting for her to answer.

"The place is marvelous, darling," Cara responded, her own face breaking out into an equally as excited grin as she started to pour the wine. It was chardonnay that smelled delicious as it filled up each of the four glasses in the center of the table. "It's in a small subdivision that's all about privacy. There's nothing but trees all around it, so I don't have to see my neighbors if I don't want to, and it has a beautiful willow tree in the front yard." Sophie tried to imagine Cara doing yardwork and raking up the leaves every autumn, but she was pretty sure that wouldn't be happening. "And inside? It's gorgeous. Very quaint, but in a good way. It's very homey, and that's exactly what I wanted." It was true! The home was not what one would expect a socialite heiress to purchase on her own, but it was beautiful in its own way.

Cara chatted away about her house, describing the beautiful blue-ish grey paint that was on it and the bright, green trees that surrounded it. Even better, however, was the big yard in the back. "It's got plenty of space for children, whenever I'm ready, and I love that about the house," she announced happily with a nod of her head. She smiled back at Sophie, who quickly nodded her head in agreement. It was perfect the way that it was. Of course, Sophie was quite confident that they'd be spending lots of time remodeling the interior. She had already listened to Cara chat her ear off about how much she wanted to change about the house. She wanted to put in a beautiful hard cherry wood into the home for flooring—she had shown pictures of Brazilian cherry wood that was absolutely gorgeous. She had also been quick to say that she wanted to paint the interior a warm creamy color that would highlight the colors of the wood. The cabinets, she had insisted, would be made of matching wood, and she wanted to get quartz counters and backsplash on the whole kitchen. She loved the idea of having this beautiful look that she could go into and enjoy—modern, but still conventionally comfortable. The appliances had to be replaced too—she wanted them to be nice, stainless steel.

Perhaps Cara's favorite part of the house, however, was the big window overlooking a beautiful yard form the window in the kitchen. The home had such great, big windows that they could see through. The windows made it nice and bright indoors, despite the greyed out surroundings most of the year. Sophie knew that Cara would be happy—she could already see the home is made up into something that would be incredibly cozy to live within. It would be warm and inviting, and it was likely to be filled in rapidly with practical, yet luxurious furniture that would bring the whole look together.

"Are you going to paint the outside?" Alyssa asked, sipping at her wine.

"Maybe—it's such a cute blue now, though!" Cara replied as she took a sip as well.

"But the bigger question," Olivia asked as she grinned at everyone mischievously, "is whether or not you are going to fill that house up with a nice man now that you're moving into your own place." She chuckled, raising her eyebrows suggestively. "It's time to settle down, isn't it? Sophie, does Felix have any brothers? Or cute single friends?"

Sophie gasped, covering her mouth as her eyes widened in faux shock. She giggled behind her hands, looking at Cara to see what her response was, and the response was quite surprising—she saw Cara chuckling, her cheeks turning red. It was hard to tell if it was the wine that was staining them or if she was actually embarrassed.

"You know, I don't need a man!" Cara announced, raising her glass to her friends. "And how could I when I have such great friends?" She tilted her head with a grin. "You all are too kind, you know? You're too great for all of this. But, you know what? You're all more than welcome to come and visit me any time you want. Besides, maybe I'll just be that cat and wine-loving aunt that never actually marries or has kids. I'll look after all of your kids to be the fun one. It'll be great! All the fun and none of the mess or responsibility!" She grinned at them all.

The truth was, Cara was nervous about finding a partner that she would need to set up such an extensive prenup with. She was worried that any man that came near her was really interested in her for the money rather than actually being affectionate toward her, and she didn't want to deal with having to figure out who was who. She wanted to have a good time with people that she could trust, and so far, she couldn't trust any of the ones who had come around. It was too easy to tell when they started having problems accepting that she didn't want to shower them in gifts constantly. She didn't want to pay for them to have a car or cover every single bill when they went out—she wanted them to offer to cover sometimes, too. Not because she believed that it was always the man's job to pay—but because she wanted to believe that she could trust him to also contribute to pay for things that mattered. She wanted to ensure that he would also cover the bills and be willing to jump in and cover things just because she believed that they ought to be a partnership rather than rely on her entirely for everything that she would do. She wanted to make sure that she was not going to be taken advantage of just due to her money.

Really, Sophie couldn't blame her for those feelings- she wasn't wrong to tell others that she wasn't going to deal with the mingling of funds that could potentially cause her all sorts of problems. She squeezed Cara's hand underneath the table in understanding and support, and Cara squeezed hers back. Before the conversation could go any longer, however, the waitress had returned with a platter of food.

Sophie had a delicious shrimp, clam, and mussel pasta placed in front of her. It smelled amazing. There was a nice red tomato sauce that smelled garlicky and slightly spicy alongside the shrimp, scallops, clams, and mussels. The mussels and clams were already opened up for easy eating, and the shrimp were decently sized—each one was about the size of her thumb. There was a nice sprinkling of fresh parsley all cross the top of the pasta as well. She couldn't believe just how amazing it smelled next to the bakery-fresh garlic bread that was placed next to her alongside a generous portion of a caesar salad.

Cara got a delicious looking stuffed lobster dish that was filled up with crab meat as well, and alongside it was a gently steamed vegetable medley. It looked and smelled just as amazing as the seafood pasta. Alyssa ordered a basic shrimp fettuccine that looked as decadent as it smelled, and judging by her total silence after she tried a bite, probably tasted just as good as well. And Olivia ordered a grilled lemon garlic salmon that was practically melting underneath her fork.

Together, they enjoyed their meal, laughing, and chatting about what they thought of Cara's house. It was a great one from what everyone gathered, and they continued to sip at wine throughout the meal. When they were all done, Cara looked around at her friends. "I've got one more announcement to make!" she told them all happily. "We're going to go to the theater next—I got us a private booth to see the new show!"
The women all cheered and piled into their cars. None of them had enough wine to be unable to drive, and they all made their way to the theater, parking, and heading upstairs. The sun was starting to set at that point as they made their way in to hand off their tickets, and they were all ushered up. They were there to see a new musical that was apparently fantastic, according to the phenomenal reviews all over the internet, and they were thrilled to get the chance to not only see it, but to see it in such a good position.

Their seats were perfect—they overlooked everything above them and allowed them to see and hear everything perfectly. It was such a great place to be, and Sophie was beyond thankful for her great friend. Together they enjoyed the show, sipping at more wine from the concessions stand and watching as everyone did their thing. She thought that the show was fantastic—just as good as everyone had said to them. Being able to see it was great.

Before long, the show was over, and they were all on their way to go back to Sophie's home. They were going to spend the night enjoying silly movies with a few more bottles of wine, ice cream, and any other junk that they wanted to enjoy. Girls' night out only happened so often, and when they had a reason to celebrate, they wanted to celebrate big and enjoy every moment of it. They wanted to feel like they were having a good time together—and they were confident that if they were together, they would do just that. It was going to be a perfect night together, celebrating their best friend's newest success.

# Story 6: Sophie Swallows the Frog

*It's a typical Monday afternoon and as much as Sophie wished that she could do something else, she found herself being resigned to her fate—she had work to do. She had a whole laundry list of errands to run, and she knows that they have to happen sooner rather than later. So, off Sophie goes, ready to take care of everything that she needs to do. Join Sophie as she goes on her way to take care of everything that she needs to do.*

With a sigh, Sophie looked out her window. Of course, it was raining. Bella was laying down next to the sliding glass door that led to outside, simply staring at the drizzle as it came down steadily. It continued to drop all around their home, constantly dribbling out of the sky and creating massive puddles. They could hear the pitter-patter of it drumming against their windows. The rain only made that Monday feel even drabber than before, causing Sophie to feel sleepy. It was something about the lack of light— whenever it rained like that, she just wanted to sleep her day away. She wanted to be able to curl up, comfy and warm, in bed, and just let the day pass her by. But, of course, the more that the rain fell, the more she knew that she couldn't do it. No matter how much she wanted to do so, she was stuck. She had to ensure that she was properly adulting as the world told her to.

So, Sophie found that she had no choice but to steal her resolve. She had to tell herself that she was going to go through the day and take care of everything that needed to be done. She was determined to make sure that she got through everything, even if she was miserable. So, she pushed herself up. She forced herself to get up and walk up the stairs. She went straight to her room, showered, and got dressed to get ready to go. "Mondays, am I right?" she muttered to herself as she trudged up the stairs, not really wanting to deal with the day. Mondays sucked, even with her untraditional job and hours. She didn't want to have to deal with everything that she was doing—she just wanted to make sure that she was responsible enough to keep everything stable.

Sophie's parents had not exactly been the best role models on responsibility—she had always been told that she had to do things a certain way, but she had also grown up believing that she didn't really have to do much in terms of making sure that they had stability. Sophie had always moved around a lot—she went from home to home because her parents had never managed to keep things consistent, and Sophie didn't want that life. But, that also meant that she didn't exactly have the best role models or experiences. She had to make sure that she was driven to do better.

Sophie pulled out her phone and looked over her list. She had a whole lot that she needed to take care of that day. She had to pay her mortgage, pay power, stop at the grocery store for food, and run Bella to the vet. It didn't sound like much fun, but she knew that it needed to be done one way or another. She put her clothes on for the day and looked down at the list of things that she had to do. The first order of business was paying those bills—and at the very least, they could be done online. She tapped in the login information and paid both of those in moments. It was nice and simple, but Sophie still had more to do. "Swallow the frog," Sophie told herself quietly as she walked down the stairs, purse over her shoulder.

Though her parents may not have been the best at making sure that she learned how to pay her bills and be responsible, they had taught her one thing: When faced with a laundry list of things that you don't want to do, the best thing to do was simply get it done. Do the worst thing first, her mother would tell her growing up. "Swallow the frog and be done with it. The more you think about it, the worse it will sound, and the more you'll procrastinate. When you stop thinking and just do it, it's easier to tolerate."

Her mother had a point—if she just swallowed the frog, things would be all over, and she'd be done worrying about what she had to do. All she had to do was get it done. She looked at herself in the mirror one last time before walking out the door. She hopped into her car, and off she went. There were a few grocery stores closer to where she lived than the one that she preferred to shop at, but she loved the one that was an extra five minutes away. It was further, but the food was better. It tasted great, and usually, the staff was better suited to helping as well. She knew that she'd get much better service there than if she had stuck around at the closing stores.

Off Sophie went, driving down the road, idly tapping her fingers along the steering wheel. It was a bit easier to feel energized when she was outside. Though it was cloudy, the light was brighter, and she felt a bit more awake. She looked at the other cars that were driving along as well. They were quickly making their way through the roads as well. Sophie liked to imagine where everyone was going as she drove the whole fifteen minutes to the store that she preferred. She looked at the first car to her left. It was a purple minivan-driving by, soaked in the rain. There was a woman driving it that looked stressed out. The expression she wore looked like she was ready to just give up on whatever was going on. She looked down at the road in front of her, biting her lip like she was trying not to cry. Sophie felt a pang of sympathy for the woman.

Was she stressed because the children in the car were causing problems? As the van passed her, she saw that the children in the back were unmoving and looking straight ahead. They looked stressed out as well. Maybe someone close to them just heard that they were sick? Or maybe someone passed away? That had to be it, Sophie told herself—someone must have passed away, and that was what caused the sadness that was emanating from the truck so palpably that evens he could feel it.

The car to her right had a much different attitude. The car itself was an older sedan, perhaps 15 or 20 years old, and it had its own fair share of dents and dings in it. It must have been caused by the young driver that was in the car. The kid must have been maybe 16 or 17 in the driver's seat, and he looked a little bit stressed out too, but his source of stress appeared to be the shy young woman sitting in the passenger's seat. It was probably someone heading off on a date, Sophie told herself with a nod and a smile. How cute. She looked so afraid to be there in the car next to him, and she imagined that they were heading to the movie theater for their date.

Sophie turned her attention right back to the road in front of her as she kept on going to the store. Before long, she was there and pulled right into the parking lot. The place was surprisingly empty for the time and she parked near the front of the lot. Yeah, parking in the back was better for the legs, but the constant drizzle convinced her otherwise. She didn't want to deal with it—she just wanted to be there to get what she needed and get out.

She booked it into the store, covering her head with her purse in hopes of avoiding the rain. Immediately, the warm scent of fresh, roasted coffee filled her nose, and she looked over at the café that was there. She smiled and nodded to herself. That sounded perfect. So, in she went to pick up a coffee to enjoy on her shopping trip. If she had to swallow the frog, at least she could do so in style and comfort with something tasty to wash it down with!

Sophie chose a chai latte to sip at, savoring the spiciness that it brought with her, and she loved just how delicious it was. As she went through the store, pushing her cart and enjoying the delicious drink, she found herself feeling a bit better. Perhaps this frog hadn't been as bad as she had thought. She grabbed her ingredients quickly. For the week, she was planning on making a nice garden salad to eat for lunch with some chicken and eggs tossed into it. For breakfasts, she grabbed a bag of bagels to enjoy with some cream cheese. And for dinners, she was going to be making a big batch of spaghetti, and later in the week, a big batch of curry. That would give her plenty to deal with to eat and enjoy as she went through her day. She just had to make sure that she got everything. Along with the ingredients for her meals for the week, she picked up several different fruits to munch on as snacks. Who didn't love having a taste of banana or watermelon sometimes?

With her cart stocked for the week, Sophie turned her attention to the checkout line and made her way over. However, she stopped as she walked past the bakery. There were some delicious cakes there, lined up and ready for someone to pick up. She just had to decide if she wanted one or not. Her eyes fell on a dark chocolate cake that looked decadently sinful. She eyed it for a moment, debating if the cake was something that would be worth the need for extra exercise or not. She deliberated over it longer and nodded her head to herself, picking it up and putting it in the cart. If she had to run errands, she wanted to treat herself! Besides, adding a treat was a great way that she could also add some pleasantries to the whole nine yards of work she needed to follow.

With her food paid for and loaded into the car, she was off once more. She had to run home to put away all the groceries so she could pick up Bella and take her to the vet. She knew that Bella would be difficult to deal with—she hated the vet and somehow always knew within minutes that they were heading there. She must have memorized the path that was taken, Sophie had told herself the last time she tried. The poor pup had to be kept buckled into a safety harness to make sure that she didn't try to run out the window or climb all over Sophie in a desperate bid to escape. Sophie hated that she'd protest so much, but she still needed her annual checkup, and she needed to get a few booster shots that year, too.

So, upon arriving home, Sophie quickly put everything away and turned to Bella. She smiled at the dog, but somehow, the German shepherd seemed to know that something wasn't quite right. "Want to go for a drive, Bella?" Sophie asked.

The dog perked up at first, but then her ears immediately fell down, and she flopped on the ground. Sophie stared at the dog and sighed. How was she supposed to lug a dog that was more than half her weight outside and into the car? She looked between Bella and the front door and shrugged her shoulders. She'd just have to force the point. "Time to swallow the frog, Bella. Let's go!" She clipped the leash onto Bella, and the dog looked up at her pleadingly, as if begging her to not take her out to the car. Of course, she did what any responsible pet owner would do, and off they went outside. They walked to the car, and the dog got in, whining softly as she listened. Sophie clipped her leash to the dog harness seatbelt and then sat next to her. "Sorry, girl, but you need this," she whispered as she patted the pup on the head.

They drove off to the vet with ease then. It didn't take them too long to get there, and before she knew it, they were off toward the vet. This time, Sophie didn't have the time to look at what everyone else was doing. She was busy looking at Bella and making sure that the dog didn't try to bound away or push off from the area. She just wanted to make sure that she didn't need to run away from there or do something that would cause them some problems. Sophie patted the dog as they pulled into the vet's parking lot. The rain was still falling, and she knew that they'd have to move quickly, or Bella would take any opportunity that she could to run away and avoid going in. So, Sophie hopped out, clipped her leash onto Bella's harness, and pulled her with her. She just wanted to get the dog in and out as quickly as possible so they would be done. She was determined to make sure that the dog was taken care of and that they'd be able to go, but she wasn't quite sure how to get through it all. So, off Sophie went, tugging Bella inside.

Bella, of course, was the picture of resistance. She pulled back. She resisted. She demanded to be left alone. But, Bella couldn't just go in to get checked out—she had to be taken in as quickly as possible to ensure that they were going to get out of there sooner rather than later. "Please, Bella? Please?? You have to get inside!" She sighed, looking over the dog that was resisting so adamantly. "You have to get inside!"

The dog looked up, and if she could pout, Sophie had no doubt that there would have been a big frown on her face. But, she had no choice—Sophie wasn't to blame here. The blame was that dogs needed to be taken care of, and she couldn't help that. She wanted to keep her best doggy pall healthy, and that meant biting the bullet, swallowing the frog, and bringing the dog indoors.

Bella seemed to sense that Sophie wasn't going to back down. Though she was still clearly hesitant, she whimpered a few times and followed her into the building without pulling back any longer. She stopped trying to get her to stay behind or let her go. As Sophie held the door to the doggy entrance open, Bella slowly went in, tail down between her legs and ears flat on her head.

"Come on, you wimpy dog. It's just the vet!" Sophie patted her head affectionately. "Don't worry so much about it and let's just get it over with already. The sooner we do that, the better. The sooner we head in, the sooner you get to go home and play. Let's go!"

So, in they went, and Sophie checked them into the receptionist. They both sat in the corner near where they were confident that the vet would come out. The vet's office was small—at least on this side. They had two different waiting rooms—one for dogs and one for cats. There were two other people sitting in the waiting room where Sophie and Bella were. Bella immediately dove to hide under the seat while Sophie sat down. There was another person sitting there with her small Chihuahua under her own seat. The dog looked just as miserable as Bella did, and Sophie felt a bit bad. She was sure that dogs hated the vet-- it wasn't like the people could explain to them that they were just there to get checked out or that things would be just fine if they went in without any protesting. They were stuck somewhere getting poked and prodded and didn't understand why. Of course, it had to happen.

There was another dog there too—this one, a puppy, falling asleep in his owner's arms. The puppy was small and red, with pricked ears that were starting to fall down and a look of utter tiredness on its face. The dog was adorable and quite calm.

Before much longer, the vet popped out and asked for Bella to head to the back. So, off, Sophie and Bella went into the back of the room. The appointment, thankfully, didn't take too long. Though Bella always put up a big stink about going to the vet, she also was quite obedient when she was told to do something. Despite the initial protests, she was willing to listen if she had to. She sat there as she was poked, prodded, moved around, and told to stop moving around so much. She was perfectly healthy, declared the vet after a few moments before giving her a quick pat on the head and a treat. Despite their attempts to convince Bella to like the vet and despite the vet's skill at giving her delicious treats every time she showed up, Sophie had never been able to get that sense that the vet was fun instilled in her dog. Maybe it was that the animals could smell that the area was somewhere scary or depressing. Maybe it was that the animals could smell that there were others there that were sick, hurt, or dying. No matter, Sophie was glad that Bella had at least mostly cooperated that day.

With the vet out of the way and feeling thoroughly drained from a day of errands, Sophie loaded Bella into the car. "Time to go, big girl," she told Bella, who eagerly hopped in, ready to get as far away as possible from that area. It was clear that she was ready to leave as soon as possible, and Sophie couldn't really fault her for that. Off they went, heading home. They were ready to eat and spend some time unwinding for the rest of the day.

# Story 7: Horseback Trail

*Time for an adventure! Felix has asked Sophie to go horseback riding with him! She has never gone before, but she is ready to get going if that is what he wants. She decides that she'll try her hardest. Besides, you gotta try something before you decide that you don't like it. Sophie may be nervous, and she may be a bit afraid of sitting atop a great, big horse, but she is willing to try if that is what it will take.*

"I promise, you'll love it," Felix practically purred as he placed a hand on the small of Sophie's back, guiding her toward a building. They were in the middle of a mountain that Sophie had never gone to before. There was a stable there that people could rent horses from, and though Sophie had never tried it before, there was a first time for everything. She was quite confident that she could have a good time if she could get over one thing in particular: Sophie was afraid of heights. The idea of sitting on a horse to ride was almost terrifying to her—she was afraid that she would fall at a moment's notice and that was horrifying for her. She was terrified that she'd be unable to keep herself up on her feet, and she knew that she'd have to cope with that fear when the time came.

Sophie nodded back in response to Felix's comment and wrapped one hand around his arm. It was more to comfort herself than to show her affection, but he appeared to take it differently. He assumed that she was simply cuddly. She hadn't told him her big problem, and instead, she nervously walked alongside him, smiling and nodding whenever he said something so that she didn't upset him. She was afraid that he would be bothered when she told him that she was afraid of horses—but she also had to remind herself that this was *Felix* they were talking about. He was so sweet. There was no way that he'd be upset or angry at her. She just had to be willing to give it a shot at least once, and he'd forgive her. ... Right?

The area smelled of farm, and as they got closer to the small building that hooked onto what looked like a large stable, Sophie noticed that there were some horses that were sitting there, watching them with interested eyes. They knew that people showing up meant that they'd get ridden, and that meant a chance to explore. Sophie, on the other hand, eyed them back uncertainly. She sighed to herself, trying to steel her resolve.

"I hope you're ready, sweetheart," said Felix as he opened the door. The interior of the building was much nicer than she had expected, and they were surrounded by chairs and a nice water fountain as well. It looked nice and quaint indoors, and behind the table, there was a nice-looking woman. She had long, red hair that she had braided into pigtails that hung down over each shoulder. Her kind face was freckled, and her bright green eyes looked at them with interest. She wore a straw hat even indoors and smiled when they made eye contact.

"Welcome to Horse Ridge Acres!" Her voice was energetic and kind at the same time. She seemed like the type that would help them with anything, or the type that would literally give someone the shirt off of her back if she had to. Sophie hoped they wouldn't have to test that theory as she looked shyly up at the woman. "I'm Anne, and I'm here to help. What can I do for you today?" Her voice had a slight southern twang to it as she spoke, and Sophie couldn't help but think back to the stereotypical southern tomboy type who had no qualms with getting dirty when they went to work.

Felix nodded his hed. "Thanks, Anne. I'm Felix, and this is Sophie. We have a two o clock appointment to go riding."

He wrapped his arm all the way around Sophie's shoulder and leaned in to kiss her on the cheek.

Anne grinned at them. "I see you right here. Looks like you have Strider and Morning Star today as your horses. Have you ridden before?" Felix nodded in response, but Sophie looked nervous.

"No, ma'am," Sophie replied, looking down.

Both Felix and Anne stared at her. "Never?" asked Felix. "Why didn't you say something about that before we came?"

"I didn't want to let you down," Sophie responded with a shrug of her shoulders. "I figured it couldn't be too hard... Right?"

Felix and Anne exchanged dubious glances, and immediately, Sophie's heart dropped. Did she need to actually do more than just hold onto the reins?

"You know," said Anne, "I've got another horse, Esprit, who should be strong enough to hold both of you up if you want to ride together. He isn't booked this afternoon. But... He is just as spirited as his name implies. Do you think you can handle him?" She looked at Felix. "You've ridden before, right?"

"Yes, many times. I used to keep horses when I was younger, but life happens, times change, and I don't have the time to dedicate to doing so anymore. But, I'm quite confident in my abilities. We'll try him." He squeezed Sophie's hand. At the very least, she had admitted her inability and inexperience prior to getting on the horse, he thought—she could have been seriously hurt trying to ride a horse without the experience.

A few minutes later, they were out in the stables, walking through to the end where the horse named Esprit was kept.

When Anne opened the gate to his stall and grabbed his reins to take him out, Sophie could hear a gruff snort and a stomp on the ground. She wasn't sure this horse was going to be willing to take them on their journey either—but they had to try at the very least.

"Here he is," said Anne, pulling him out. He stared at her as if debating defying, but followed around. "You'll have to be careful with him, though," she told Felix, passing his reins off.

"I've got it," said Felix with a nod. They walked outside and fitted the horse with a nice double saddle so Sophie would be able to sit comfortably. Before long, they were getting ready to mount him. "I'll go first, and then you come up after," he told Sophie, climbing up and throwing a leg over the horse. He put out his hand and pulled Sophie up as well.

Sophie looked down at the ground and felt her head swimming. She clung to Felix nervously, wrapping his shirt in her hands and squeezing her eyes shut. Felix sensed her shifting and instability. "Are you okay?" he asked, glancing over his shoulder at Sophie. He was holding the reins firmly and the horse was not yet moving.

Sophie nodded her head against his back, eyes still tightly shut. She was nervous and afraid—but she had no choice. She had to try. She stabled herself and looked around. The height was intimidating—but she didn't want to hold them back. She wrapped her hands around Felix's waist. "Let's go," she said, her voice trembling.

"Are you sure you're okay?" Felix's voice was full of concern.

"Yes," she said in reply, steeling herself a bit more. "I'm okay."

So, they began to ride the horse, slowly at first. Esprit seemed eager to run off, but under Felix's firm guide, he followed instructions relatively obediently. They walked at a slow trot along a trail, and Sophie looked around, trying to focus on anything but the height around them. She looked at just how high up they were and then looked down again. She looked at the fields of flowers that were growing all around them. The fields were almost brownish in areas, but they still had great, big flowers that were sprouting out. There were green leaves in some places, and there were others that were just fields of wheatgrass waving in the winds. There were big yellow flowers that they could see as well that looked great. Sophie could see the great, big sky, too, with massive white clouds billowing around them. There were also trees lining the path.

The longer they rode, the calmer Sophie started to feel. She was trying her hardest not to focus on the height that she had and soon, she began to smile a bit. "I'm sorry I didn't say anything earlier," she told Felix as she watched a few birds flying over their heads. "I should have, but I was afraid that you'd be upset. I mean… We seem so different. I don't want you to feel like I'm not good enough for you."

That was enough to make Felix stop in his tracks. He pulled the reins, and Esprit came to a stop. Felix looked over his shoulder at Sophie. "Honey, of course, you're good enough. You don't have to share all of my likes and dislikes for us to get along. You can be yourself. I don't mind at all. Don't try to change who you are for me. Just be who you are, and I'll be happy."

Sophie nodded her head. "It's just… You love the outdoors, and I…"

"Don't?" finished Felix as Sophie's voice trailed off.

Sophie chuckled and nodded her head weakly. "Yeah," she replied. "I mean, I can have fun, and I really love all of the places that you've taken me, but… I'm also happy spending my time inside with a good book or a movie. And I feel like you might want someone that wants to be a bit more outdoorsy.”

Felix shook his head. “Sophie, that’s nonsense.”

“Are you sure?” Sophie asked him, looking up with big, worried eyes.

“Of course.” He nodded his head solemnly as he looked at her. “You’re the only one for me, Sophie. You just have to see that and accept it for what it is. If you can do that, we’ll be much happier, I think. Just because I want to do something doesn’t mean that we have to. Tell me if you don’t so we can find something that we both love to do. I want to make sure that you’re happy too, and if that means that sometimes, we go to a movie instead of doing what I want to do, that’s fine too.”

Sophie nodded her head, feeling a bit more comfortable with the whole talk. “Thanks, Felix... The truth is, I’m scared of heights.” She finally managed to blurt out what she had been thinking. “So, this whole time, I’ve been trying not to look at the ground underneath us because it makes me nervous. I’m the kind of person who’s passed out looking down. The Space Needle in Seattle? Nope, not gonna do it. I can’t look down on the elevator going up!” Sophie laughed nervously. “I just didn’t know how I could tell you this all without upsetting you or feeling like a failure. I’m sorry.”

Felix shook his head. “Don’t apologize so much!” he insisted. “You’re fine. How about we head back and go do something that is a bit more enjoyable for both of us, then? I know we passed a few towns on the way here, and I bet we could find a movie theater or a restaurant for dinner instead if you want.”

“Smelling like horses?” Sophie laughed. There was definitely a distinct smell when they wandered around with the horses. Sophie wasn't sure she wanted to bring that into any restaurants that they went to.

"Definitely!" Felix said with a chuckle to himself. "Or we could head back to your place, change, and spend a day in. I'll order takeout sushi or something."

That sounded like much more fun to Sophie than continuing on that trail with the horse that looked like he was ready to bolt at any moment in time. She nodded her head back. "that sounds perfect," she told him with a hug. Her heart was full as they retreated back to the barn that they had gone to originally. They made their way back slowly, but then, something happened, and Esprit bolted away. Sophie screamed from her position on top of him, but that seemed to only embolden the horse even more, and he ran faster. Sophie squeezed onto Felix's waist and closed her eyes as tightly as she could before they made their way back. Felix somehow managed to get him under control after a moment or two, but Sophie was terrified.

She rested her head against Felix's head and shook as they ran by. As the horse finally came to a slower pace before stopping, she peeked her eyes open, peering about them. They were back at the barn by some miracle. Felix laughed. "He probably wants a rider that will take him for a real run," he told her as he slid off, holding his hand out for Sophie to climb down as well. Sophie took his hand, her own, trembling in fear, and she saw a flash of concern across Felix's face. "It's okay," Felix told her, squeezing her tightly.

So, they went inside, returned the horse, signed the paperwork, and off they went back home. Sophie spent the whole drive staring at the window, shaking slightly as they went. She was willing to chat back here and there when Felix had something to say, but for the most part, she was quiet. Before long, they were back at home, and Sophie couldn't have been happier. She was relieved that they were back and on her own ground. She hugged Felix tightly. "Thank you," she told him as they headed into her house.

Felix smiled and kissed her head. "You still smell like a horse," he replied, squeezing her tightly. "But that's okay because you're still my smelly, Sophie." He laughed and kissed her on the lips. "I'm just glad to be here with you, no matter what we're doing. And you know what? No more horses in the future." He grinned. "I've got friends I can go riding with. We'll stick to less strenuous trips in the future!"

Sophie smiled and nodded her head thankfully. She could live with that. So, she went upstairs to get herself all cleaned up and de-horse-ified, and Felix got to work ordering food for their date that night. As Sophie washed clean, she couldn't help but feel beyond thankful for such as a loving and caring partner to have. She was so happy that he was willing to do that for her. He seemed to really care about her for her, and that was enough.

# Guided Meditation 1: Stream of Thoughts

*Have you ever felt like your mind was racing within you, and there was nothing you could do about it? Have you ever felt like no matter what you did, you couldn't slow down those thoughts that continued to whirl around within you, flying about and leaving you utterly overwhelmed? Stress... Anxiety... Fear... Sorrow... They can all hold you back if you don't know how to take a step back from them. In this story, you will enjoy a peaceful trip to your own personal stream of thoughts, learning to watch them go by without reaching out to them to interrupt. You will be mastering the art of passive thought observation and eventually letting them go so your stream can run empty, and you can finally drift off to sleep.*

Close your eyes, and settle yourself into bed. Get into your most comfortable position as you prepare to be gently guided off to sleep. Take in a great, big, deep breath through your nose. Feel it flowing through your nostrils and down into your lungs. Is it warm? Cold? Just right? What smells does it carry with it? Focus on those smells. Focus on the sensation of your air as it fills up your lungs with air. Your lungs are like balloons, filling up and swelling up until they are full, and there, they give you the energy to live. Graciously thank the air in your lungs for providing you with the oxygen you will need and exhales slowly. Feel the air, warmer now, as it gently whispers over your lips. Does it dry them out? Does it feel gentle? With every breath that you take, you can feel yourself releasing tension and feeling more at peace.

You will breathe in... And out... On counts of five.

You take a deep breath in...

One... Two... Three... Four... Five...

And out...

One... Two... Three... Four... Five...

Your breath helps you to center yourself. You feel yourself relaxing as your breath slowly and gently calms you down. You feel yourself feeling more connected, more at peace, more aware of everything that you do. You are becoming aware of yourself, what you do, and how you feel.

You take a deep breath in...

One... Two... Three... Four... Five...

And out...

One... Two... Three... Four... Five...

Now, focus on the tension in your body. Become aware of any tension you are holding in your head and face. As you breathe in, imagine that you are pushing the tension within your body and down to the center point above your belly button. Let it gather there. Now, feel the tension in your shoulders. Focus on that stress and tension and as you breathe in, feel it moving down to your center. Let it gather there, imagining your tension and stress all becoming balled up in the center. Feel the tension in your arms and hands gathering and flowing in to your center. Feel that center growing with the tension and allow it to build up. Then, take the tension from your chest and upper back, and flow it down toward your center.

Then, go down to your toes and feet, identifying the tension that is there. Push it up, feeling it flowing up your legs, through your pelvis and belly, and noting it as it arrives in the belly. Focus on it as it grows within you and allow it to flow.

Feel all of the tension in your body, all boiled up into one big ball in your core. You've pushed away all of that tension away from yourself, so you can better focus on Allow yourself to feel the weight of that tension and the burden that it has been putting on you. Feel the heaviness on yourself. That tension in your core begins to transform, and you find yourself laying there, with butterflies all over your body, holding you down. You feel them, holding you, pressing against you, and keeping you down. You are trapped by your tension, burdened. It's keeping you awake, lost in your mind...

You take a big, deep breath into your chest. And you breathe out deeply...

As you exhale, all of the butterflies suddenly fly away. They all push off from you suddenly, and they all flutter away, one by one, disappearing into the sky. As they all disappear, you start to feel lighter. You feel more comfortable, more content. One by one, you feel your tensions fade away. You feel more relaxed. You watch each butterfly take away one of your concerns for the day. You watch each butterfly disappear with your stress, and you feel lighter.

You feel like you can move again.

You feel relaxed.

You feel at peace.

Now, in that space where you pulled the tension away, in your center, imagine that peace and calmness flows into you. It is slowly manifesting within your core, filling you with peace, comfort, and the feeling that everything will be okay. You have a big, shining silver ball of peace and relaxation within your core. Breathe in... One... Two... Three... Four... Five... And out... One... Two... Three... Four... Five... As you breathe in, imagine the feeling of relaxation extending throughout your body. Feel it in your head. Breathe in... and out... Feel the relaxation pulsating in your shoulders and arms... Feel it spreading throughout your chest. Feel it spread down to your legs and feet. It fills your whole body, bringing you utter peace and relaxation. Your mind feels incredibly open and ready to go on a peaceful, relaxing adventure. Your body is ready to fall deeper and deeper into your relaxation so you can become more and more relaxed, with the ultimate goal being to help you to fall asleep.

Your mind is at ease, and you continue to breathe deeply. You breathe in... And out... And in... And out... You look all around you, and you realize that you can see something through the darkness. In front of you, a little speck of blue manifests far off in the distance. It scoots closer and closer to you, flowing. It's fluid as it gets closer to you, and you can hear a babbling sound in the distance. You can see it getting closer and closer to you. As it approaches, you realize that it is a little stream. As the stream approaches you, flowing more and more across the vastness of your mind, you can see that there are little specks of something floating across the top. There are hundreds of them, whatever they are, and you move toward them.

Grass starts to sprout around the stream, slowly stretching out from the water and blanketing the vastness of your mind, filling in the dark expanse of nothing that you had found yourself floating within. You see it getting brighter and brighter within yourself. It grows underneath your feet and leaves you feeling treat. You feel happy and content. You feel at peace where you are. You approach the stream. You kneel down and dip your hand into the water. It is coolly refreshing, lightly trickling around your hand. The water flows between your fingers, and you enjoy the feeling. It's not too hot and not too cold—it is pleasantly cool.

You take a deep breath in...

One... Two... Three... Four... Five...

And out...

One... Two... Three... Four... Five...

You watch the water beneath you. You can see that the water is filled up with tiny fish that swim about happily in the short reeds growing underneath it. You can see them darting about, looking for food. They are small and silvery, maybe the length of your knuckle. They look perfectly content as they go about, darting around, and you feel a wave of happiness within yourself. You feel calm. You feel at peace. You feel like you are ready to make some very real progress.

You take a deep breath in...

One... Two... Three... Four... Five...

And out...

One... Two... Three... Four... Five...

Now, you turn your focus to the things floating atop the surface. You see pink flower petals, all lazily drifting in circles as they float down the stream. They are tiny—the size of your pinky nail, and are so powdery pink that they almost look white where they are. They are beautiful, and there seems to be an endless supply of them all. You start to wonder where they are all coming from. You look around, turning to look upstream, and you decide to walk that direction. You pull your hand out of the water and stand up, seeing that the entirety of your surroundings has transformed into something that is full of so much more than you had seen before. You can see that there are trees and grass and hills. There is a sky overhead, a soft, crystal blue color, and you can see great, big, fluffy clouds, slowly floating. They move through the sky lightly, without a care in the world, and you feel at peace too. You feel like all of your negative feelings are fading away. They float away with the clouds.

You take a deep breath in...

One... Two... Three... Four... Five...

And out...

One... Two... Three... Four... Five...


And again, take a deep breath in...

One... Two... Three... Four... Five...

And out...

One... Two... Three... Four... Five...

You turn your attention back to the stream and start to walk along with it. You walk, step by step. The grass is just as lush and thick the further that you go, and you realize that there is no shortage of the little pink petals. You continue walking along, watching them lazily floating. You feel surprisingly calm as you go as if your core were radiating peace out to you so that you could feel as good as possible for yourself. The sound of the water gently babbling over rocks brings you peace, and you can hear a bird singing in the distance somewhere.


You take a deep breath in...

One... Two... Three... Four... Five...

And out...

One... Two... Three... Four... Five...

Soon, you start to smell something softly sweet. It is a beautiful smell, soft and pleasant. You can't quite place your finger on it, but it is a fragrant, floral scent that brings you another wave of peace as you smell it. You notice a small tree just in front of you. The tree is maybe ten feet tall with long, knobby branches that reach out to you. The wood is a deep, inviting brown, and the whole tree appears to be covered entirely in flowers. The flowers are tiny pink blossoms with five petals each. They have little yellow pistils within them, and they smell amazing. The flowers grow in little clusters with each other nearby. They reach out in all directions. You feel uplifted as you see the flowers on the tree. They are cherry blossoms and they smell so inviting as you approach them. They look beautiful, and you want to reach out to touch them all.

You take a deep breath in...

One... Two... Three... Four... Five...

And out...

One... Two... Three... Four... Five...

You take a deep breath in...

One... Two... Three... Four... Five...

And out...

One... Two... Three... Four... Five...

You can't help it—you feel like you have to reach up and touch them, and you do it. You reach out to touch the tree, and you realize that the petals feel just as soft as they look, and they smell twice as good, too. Suddenly, as you touch the petal, it falls down, drifting down, down, down, until it lands atop the stream in front of you. As it lands there in front of you, you are distracted for a moment—you realize that you are thinking about something. Identify that thought that just went through your mind. What was it? Allow yourself to think about it as it goes by until it fades away.

You take a deep breath in...

One... Two... Three... Four... Five...

And out...

One... Two... Three... Four... Five...

Another petal falls down from the tree, drifting just as lazily. You watch it, breathing slowly and deeply as it makes its way, slowly, down to where it needs to be. It works its way down and eventually lands atop the water, making tiny ripples where it lands. You look at the petal as it sits there. Suddenly, you are thinking about the worst part of today. What happened? Allow yourself to think about it. What was so bad about the day? What made it so frustrating or upsetting? What made it easier to deal with? Let yourself continue to ponder the moment, watching as the petal slowly is carried away by the current. Don't fight it as it does—just watch it make its way down into nothingness.

Soon, it disappears out of sight, and as it goes, you allow your thought to go with it. You let go of the thought and the worry that came with it. You let go of feeling like you need to be so frustrated or upset with the moment. You stop caring about the moment—you let go of the anxiety. You are free.

You take a deep breath in...

One... Two... Three... Four... Five...
And out...

One... Two... Three... Four... Five...

You look back up at the tree and see another petal falling
down to the surface of the stream, and just as it touches the
water, you realize that you are thinking about another
thought. You allow the thought to continue its way
throughout your mind without interrupting it. You let
yourself think about it. You let yourself worry and wonder
about it, and once that petal is out of sight, you let it go
instead.

The more petals fall in front of you, the easier it becomes to
let go entirely as the thoughts flow. Every time you see a
petal falling to the surface of the water, the thoughts come
and go. Each and every petal is one of the thoughts that go
through your mind. Each and every petal is different, and
each one will take your mind to different places. Each place
that you go to will fill you with different feelings. Some of
them will be good, and others may not be. No matter the
thought, let it come. Let the thoughts come and
acknowledge each and every one as they pass through your
mind in the stream. You are looking at the stream of
thoughts within your own mind. They are all unique. They
are all different. They are all meant to do something
different. Even the thoughts that may not be as pleasant still
have their own inherent value that matters. Every thought,
no matter whether it is positive or negative, maters to you
and will help to drive you. Each thought does something on
its own. Each thought will allow you to have something
more, something better. They are good to acknowledge, and
you do not have to shy away from them.

When you find yourself immersed in a negative thought, it
is okay to tell yourself to let it go. It is okay to sit back,
watch, and allow it to fade away. It is okay to allow it to

dissipate over time. It is okay to acknowledge the thought but not react to it. As you watch the petals go by in your own mind, remember that they are just thoughts. They are just passing by on your stream of thought. They are not able to hurt you. They are not able to take control of you or who you are. They are not able to hold you back. They are simply thoughts—they are petals floating atop a river, and they will not harm you.

You take a deep breath in...

One... Two... Three... Four... Five...

And out...

One... Two... Three... Four... Five

You sit there for a while—you can sit there for as long as you would like. You can sit back and enjoy the moments as they pass through. You can sit back and watch as your own trains of thought change over time. They may be positive today as the petals float by, or they may not be, and that's okay. Let the thoughts go. Let the thoughts fade by. Let the thoughts disappear. You will feel more at ease over time. Just let them go.

You find yourself leaning against the trunk of the cherry tree, watching the blossoms and petals float away. It seems like there will be an endless supply of them—and there may very well be. However, you can slow your mind down as well. As the thoughts go, focus on how sleepy you become. Let yourself feel at ease.

Breathe deeply again. In... And out...

Now, focus on your breath again. You are shifting your attention from those thoughts back to your breath. You no longer need to focus on the petals. Now, it is time to relax.

You take a deep breath in…

One… Two… Three… Four… Five…

And out…

One… Two… Three… Four… Five

How does the breath feel? How does the air smell? Can you smell the cherry blossoms? Focus on the scent and embrace it.

You take a deep breath in…

One… Two… Three… Four… Five…

And out…

One… Two… Three… Four… Five

Hear your breath coming in and out of your chest, and do not turn your focus away. Focus on a point in front of you, but do not pay attention to it. Allow your eyes to gently rest there, and listen to your breathing.

You take a deep breath in…

One… Two… Three… Four… Five…

And out…

One… Two… Three… Four… Five

You start to feel calmer as you breathe deeply. The worry that may have set in from the thoughts starts to fade away. You are at peace. You are at ease. You do not want to respond to the world around you any longer.

You take a deep breath in…

One... Two... Three... Four... Five...

And out...

One... Two... Three... Four... Five

You feel the anxiety fade, and you are left instead with a feeling of peace within yourself. You feel yourself feeling at ease at the moment. You feel like you are totally at peace. You feel totally content in the moment. You feel ready to rest. You realize that your entire body is feeling very heavy. It feels ready to sleep. It feels ready to rest and relax without any interruptions.

You take a deep breath in...

One... Two... Three... Four... Five...

And out...

One... Two... Three... Four... Five

Your sleepiness is starting to become entirely overpowering. Your breathing grows slower... Deeper... More peaceful... You are ready to fall asleep.

Repeat these thoughts to yourself:

"I am ready for a restful, peaceful, and wholesome night of sleeping in my bed."

"I am safe where I am, and there is nothing to worry about where we are."

"I am at total peace in my bed at this moment, and there is not anything in this world that could keep me away from the sleep that I am about to enjoy."

Breathe again to yourself.
You take a deep breath in...

One... Two... Three... Four... Five...
And out...

One... Two... Three... Four... Five

Focus on the breath again. How does it feel? You realize that each breath is making you sleepier. You know that you will not be able to fight it any longer. Soon, the petals stop falling into the stream. The water runs clear, perfectly blue as it gently flows past you. The blossoms all fade out of sight.

You take a deep breath in...

One... Two... Three... Four... Five...

And out...

One... Two... Three... Four... Five
With that breath, the tree behind you starts to fade away slowly as well. It is hazy at first but slowly starts to disappear. It starts to become less and less present, and then you realize that you can't rest your back against it anymore. That's okay though—you allow yourself to gently sink back to lay in the softest, plushest grass that you have ever felt. You are comfortable. You are at ease.

You take a deep breath in...

One... Two... Three... Four... Five...

And out...

One... Two... Three... Four... Five.

With that breath, the blue sky starts to fade away. First, it is a brilliant blue, and then it becomes alight with the impending sunset. You see the sky turning a beautiful fiery color as the sunset blazes along the surface. You see it fading away, little by little. The fiery blaze of sunset slowly becomes darker and darker, until finally, the light from the sun is gone.

You take a deep breath in...

One... Two... Three... Four... Five...

And out...

One... Two... Three... Four... Five

In that dark, night sky, you realize that there are millions upon millions of stars, all lit up around you. They are brightly shining. They are peacefully twinkling. There are more than you can possibly count up there in the sky above you, and you lose yourself in watching them. Their twinkling is peacefully lulling you deeper into your own sleep. You feel more and more tired. You feel ready to fall asleep entirely.

You take a deep breath in...

One... Two... Three... Four... Five...

And out...

One... Two... Three... Four... Five.

With that breath, even the stars start to grow hazy. They start to fade out of sight as you stop focusing your vision on anything around you. You let go of the need to focus. You let go of the need to see. You let go of your need to think.

You take a deep breath in...

One... Two... Three... Four... Five...

And out...

One... Two... Three... Four... Five

The grass beneath you starts to fade away into nothingness as well. You lose your awareness of the sensation of the grass against your back and you let that go. You let go of the need to focus so much upon it. You let it go and get ready to sleep.

You take a deep breath in...

One... Two... Three... Four... Five...

And out...

One... Two... Three... Four... Five.

You take a deep breath in...

One... Two... Three... Four... Five...
And out...

One... Two... Three... Four... Five

You take a deep breath in...

One... Two... Three... Four... Five...

And out...

One... Two... Three... Four... Five

You are ready to sleep now. You continue breathing, softly and quietly, until your mind is gently enveloped by the wonderful cushion of sleep.

Good night. Rest well.

# Guided Meditation 2: Hot Air Balloons

Close your eyes, and settle yourself into bed. Get into your most comfortable position as you prepare to be gently guided off to sleep. Take in a great, big, deep breath through your nose. Feel it flowing through your nostrils and down into your lungs. Is it warm? Cold? Just right? What smells does it carry with it? Focus on those smells. Focus on the sensation of your air as it fills up your lungs with air. Your lungs are like balloons, filling up and swelling up until they are full, and there, they give you the energy to live. Graciously thank the air in your lungs for providing you with the oxygen you will need and exhales slowly. Feel the air, warmer now, as it gently whispers over your lips. Does it dry them out? Does it feel gentle? With every breath that you take, you can feel yourself releasing tension and feeling more at peace.

You will breathe in... And out... On counts of five.

You take a deep breath in...

One... Two... Three... Four... Five...

And out...

One... Two... Three... Four... Five...

Your breath helps you to center yourself. You feel yourself relaxing as your breath slowly and gently calms you down. You feel yourself feeling more connected, more at peace, more aware of everything that you do. You are becoming aware of yourself, what you do, and how you feel.

You take a deep breath in...

One... Two... Three... Four... Five...

And out...

One... Two... Three... Four... Five...

Now, focus on the tension in your body. Become aware of any tension you are holding in your head and face. As you breathe in, imagine that you are pushing the tension within your body and down to the center point above your belly button. Let it gather there. Now, feel the tension in your shoulders. Focus on that stress and tension and as you breathe in, feel it moving down to your center. Let it gather there, imagining your tension and stress all becoming balled up in the center. Feel the tension in your arms and hands gathering and flowing into your center. Feel that center growing with the tension and allow it to build up. Then, take the tension from your chest and upper back, and flow it down toward your center.

Then, go down to your toes and feet, identifying the tension that is there. Push it up, feeling it flowing up your legs, through your pelvis and belly, and noting it as it arrives in the belly. Focus on it as it grows within you and allow it to flow.

Feel all of the tension in your body, all boiled up into one big ball in your core. You've pushed away all of that tension away from yourself, so you can better focus on Allow yourself to feel the weight of that tension and the burden that it has been putting on you. Feel the heaviness on yourself. That tension in your core begins to transform, and you find yourself laying there, with butterflies all over your body, holding you down. You feel them, holding you, pressing against you, and keeping you down. You are trapped by your tension, burdened. It's keeping you awake, lost in your mind...

You take a big, deep breath into your chest. And you breathe out deeply...

As you exhale, all of the butterflies suddenly fly away. They all push off from you suddenly, and they all flutter away, one by one, disappearing into the sky. As they all disappear, you start to feel lighter. You feel more comfortable, more content. One by one, you feel your tensions fade away. You feel more relaxed. You watch each butterfly take away one of your concerns for the day. You watch each butterfly disappear with your stress, and you feel lighter.

You feel like you can move again.

You feel relaxed.

You feel at peace.

Now, in that space where you pulled the tension away, in your center, imagine that peace and calmness flows into you. It is slowly manifesting within your core, filling you with peace, comfort, and the feeling that everything will be okay. You have a big, shining silver ball of peace and relaxation within your core. Breathe in... One... Two... Three... Four... Five... And out... One... Two... Three... Four... Five... As you breathe in, imagine the feeling of relaxation extending throughout your body. Feel it in your head. Breathe in... and out... Feel the relaxation pulsating in your shoulders and arms... Feel it spreading throughout your chest. Feel it spread down to your legs and feet. It fills your whole body, bringing you utter peace and relaxation. Your mind feels incredibly open and ready to go on a peaceful, relaxing adventure. Your body is ready to fall deeper and deeper into your relaxation so you can become more and more relaxed.

You can feel your body's tension all fading away, little by little, pushing it further and further from yourself. It dissipates as it emanates away from you, and the more that you sit at rest, the more that you feel like you are able to be comfortable in your spot. The more that you are calm and in control, the more you feel ready to relax.

You can feel yourself growing distant from the tension and worries. You feel yourself drifting away, little by little, moving further and further out and free from those worries and fears that hold you back. You feel like you are almost weightless—and you can be. You can allow yourself to be drifted away to glide through the sky, free from the weight and gravity of your stress that you are experiencing. But, before you do that, you must release the corporeal stressors and worries that you have that are holding you down. You must let go of the pain, the discomfort, and the doubt that will hold you back, and you must do so carefully and willingly.

To achieve that inner peace that you are looking for, you must begin on the ground. If you want to free yourself from the doubt, fear, anxiety, and insomnia, you must first learn to release it all and let it stay away from you. In releasing that fear and anxiety, you can become much more comfortable with yourself. You can begin to drift into comfort, and that comfort as you drift lazily about yourself will help you achieve that relaxation and freedom that you seek for yourself.

You are lighter than you realize. You do not have to be pulled back down to earth, not just now. You can let yourself drift off and fall asleep. All you have to do is surrender yourself to the currents of the air, and you will find yourself floating. Envision yourself for a moment, sitting in a wicker basket. The basket is brown and woven carefully all around you. It is a warm, oak color, and it feels smooth to the touch. You can see that it is carefully and tenderly constructed with each and every fiber right where it should be. The surface of the wood is warm to the touch from the sunlight beating onto it. You focus on the woven basket, looking at the intricacies. Individually, each and every one of those fibers may not be very strong, but when they all come together, they create something powerful— something that can support even your entire weight. You focus on the entire basket now, and you can see that each of the corners of the basket is bracketed and attached to something.

Laying on the ground next to the basket, you realize, is a great, big, limp, deflated hot air balloon. The balloon itself is a vibrant rainbow color. It has geometric patterns of rainbow colors, starting at red, then turning orange, yellow, green, blue, and violet before repeating. The colors ripple across the balloon, brightly creating the entirety of the balloon.

You breathe in... And you see the flame above your head flicker to life. Suddenly, the fire starts to burn, warming the air that funnels into the hot air balloon. With every breath you take, you are going to warm the air that your balloon needs to begin to lift off. You breathe out... And in... And out... And in... And every time that you breathe out, you see the fire continue to burn. It is filling the balloon up, and you can see the great, big, deflated sack slowly start to fill and inflate. You can see it slowly working to create that balloon that will carry you away.

Every breath you take brings you back to that state of inner peace. It helps you to feel like you are right where you belong. It helps you to feel at ease in your skin. Each and every breath fills you up with that utter peace of mind that you were looking for.
Every exhale that you take releases some of your anxiety and stress. Your tension is channeled into the hot air balloon, filling quickly in front of you. It fills rapidly as you breathe. It fills up more and more, and before you know it, the balloon is right over your head. It is not quite filled up enough for you to float away, but you can see it getting close. You can feel the nearly-weightlessness as you sit there inside of the basket, breathing deeply.

And with one final breath, you let go. You release that tension and revel in the moment of utter peace for a moment. And, as you do so, you feel your basket break free from gravity. You feel the gentle bob and sway as your basket slowly starts to pull away from the ground. The flame above you continues to burn brightly, releasing your tension and giving yourself that space that you were looking for. You notice that you begin your ascent into the sky, and every breath brings you just a little bit higher. You are comfortable in the basket and lay down inside of it, looking up at the bright, rainbow-colored balloon that pulls you higher and higher. You allow yourself to watch the rippling of the fabric as the flames warm the air within them. You watch the gentle bobbing of the balloon and feel the swaying yourself as you go.

You cannot see the ground as you look up at the sky, but you are certain that you have floated up quite a ways. You look up at the sky and smile—you are comfortable. You are content where you are. You are enjoying the moment as you continue to breathe, and at the moment, you allow yourself to fall still. You know that if you move too much, you will shake up the basket, and you do not want to do this. You instead gently settle yourself down into your position. You look up at the sky above you, beyond the basket. You look at everything around yourself, and you feel calm.

The sky is a beautiful shade of blue. It is clear and vibrant alongside the rainbow hues of the balloon above you. There are puffy white clouds slowly catching a ride on the current, just like you are. You and the clouds are the same in that moment, allowing the will of the universe to take you wherever it will take you, and you do not feel the need to resist. You do not feel the need to fight the current at all— you exhale and allow yourself to slowly drift about. Your tension is practically nonexistent now as you remain floating in the air.

In the moment, you can feel just how connected you are. You are connected to yourself—your mind, your body, and your spirit are all at ease with each other in that moment.

All of you are able to feel entirely comfortable at the moment. You feel at ease. You feel content—true contentment—emanating from within you. You can feel yourself warming up within yourself. You can feel yourself becoming calmer and more relaxed as you sit there. You can find yourself embracing your connection to yourself.

You are connected to the universe as well. Like the clouds above you, you are simply drifting along on air currents that are entirely outside of your control. You are floating among them, not bothering to move at all. You do not fight them—you simply allow them to continue on as normal. You allow yourself to ride along those currents and see where the world and life take you. the more that you do this, the further that you will get.

You breathe deeply again, and you feel yourself freeing yourself from the anxieties of your day. Work doesn't matter when you are hundreds of feet above the ground. Deadlines don't matter when you are too far away from meeting them anyway. You are too far away from these issues to feel attached or bothered by them. They are as small to you as the winding roads that you would see if you peered over the edge of the basket, seeing them, barely visible on the ground beneath you.

You are at ease as you distance yourself from everything. You grow further away from the worldly complaints and closer to your ability to accept yourself and love yourself. You feel yourself growing attached to yourself and who you are. You feel yourself feeling driven toward embracing the situation that you are in. You feel yourself feeling driven to embrace yourself. You feel content. You feel comfortable and happy. You feel ready to rest and ready to embrace yourself.

You are drifting along now, no longer ascending higher into the sky. Now, you are simply pulled about by the currents. You are at peace where you are. You are content with where you are in the moment, and that is enough. Breathe and enjoy the moment. Allow yourself to revel in the contentedness. Embrace the joy that is starting to spread within you. With each breath in, you draw in more peace and contentment. Your body is completely relaxed at this point—there is no more tension holding you back. You feel happy. You feel ready to rest.

The hot air balloon starts to drift downward. It starts to descent toward the ground. The descent is gentle and smooth. You feel your relaxation spreading as you get closer and closer to the ground. Each breath brings you just a bit closer to the ground. It brings you just a bit closer to being back down to earth.

You take the time to peak over the basket now and the sight is absolutely breathtaking. All around you, you can see gently rolling, green hills. There are patchwork farms on the ground beneath you, and you can see endless sky all around you. In the distance, you can see the silhouette of the mountains looking over everything, faint, but present. You can see that there are people along the ground—cars look as small as beetles crawling across the ground. The roads look like tiny lines scrawled across paper by a child. The houses look like little more than blocks on the ground. You can see that they are there, but they look almost fake.

A little river runs along the ground underneath you as well, snaking gently across the hillsides and winding along the ground. The water reflects back the shining sun in places, and it shimmers as it cuts through the green. The trees look like tiny puffs, hardly bigger than broccoli florets as you remain there in your basket.

You breathe in... And out... and you look down underneath you. You can see the shadow from your balloon lazily dancing about on the ground, flickering and fluttering about as you continue to make your way across the sky. You feel the basket sway underneath you, but you do not mind. You do not mind the fact that the wind tousles through your hair.

Suddenly, you feel the air grow colder. It suddenly embraces you—chilly and washing over you. It isn't unpleasant—just cool, and when you look, you see why: All around you is a giant cloud of mist floating toward you. It is massive as it makes its way toward you, hulking and floating closer and closer. You look at it for a moment, wondering if you should move away from it or embrace it head-on and decide that you will go straight through it without fear. It is cool, but not unpleasant.

The cool cloud leaves a fine layer of moisture on your skin, and you feel the hot air balloon dip a little bit more as the temperature drops. It is not too bad—you accept and embrace it anyway and keep moving forward. You decide to keep on going along without concerns, and you enjoy it. You don't mind letting the atmosphere take you where it will.

You realize that the air is nice and fresh where you are. It is crisp and cool. It is refreshing as you breathe it in through your nose. It smells lightly of rain and of freshness, far from the hustle and bustle of daily life or the pollution that the day may bring with it. It is gently enjoyable to breathe in and the more that you do, the calmer you feel.

You are completely relaxed as you breathe on, beholding the beautiful scene in front of you. You can see for miles and miles, and it is the most breathtaking site that you have ever seen. You are high above the ground and just as high above all of the problems that you are facing. You are high above it all, able to gently drift away, free from everything that would ordinarily bother you. You are free to enjoy the moment. You allow it to bring you calmness and serenity.

You let yourself breathe out any remnants of tension that fill you up inside. You allow it all to fade away, burning as fuel for the hot air balloon. You allow it to continue to burn away as you slowly drift. The balloon continues to descend gently in the air, slowly and carefully moving about until it is finally starting to approach the ground.

You breathe in deeply and breathe out your concerns for the day. Your worries for the future dissipate. Your deadlines and your struggles are all fading away, and you feel at peace. You feel at ease. You feel ready to tackle it all, and all you have to do is choose to keep moving forward. You choose to do so. You choose to embrace it once and for all, and you are glad that you did.

The hot air balloon eventually touches down on the ground, and you are at peace with yourself. You are at peace with the world. You feel free from the struggles of the world around you and free from having to struggle so much in general. All you have to do is breathe.

# Description

*Bedtime stories aren't just for kids anymore...*

Do you find that you struggle to sleep, no matter how hard you try to cope with it? Are you always exhausted even though you know that you shouldn't be? If you find that bedtime is impossible for you to cope with, then this book is for you!

As you read through this book, you will build off of the skills from the previous two books, mastering the concepts of mindfulness so that you can feel far more capable of navigating your own difficult feelings with ease. There is a reason that bedtime stories are so recommended for getting children to sleep; after all—having time to enjoy a story allows your mind to relax and allows you to begin to focus more on the moment. You may be pleasantly surprised and discover that through reading these bedtime stories, you will help your mind relax and ease off to sleep.

In this book, you will continue the use of meditation that has been built in the previous books. Then, you will be provided with several options for bedtime stories. Each story is designed to be a calming slice of life story about the various adventures (and sometimes misadventures) of Sophie Rogers, a young woman that lives in the Pacific Northwest with her German shepherd pal, Bella. Together, and sometimes separately, they get out and enjoy their lives and the stories of her day to day life can help you to relax and soothe yourself into a state in which you will be able to relax. As you read, you should find yourself calming down and preparing for a night of sleep. Each of the options that are provided to you should be fun and engaging without keeping you up at night.

Finally, at the end of the book, you will be given two more traditional mindful meditations that are designed to trigger that state of mindfulness within yourself so you can then begin to relax and enjoy a restful night's sleep. When you utilize these techniques, you can calm yourself down when you need to, allowing yourself to finally fall asleep.

If you're ready to start sleeping better, then you are in the right spot. This book may be able to help you relax enough to fall asleep! As you read, you can expect to see:

- An adventure in which Sophie builds herself a new garden in her yard
- A day trip to go fishing with Sophie's boyfriend
- A horse and carriage date through a beautiful Christmas town
- A scuba diving adventure vacation on a cruise
- Girls' night out to celebrate Sophie's friend's new house purchase
- A day of errands in which Sophie has to force herself to just take care of business and do what needs to be done
- A trip by horseback into the mountains
- Two guided meditations to help you fall asleep with ease

If you're ready to fall asleep, then don't let another day pass you buy. Enjoy these stories and see if sleep is more within your grasp than you realized!